Advance Praise for *Love, Reality Style*

"*Love, Reality Style* by Judith Natelli McLaughlin shows readers what real love in the real world is like. It's funny, sweet, frustrating... McLaughlin knows how to paint a stunning yet realistic portrait of love and marriage. She brilliantly takes readers on the roller coaster ride of a lifetime. This tale was romantic and funny. *Love, Reality Style* is definitely one romantic comedy that readers everywhere will love. Overall, I highly recommend this title to readers worldwide." 5/5 stars
- Danielle Urban, *Universal Creativity Inc.*

"I loved this story and am thrilled to have had a chance to read it. The writing was fabulous and funny with witty conversations... for those who just want to read something that makes you smile, cry, and laugh out loud, read this adorable, true to life story." 5/5 stars
- Ruby Blotzer, *Goodreads* reviewer

"5 stars! I loved this book! I cannot wait to pick it up and read it over again! This book is so on point and current. Reality TV has taken over how we watch television. To put this as the theme in the book is genius. It is not something I've read in any other book. It is a modern day love story. I highly recommend it!"
- Robin Handwerger, advance reader

"What makes [*Love, Reality Style*] different from similar stories is the rather unique course of action the unsuspecting couple take. I liked this book, and any lead protagonist with a serious cake addiction is a friend of mine." 4/5 stars
- Michelle Simons, book reviewer

4/5 stars
- Ilene Bieleski, *A Bookworm's Reviews*

Copyright Information

LOVE, REALITY STYLE

By Judith Natelli McLaughlin

To Joyce

I hope you enjoy LRS!

BlueMoon
PUBLISHERS

For Brian

CONTENTS

ACKNOWLEDGEMENTS

I couldn't write without the love, help, support, insights, enthusiasm, affection, and dedication of my family and friends. You all keep me happy, humble, and grateful. If I begin naming names, I am just that neurotic that I'll start to lose sleep at night, fearing I left someone out. Best to say, "You know who you are." I hope you do!

Special thanks go to my very first editor, Brent Taylor. He added such value to this novel and his favourite line became part of the Book Club Guide. Hope you are smiling, Brent.

And finally, to my team at Blue Moon Publishers, especially Talia Crockett, my editorial coordinator, thanks for the brilliant insights. And even more than that, thanks for believing in my work.

CHAPTER ONE

"Vegetables are a must on a diet. I suggest carrot cake, zucchini bread, and pumpkin pie." JIM DAVIS

Ralph Ichy was certain he would do it this time despite having failed miserably on his last two attempts. He should have seen it coming. The first time anyway. It was like he was predestined to crash and burn at everything from sex to grocery shopping, a virgin at both until his mid-thirties. He knew why. A person doesn't always need a degree in psychology to figure out the genesis of their sweat-inducing, leg-tapping neurosis. His father dying young, and his brother Walter—he still couldn't talk about it—left him to be raised by a single, overprotective mother. But he carefully avoided thinking about the whys and instead focused on the failures themselves. At least two of them, anyway.

That first time he tried, the results weren't pretty. His heart was racing at panic attack speed. He swore when he looked down he could see the white T-shirt he wore to the gym rising and falling to the beat of his heart. Ba boom. Ba boom. Ba boom. Easily one hundred beats per minute. Sweat was pouring off him, running down the sides of his china white face until it dripped, plopped, to the ground. All of that perspiration and he hadn't even stepped foot onto the treadmill. He pulled a clean towel out of his gym bag and wiped his forehead, then dug for his bottle of Purell. He gave himself a quick squirt, rubbed his hands together, and then took a whiff, using the aroma as some sort of therapeutic, muscle relaxing treatment.

Mixed in with the antiseptic scent of the hand sanitizer was the distinct odour of fat frying. *Probably bacon*, Ralph thought, as he recalled the proximity of the diner. Bacon frying, eggs being scrambled in lard, grease-filled sausage links dancing in pans. These aromas unwillingly led him to thoughts of his mother, and all the ever-loving hearty breakfasts she cooked him because she never wanted him to be hungry. Or cold. Or tired. Or hot. Or dirty. Or sick. Or anything but totally and perfectly fine. It was understandable, after all she had been through.

I don't want to be analyzing that right now. I've got a task to accomplish and I am going to do it. He stood outside the glass door to the gym, watching and waiting. Pacing back and forth on the cement sidewalk, he made himself available to open the heavy glass door for the early morning exercisers, just so he would have something to do. *I'm going to do it*, he repeated, not letting the smells of the diner infiltrate his nose. *For God's sake, this isn't a bank heist. I'm going to do it.* Splat. Another bead of perspiration hit the pavement, leaving a prominent circle at his feet—a memorial to his sweat. He grabbed a new towel from his gym bag and once again wiped his face.

"Forget it," he whispered to himself, yanking the door open and entering the gym, walking heavy-footed to the treadmill room. "Just forget it."

The second time he failed, at least he had gotten a bit closer. This time he wasn't outside some smelly gym, at an ungodly hour of the morning, waiting for his girlfriend. This time she arrived at their predetermined destination first. She was seated at a table patiently waiting for him. Ralph knew, because they had just talked on their cells. "I'm in the back," she had said. "And it's dark in here, so just walk to the little room in the rear of the restaurant, turn right, and you'll see me."

It was dark. The lack of light added another dimension of mystery to the evening. Ralph liked it. He also liked the dark because it made his bald spot less visible. But the dim light soon worked against him as he tripped on the slightest of steps that led to the back of the restaurant. Now on his hands and knees, he looked up fast, turning his head right and left, trying to determine if anyone, especially his girlfriend, Mary Grace, had witnessed his act of clumsiness. When he was certain only he and the hostess were privy to his gymnastics, he got up, breathing a sigh of relief while wrenching his neck at the same time. Just like that, he lost the mobility in his neck. He tried to remain positive. *Tonight's the night*, he told himself, though his internal voice was weak and unconvincing.

"Hey," he said when he saw Mary Grace, a forced grin spreading across his face. He tried to sound cool and walk normally, but his careful steps toward the table were a dead giveaway. Ralph noticed his girlfriend's head tilt to the left, and saw the curiosity filling up her eyes.

"Why are you walking like that?"

"Like what?" He pretended nothing was wrong, concentrating on his easy-breezy grin instead.

"Like a petrified zombie."

And that was it. Any shred of hope was all but gone.

Appetizers turned into salad and then salad turned into dinner and then dinner turned into dessert and before he knew it, he asked the wrong question. "Mary Grace, will you share my dessert with me?" he asked, completely disgusted with himself and still acutely aware of the sharp pains in his wrenched neck.

"No," she said, her voice carrying a hint of annoyance. "I'm getting my own piece of cake." And she did.

And Ralph didn't share one bite of it. His mission remained unaccomplished.

Ralph swore this time he would do it. *Third time's the charm*. In his faded blue, rusted-out Honda Accord, he picked Mary Grace up from the elementary school where she worked as a third-grade teacher. The left fender of the vehicle was dented, a fact he only started caring about when he and Mary Grace began dating. *At least she'll always enter on the passenger side*, he thought, trying to convince himself a fender-bender car was no deal breaker.

Today Ralph was driving Mary Grace to the gas station where her car was receiving a new transmission. *A gas station. This is even less romantic than the gym.* But Ralph didn't care. He just wanted to get it over with. So, like a mantra, he repeated reassurances in his head. *Do it. Do it. Do it.*

As Ralph waited in front of the building for Mary Grace to exit, he saw a pack of school kids leaving. Boys and girls laughing, skipping, calling for play dates and lingering in groups, waiting for their mothers to pick them up. Then, from the brick building, a boy emerged alone. He was small, but the size of his backpack made Ralph assume he was older than a kindergartener. The sight of the boy shot a pang of sorrow through Ralph's heart, reminding him how many times he had exited elementary school by himself. And middle school and high school, for that matter. But thoughts of the boy faded fast when Ralph saw Mary Grace walk through the school's door. When Mary Grace caught Ralph's eye, she smiled. It was a smile that gave Ralph some sort of false sense of security. He tried to smile back, but it didn't work. If he had looked at himself in the mirror, he would have been able to tell that he appeared more constipated than happy. Mary Grace halted for a moment, furrowed her brow, and then took the few more steps she needed to get to the car. She opened the door and entered in one swift move.

"You okay, Ralph?" She didn't give him time to answer the question. "Thanks for getting me. I just called the station and my car is definitely ready, so we won't have to wait or anything. You okay?" She cocked her head. He felt like she was examining him. It was a long minute. "You have a bad face on."

"Will you marry me?" *There, I did it.* He exhaled one huge long breath. *Oh my God. I did it.* The knots in Ralph's stomach got surprisingly tighter. *I might actually throw up.* Getting the words out, unexpectedly, was no relief at all. Pushing them out of his mouth only set him up for more failure. Bigger failure. *Why didn't I see this coming?* The fear of rejection was so strong it produced a sour odour, one only Ralph's sensitive nose could detect. He couldn't help but scrunch his face.

"What?" Mary Grace's right hand immediately rose to her head, pulling at her short brown curls. She looked at Ralph with what appeared to him as intense scrutiny mixed with equal parts confusion. Or was it disgust?

His smile was crooked and his movements awkward as he tried to readjust himself in the seat. *I'll try to be less awkward. I'll forever be faithful. Marry me, please.*

There was silence. Ralph let it linger momentarily before asking again.

"Mary Grace, will you marry me?"

He opened a velvet box he pulled from the car's console, exposing a brilliant diamond ring. The stench of what was turning into his most epic fail became overwhelming. He tried not breathing for a moment.

"Oh."

"Oh yes, or oh no?"

"I don't know," Mary Grace said. "Where did this come from? I thought you were taking me to get my car. I'm sorry, Ralph, it's just that, you kind of surprised me here."

"I didn't mean to. It's just that..." Ralph said, repeating those same three filler words Mary Grace had used only seconds ago. He took one long, deep breath, afraid if he didn't he would start hyperventilating.

"...oh, Mary Grace, will you please marry me?"

CHAPTER TWO

"There is no problem in life that can't be solved with a good piece of cake." ANGELA FALCONE

There was a magnet on Mary Grace Falcone's refrigerator given to her by one of her two best friends, Annie. Annie also bought one for herself, and one for the third in the trio, Jayde. The girls laughed when Annie gave them their gifts because the quote on the magnet summed up their friendship in less than fifteen words.

"I don't know how anyone can be so smart, and so spot on, with so few words," Jayde said upon receiving and reading the magnet. "Here's to Virginia Woolf."

"And here's to Annie for giving these to us," Mary Grace added.

Annie glanced from Jayde to Mary Grace, and then raised a glass. "Some people go to priests; others to poetry; I to my friends," she said, quoting the Virginia Woolf magnet.

The girls toasted with their frothy margaritas and, like usual, talked the night away.

After the marriage proposal, Mary Grace needed a chat session like that. *Should I marry Ralph? Should I say yes?* These were not questions she could answer by herself. *A meeting,* the trio dubbed it, with MexTexas acting as their boardroom. The loud buzz and frenetic pace of the restaurant made it a great place for private conversations in social settings, and quickly became their spot.

Mary Grace called Annie and Jayde, and then was off to MexTexas to figure out if she, Mary Grace Falcone, would soon become Mary Grace Ichy. *Seriously? Say it incorrectly and it sounds like you suffer from psoriasis. Say it correctly and you just sound gross. Why couldn't his name be Smith?* She let out a disgusted sigh.

The reds and yellows that splashed the restaurant's walls with big blocks of colour were as alive and vibrant as the patrons inhabiting the joint. The chatter in MexTexas was loud, no doubt helped by the potent margaritas and throngs of thirsty customers at the bar. The smells of sizzling peppers, onions, and strips of frying steak and chicken made hungry people starving. Like bumper cars at an amusement park, waiters and waitresses scrambled to serve their customers and reap the rewards of generous tips.

"Okay, so are you guys ready for this one?" Mary Grace leaned on the round wooden table she shared with her friends. She pushed the curls of her close-cropped hair off her face, more out of habit than necessity.

"That good, huh?" Jayde took a gulp from the salted rim of her Margarita glass. "Mmm. Delicious."

"Ready for what?" Annie wore a quizzical look while shoving a hunk of nachos grande in her mouth.

"My news. My big news. The reason I called our meeting tonight," Mary Grace said.

"Right. Sorry," Annie replied. "I'm with you. It's just these nachos are so good. And it is such a treat to get away from the twins. I got lost in the cheese for a second."

"They're the same nachos we eat every time we come here." Jayde scratched her head, letting her dark, polished nails comb all the way through her long, straight, black hair.

"I know, but they're especially good because I ate nothing but shredded wheat and apples all week. This, my friends, is the food of the gods." Annie offered up a slab to the heavens. "And in honour of you, Mary Grace, I'm ordering the biggest hunk of cake for dessert," she said. "You've really rubbed off on me. Or maybe I should just blame this on the twins." Annie patted her belly with a self-deprecating head nod and grin to match.

Mary Grace could feel her eyebrows wrinkle together as she stared at Annie for a moment. She had known Annie for over ten years now. They had started their teaching careers together and became fast friends the day they walked into South Mountain Elementary School. They were first time third-grade teachers, wearing identical outfits: brown prairie skirts, white T-shirts, tan sandals, and some sort of chunky necklaces. *Boy, were the kids confused*, Mary Grace recalled with an internal chuckle. Her outfit had been complements of Jayde's fashion advice. It turned out Annie got hers with no aid from any consultant. Mary Grace had been more than impressed.

The two had helped each other with third-grade lesson plans and navigating the political life of an elementary school teacher. Together they discovered, in those uncharted waters, it was the parents, not the children, who created the biggest waves.

Annie had left teaching behind after her twins were born, electing to be a stay-at-home mom. Mary Grace expected this to happen, but still missed her friend at work. It helped that she was busy, agreeing to become the school's lead third-grade teacher—a position she discovered was considerably more challenging. But when she spent time with Annie and the twins, Mary Grace forgot about work and instead felt a distinct ache in her heart, wondering if motherhood was in her future. When Jayde, on the other hand, joined Mary Grace, Annie, and the boys for a lunch in the park, the twins appeared to disgust Jayde, with their spit-up, burping, and constant crying. "Motherhood is not for me," she had said with a roll of her eyes.

Mary Grace didn't believe Jayde. She had been mothering Mary Grace since they were six. It all began on the kindergarten playground when Cynthia Martin called Mary Grace "four eyes." Jayde marched right over to Cynthia Martin, looked her in the eye, and said, "Beat it. No one cares what you think. C'mon, Mary Grace. Your glasses make you look smart." Jayde pulled Mary Grace by the arm, practically dragging her to the hopscotch board. "Let's play," Jayde had said, throwing a stone onto the number one.

Oh contraire. Jayde was the mothering type, and from that moment on, Mary Grace had allowed it.

But now in MexTexas, Mary Grace needed her friends and their advice. She had news, damn it, but it seemed all Jayde and Annie were interested in were nachos and tequila.

"Hello!" Mary Grace shouted, louder than she meant to as evidenced by the couple at the table next to them, who conspicuously stared in their direction. "Hello," she said again, a bit softer this time. "I'm waiting."

"There's your teacher's voice." Jayde laughed at Mary Grace, then looked at Annie. "She's got to stop using her teacher's voice on us."

"I know. If we don't let her talk, I'm afraid she's going to send us to the principal's office. You know, back in the day, Mary Grace and I actually practised our principal voices," Annie said.

Jayde raised her perfectly arched eyebrows not only in response to Annie's comment, but also due to the mental picture of Mary Grace practising such a voice.

"Well, if you don't care to know, I'll just call for the cheque," Mary Grace said.

"We're kidding," Jayde said. "Tell us the big news."

"He asked me to marry him!" Mary Grace practically spit the words out.

"What?" Annie was too excited to even wipe the cheese off her lip.

"Ralph! He asked me to marry him!"

"Congratulations!" Annie said.

"Where's the ring?" Jayde's voice was filled with all the joy of a root canal.

"Here." Mary Grace plunged her hand into her big brown purse, pulled out the black velvet box, and opened it. Then she modelled the sparkling one-carat diamond ring for her friends, stuffing the black velvet box back in her purse.

"It's beautiful," Annie gushed. "Why aren't you wearing it?"

"Don't be so obtuse," Jayde said. "She obviously didn't say yes. You didn't say yes? Did you? Tell me you didn't say yes!"

"I didn't say yes," Mary Grace confided.

"Then why'd you get to keep the rock?"

"He wanted me to hold it. Wear it. Love it. And then say yes. Should I? Should I say yes?"

"Yes!" Annie chimed in. "Of course you should say yes. Why wouldn't you say yes?"

"Why *wouldn't* she say yes?" Jayde squinted with purpose, shooting mental missiles at Annie. "The question is more like why *would* she say yes? For Christ's sake, the man didn't have sex until he met her, and it's not like he was studying for sainthood or something."

"You don't study to be a saint," Annie said.

"Whatever." Jayde rolled her eyes. "He chose not to have sex and now he's thirty-four years old. Did you hear? They're making a sequel to *The Forty Year Old Virgin*. It's called *Ralph*."

"Shut up, Jayde. Everything has to be so conventional with you. One small eccentricity, like celibacy, ruins an entire human being for you," Annie said. "We can't all be perfect human specimens like you." Annie avoided eye contact, choosing instead to stare directly at Jayde's perfectly manicured nails. *What the hell colour is that? So dark it's almost black. Must be in vogue.* She touched her own nails, which were chewed to the quick.

"C'mon, Annie. Don't be so blind or naïve or sentimental or weak or I don't know. Just don't be it. You honestly can't believe she should marry him. Besides—" Jayde stopped talking, mid-sentence, pausing for a moment before pushing the next words out of her mouth in a whisper. "I think he's gay."

"He is not gay." The look in Annie's eyes and the tone in Annie's voice told Jayde the question of Ralph's sexuality was off the table. "He just asked Mary Grace to marry him. And yes. I think our Mary Grace should marry Ralph."

"Still here." Mary Grace waved her hand in front of her friends' faces. "And no. Ralph is not gay." Mary Grace stared Jayde directly in the eyes and held that gaze for a long second. With a flick of her wrist, Mary Grace continued.

"And don't talk about this like I'm not even here. This is about me. Remember me?"

"Sorry, honey. Of course this is about you," Annie said. "Marry him. Marriage is so wonderful. Trust me, I'm the one with marriage experience here."

"Oh God, Gracie." Jayde swallowed hard, hoping the use of Mary Grace's childhood nickname would knock some sense into her. "Please don't marry that man. He doesn't have the Jane Asher Factor."

"What are you talking about?" Annie's eyes darted between Mary Grace and Jayde.

"You don't know about the Jane Asher Factor? Mary Grace, how could she not know about the Jane Asher Factor?" Jayde said.

"C'mon, Jayde, I haven't used that expression since high school."

"Not true. You used it when I was dating Robert Altmann. It wasn't *that* long ago. I asked you if he had the Jane Asher Factor and you told me he did."

"Yeah. And you broke his heart anyway. But that's not the point. The point is you used the expression, not me. I just answered your question," Mary Grace said.

"Semantics," Jayde said.

"Will somebody please tell me what the Jane Asher Factor is?" Annie was a bit exasperated, having followed the banter of her friends like a baseline tennis match.

"I will." Jayde spoke with no protest from Mary Grace. "Back in middle school, Mary Grace suffered from this obsession with the Beatles. I don't know, she must have found one of my brother's albums lying around the house."

"It was *Meet the Beatles*," Mary Grace remembered with a smile. "And your brother gave it to me."

"Whatever. Anyway, we played that one album on my brother's turntable until it practically became see-through. From then on, all Mary Grace cared about were John, Paul, George, and Ringo."

"An innocent and quite common obsession. But what does that have to do with the Jane Asher Factor?" Annie's tone held more than a hint of annoyance.

"I'm getting to that part," Jayde said. "You see, Jane Asher was Paul McCartney's first serious girlfriend. One of the beautiful people, right, Mary Grace?"

"Yes, Jayde. They were referred to as 'the beautiful people.'"

"But Paul didn't end up with Jane Asher, did he?"

"He did not."

"Who did Paul end up with?"

"Linda Eastman."

"Correct. Paul McCartney wed Linda Eastman. But Mary Grace always believed his true love was Jane Asher. According to Mary Grace..." Jayde stopped in mid-sentence and stared directly at Mary Grace, then tucked her long hair behind her ears before finally continuing. "Paul and Jane should never have split up."

Mary Grace nodded, agreeing more with the memory than the relationship status of Paul McCartney and Jane Asher.

"More than that," Jayde added, "Mary Grace needed to believe he only wed Linda to get over Jane."

"Is that true?" Annie asked.

"Not necessarily; it's just what Gracie thought. So, after we discussed the hell out of that topic, the Jane Asher Factor became synonymous with true love. If you are in true love, the person with whom you are in love possesses what Mary Grace dubbed the 'Jane Asher Factor.' Right, Mary Grace?"

"Yes, Jayde."

"I don't know why you are so disturbed by all this." Jayde's voice was flat and unaffected. "You made the whole thing up."

"Like twenty years ago," Mary Grace reminded Jayde. "I don't think it even applies anymore. I mean, how do you explain Heather Mills, or Nancy Shevell, for that matter? Shouldn't Paul have married Jane Asher instead?"

"I don't know. Couldn't Jane be happily married by now?" Annie asked.

"I suppose." Mary Grace closed her eyes and shrugged her shoulders.

"I kind of like it," Annie said. "The Jane Asher Factor. It's clever. I think Ralph has it."

"No. No, he doesn't," Jayde said. "You are not the Jane to Ralph's Paul, Mary Grace. Because Ralph does not now, nor will he ever, possess the Jane Asher Factor."

"What makes you the expert?" Annie demanded.

"Life. Mary Grace, please don't marry that man."

CHAPTER THREE

"For me, the cinema is not a slice of life, but a piece of cake." ALFRED HITCHCOCK

As Mary Grace slid through the entrance of her apartment, she noticed the effects of her two margaritas were wearing off. On the last legs of her buzz, she stood in child-like awe, observing the China Blue walls of her living room. Her living room. Her colour choice. Her decisions. *When did I become a grownup?* She chose China Blue because it was a cool colour that was supposed to be soothing, but at the moment it wasn't doing its job. She felt a dull pulse behind her right eye and realized all that was left of her meeting at MexTexas was a headache and the differing opinions of her two best friends. *Marry him. Don't marry him. Does he have the Jane Asher Factor or not? Why did Jayde have to bring that stupid thing up? The Jane Asher Factor.* Mary Grace was disgusted with herself for ever coming up with such inane mumbo jumbo. And even more disgusted with Jayde for remembering it.

Mary Grace glanced down at her finger and noticed the engagement ring. She was still wearing it. Using her thumb and pinky, she flipped the ring around in circles, playing a *now-you-see-it, now-you-don't* kind of game with the diamond. When she "saw it," she thought it was beautiful. Ralph—with his crooked smile and awkward movements, which had slowly endeared him to Mary Grace—picked out the exact ring that, if given the opportunity, she would have picked herself. *That ought to prove something about our compatibility, shouldn't it?* It was one big, shiny diamond. And, it looked very much at home on its white gold band, not to mention very much at home on her finger. *But marriage?*

Done with the ring game, Mary Grace flopped into her oversized, overstuffed beanbag chair. She picked the remote up off the floor, turned on the television, and began mindlessly flipping through the channels. A couple of reality shows and lose-weight-now infomercials were the runners up to the cooking show she favoured. She got sucked in to watching Guruli Smith make homemade pizza topped with fresh arugula. "Notice how the lettuce wilts when placed on top of the hot pizza," Mary Grace said in her favourite made-for-television voice. She followed it up with a huge, "Ugh!"

At the commercial, Mary Grace checked her answering machine. A red number two was blinking, blinking, blinking. She suddenly remembered she was supposed to call her mother tonight. She pressed the button to retrieve her messages.

"Mary Grace. It's your mother. Mary Grace? Are you there? It's your mother. I know you're there. Oh my God, you're not drowning in the bathtub, are you? Answer the phone, Mary Grace. It's your mother. I guess you're not there. Call your mother."

"I wasn't drowning, Mom," Mary Grace said out loud to nobody. "I was out." Next message.

"MG. It's me. Did you have a good time with Jayde and Annie? Did you tell them our news? Is it our news? Or is it just my news? I mean is it the news that I asked? Or is it the news that you said yes? I still don't know, Mary Grace. Call me. I love you."

Mary Grace stretched for the phone, but didn't have the energy required to make either phone call. Each would take so long, and she did have to teach her third graders in the morning. No, she would call her mother tomorrow, she decided. Before work. She would make her day and tell her all about Ralph's proposal. When her mom went on and on about their wedding, which she would begin planning because she wouldn't hear Mary Grace tell her that she hadn't said yes, she would hop off the phone so she wouldn't be late for work. *Brilliant.* The second phone call, the one to Ralph, she would make during her lunch break.

Mary Grace pushed herself out of the beanbag chair and shuffled to her bedroom, undressing along the way. She dropped her clothes like a trail of breadcrumbs behind her. *These are the sorts of things you can do when you live alone.*

She climbed into bed in just her bra and panties, cozied herself under her comforter, and clicked on the bedroom television, happy to see she hadn't missed much of Chef Guruli's dessert. It was easier to think about brownies than her marriage proposal from Ralph. She let herself think about the brownies. *Nuts. Ice cream. Whipped cream. Cherries. Pretty parfait glasses.* She would serve them at her next party. She was so deep in a brownie world that when the phone rang her heart skipped a beat. *Who is it? Mom or Ralph?* She checked her caller ID and then picked up.

"What now?" Mary Grace answered.

"Nice greeting," Jayde said. "Listen, Gracie, I think it's wrong for you to marry anybody whose penis I dicknamed the Bruised Banana."

"That's your issue. Not mine." Mary Grace felt a smile involuntarily forming on her lips as she recalled a few of Jayde's more infamous dicknames: the Shrivelled Orange and the Torpedo.

"Gracie, he uses Purell like it's his job. He might as well be the CEO of Antiseptic Hands."

"I know. It's weird. I know."

Mary Grace couldn't stop tugging at her curls.

"I don't think you do know. He lives with his mother. He is a thirty-four-year-old man making a decent living as a teacher, and yet he can't, or won't, cut the cord."

"She's not well," Mary Grace said. "He lives with her because she's not well."

"Play your cards right and the two of you will be living with her."

"Bite your tongue, Jayde Anderson."

"He was a virgin until he met you. Doesn't that scream crazy? Why, Mary Grace? Why would you marry him?"

"Because I love him?"

"Is that a question or an answer?" Jayde asked.

"Answer." Mary Grace's voice wasn't convincing.

"Just think about what I said. And get some sleep."

Click. No other words. No other noise. Just silence on the other end of the receiver. Mary Grace pressed the off button on her phone before placing it on her nightstand, not bothering to set it in its cradle. *Why does Jayde always get the last word? And why does she always think she's right? Because she always is.*

Mary Grace turned the television off and pretended to fall asleep.

CHAPTER FOUR

"A great empire, like a great cake, is most easily diminished at the edges." BENJAMIN FRANKLIN

The next night was Friday; typically a relief to Mary Grace after the long week with her young students, but with life-altering decisions looming on her horizon, this Friday night was no relief at all. In fact, this Friday night made her sixteen third graders, including Hazel Browne who still liked to eat glue and Connor Williams who cried when she did, seem like tranquility at its best. Longing for the students, Mary Grace tried with all her might to relax on her living room couch with Ralph.

"You're so beautiful."

"Thank you." Mary Grace made the statement more of a question, her heart feeling tight in her chest.

"I love you." Ralph picked at the curls of her chestnut hair, pulling them straight and then letting them go, watching them spring back to shape. "You're just so beautiful," he repeated.

"It's your bad eyes," Mary Grace replied, splayed on the couch, her head fitting in Ralph's lap like a well-worn T-shirt you don't have the heart to throw away.

"In case you haven't noticed, I'm wearing my glasses." Ralph let his hand spend some time massaging her shoulder.

"I see." Mary Grace stared up at the thick black frames that encircled Ralph's light brown eyes. They covered his eyebrows, making it appear as if he could have been the newest character in a series of superhero nerds. *Eyebrowless Man. Why those frames?* Mary Grace often wondered. *They look good on, say, Elvis Costello. But on Ralph or practically anybody else, they look ridiculous.* And yet, somehow, Ralph and his ridiculous glasses had worked their way into Mary Grace's heart. She reached her hand back and gave his hair a stroke. Ralph continued massaging her shoulders, moving his hand a bit left, kneading her soft skin as he shifted.

Mary Grace winced. "Ooh. Right there," she said. "You are right on my worst knot. That feels good. My kids really got to me today. I was peeling Liza Goodwin from the ceiling and prying the glue from Hazel Browne's wily clutches. You can tell these kids are more than ready for summer vacation. And their teacher, too."

"You love those kids, Mary Grace. It's not the kids that have you all tied up in knots. It's my question. Why can't you answer my question?"

Mary Grace tensed up. Ralph could feel her muscles tighten beneath her clothes. "I love you," she said.

"So say yes."

"I'm just not ready. When I say yes, I want to really know I mean yes."

"It's Jayde, isn't it? Jayde is filling your head with all those things about me that are—"

"Odd?" Mary Grace said, finishing Ralph's sentence. "Of course she is. But that's just Jayde. I take what she says with a grain of salt. We're all odd. I mean, look at me. I eat dessert before dinner."

"That's not odd," Ralph said.

"In some circles it would be considered odd. Or at least unhealthy."

"So I don't bother you?"

"I didn't say that. Of course you bother me. But what I'm trying to say is nobody is perfect."

"I bother you?"

"Oh, Ralph, I didn't mean you bother me. Can we just eat, please? I'm starving. I have a nice chocolate cake we can start with." Mary Grace jerked her body up and popped off the couch, making her way to the kitchen.

"Nice avoidance, MG," Ralph said, following her to the kitchen. "I know what you just did there."

"Good for you, Ralph. Good for you. All that therapy has paid off. You can spot avoidance."

"You don't have to get nasty." Ralph reached for a squirt of the Purell sitting safely on his girlfriend's countertop.

"You're right. I'm sorry. Here. Have this cake." Mary Grace pushed a piece of double chocolate cake in his direction while shoving a huge bite into her own mouth. "It's good," she mumbled, her mouth full.

Mary Grace took her second bite of cake when the phone rang. She checked the caller ID. It was her mother.

"I have to get this. Hello?"

"Mary Grace, it's your mother."

"I know, Mom. I know it's you."

"Why haven't you returned my calls? I've been calling you. I was starting to think you were dead. You don't return my calls, what is a mother to think? Her daughter is dead in a ditch."

"Mom, move on. I'm not dead. I just talked to you this morning."

"So now you're too busy for your mother, Mary Grace?"

"I didn't say that. I..."

"What is this world coming to when a woman's only daughter is too busy for her own mother?" Angela said, not allowing Mary Grace to finish her sentence. "A mother who, by the way, has some news."

"Oh God, Mom, I don't know which issue to address first." Mary Grace rolled her eyes for Ralph's benefit. He returned the eye roll, smiled, and ate another bite of his cake.

"Don't be fresh, young lady. Just because you're engaged doesn't mean you can be fresh."

"I'm not engaged, Mom."

"Don't tell me you didn't say yes yet?"

"Oh, so you DID hear me."

"I hear everything, Mary Grace. You're the one who needs to listen. You have a fine man who wants to marry you. I can die knowing you are taken care of. And you don't say yes? That's not the way I raised you, Mary Grace. My news will help that."

"News?"

"Yes. You know my friend Mrs. Lunt?"

"News, Mom, get to the news."

"I am. Don't rush me. I'm nearly seventy years old."

"Mom. Focus. News?" Mary Grace didn't bother to hide the aggravation in her voice.

"Don't talk to me like that. I'm your mother and I'm almost seventy-five."

"Just a second ago you weren't even seventy. Please." Mary Grace's voice was pleading. "Just get to the news."

"Right. My news," Angela said with a laugh. "Remember Mrs. Lunt's daughter? Her name is Tess. Anyway, Tess is this great, big television producer."

"So?"

"So, Tess told Mrs. Lunt and Mrs. Lunt told me her daughter is in a bit of a pickle. Ratings are down on her show."

"What show?"

"*I Do.* She is the producer of the show *I Do.*"

"*I Do?*"

"Yes. The one where America plans the couple's wedding in its entirety, from invitations to the honeymoon. It's kind of like a modern version of Jim Lang's *Dating Game.* Remember the *Dating Game*, Mary Grace?"

"Yes, I remember Jim Lang's *Dating Game*, Mom. And Bob Eubank's *Newlywed Game.* And I also remember Billy Preston was the fifth Beatle."

"Billy who was what? You make no sense, Mary Grace. No sense whatsoever. Now listen to me. I wonder what Jim Lang did when his ratings were down."

"I don't know, Mom."

"I know what Tess Lunt did. She asked her mother for help."

"Good for her, Mom. Good for Tess Lunt."

"You could learn from Tess, Mary Grace. I'm a problem solver too, you know. I can help with problems."

"I'll keep that in mind," Mary Grace said.

"So Tess told Mrs. Lunt and Mrs. Lunt told me that *I Do* is in trouble. So I told her my daughter just got engaged and she and her fiancé would be just perfect for the show."

"You didn't."

"I did. And she practically begged me to get you on the show. Begged, Mary Grace. And then she started to cry. She said if you and Ralph don't go on the show her daughter's career will be over. Over, Mary Grace! You couldn't live with that on your head, could you?"

"You're crazy, Mom. Number one, I don't believe you. Number two, I told you, I'm not even really engaged yet," Mary Grace said, once again rolling her eyes for Ralph's benefit. "And number three, even if all this were real, Ralph and I couldn't save Tess Lunt."

"Mary Grace, you're not calling your mother a liar are you? You know, that kind of talk…"

Mary Grace bit her lip and put the phone down on the kitchen table. Ralph gave her a puzzled look she brushed off with a wave of her hand. She couldn't bear to listen to her mom go on. Besides, she was confident that her mother would still be talking when she returned. She was equally as confident that her mother forgot the time she faked a sprained ankle just to get Mary Grace over for dinner, or the time she fibbed to the teachers and kept Mary Grace home from school to watch soap operas—Luke and Laura's wedding. Mary Grace walked to the refrigerator, glanced at her Virginia Woolf magnet, and smiled. She opened the door, grabbed the milk, plopped it on the table, and picked up the phone, returning to her jabbering mother.

"…I didn't raise you that way. Mary Grace? Are you there? Why aren't you saying anything?"

"Still here. Didn't mean to call you a liar, it's just that…"

"Good. It's all set then. They tape in the summer. Which is perfect for you and Ralph, my little engaged teachers. And, they pay for everything. You get the wedding of your dreams at no cost. And it's not like those other bachelor shows. You get to pick your own husband; they just throw you the wedding."

"Mom. You're not listening to me. I am not doing it."

"Just think about it, Mary Grace. This is your big chance to get everything you ever wanted. A husband. And the perfect wedding."

"Everything I wanted? I wanted, Mom? It sounds more like everything you ever wanted."

"Just stop it, Mary Grace. You're overreacting. Besides, doing this will save the life of my dearest friend's daughter."

"Dearest friend? I'm hanging up now, mother. Ralph and I are leaving for dinner."

"So you'll do it, Mary Grace? You'll go on *I Do*?"

"I didn't say that, Mom. I said I don't. Not I do."

"Good. I'll call Mrs. Lunt with the news. You won't be disappointed, Mary Grace."

"Mom!" Mary Grace said into the receiver, but the only sound she heard was that of a dead line. She stared at the phone for an eternal second before hanging it up. Her cheeks were flushed and she felt her forehead with the palm of her right hand. It was on fire.

"I think my mother just hung up on me."

"Why? What was that all about?" Ralph asked.

"My crazy mother being my crazy mother. C'mon. Let's get something to eat. And drink. I need a drink."

CHAPTER FIVE

"Dost thou think, because thou art virtuous, there shall be no more cakes and ale?" WILLIAM SHAKESPEARE

Mary Grace was finally alone in her apartment, surrounded by nothing more than her personal belongings. The vacuum of her mind kept sucking up and spitting out her thoughts, leaving them in total disarray. In this state of confusion, she felt like a bird that had forgotten to fly south for the winter, abandoned by all those dear and familiar to her. But despite her confusion and loneliness, the solitude was a curious relief.

The dinner with Ralph was over and Mary Grace refused to invite him back up to her apartment. He gave her his puppy dog eyes, pleading her to allow him into both her apartment and her. Because when Ralph finally discovered sex, he also discovered he liked it. A lot. *Gay.* Mary Grace chuckled, remembering how Jayde had been grasping at straws. *Definitely not gay.* Then Mary Grace shook her head, thinking of how she almost gave in and let Ralph up. *Maybe sex was the answer.* Instead she stood firm, knowing, more than sex, she needed time alone to sort through the events of her day, or week, or life.

Inside her apartment, Mary Grace made a beeline to the kitchen for more cake. Her eyes zoomed in on the big bottle of Purell sitting on the counter and she sighed. *Why me?* She shook her head. *The only man who wants to marry me, and what does Jayde call him? The CEO of Antiseptic Hands.* She reached for the Purell and threw it in the trash. A loud *thud* bellowed when it reached the bottom. The sound made her smile. She felt childish, like one of her students, but surprisingly good at the same time. Next she cut her third slice of cake of the day. With her cake and milk in hand, she eased her way to her favourite beanbag chair, sat down, and allowed it to envelope her.

One bite and she was little again, eating her mother's chocolate cake, sitting at the kitchen table with her father.

"Mommy got so mad at me today."

"I know, Gracie, she told me. But remember, you're such a good little girl."

"Mommy doesn't think so. But I wasn't cold. I didn't need that sweater. When *she* is cold why does she make *me* wear a sweater?"

"Think about it, Gracie. Use your good brain and think about it. Why does it matter? If a sweater makes your mother happy, just take the sweater. Is it worth such a big fight? It's only a sweater."

"Why don't you tell her that?"

"Now Gracie, don't be rude. She is your mother and she loves you. Everything she does, she does because she loves you. Don't give her a hard time."

"You mean take the sweater?"

"Yes, Gracie, take the sweater."

"Do I have to wear it?"

"If you repeat this, I will deny it, but you only have to wear it in front of your mother. Get it?"

"Not really."

"If you wear the sweater, your mother will…"

"Be happy?"

"Exactly."

"So keep Mommy happy?"

"You are a smart little girl. Now eat your cake. Your mother makes the best cake, doesn't she?"

The grown up Mary Grace ate her cake. It wasn't exactly like her mother's cake. Angela never used a mix or pre-packaged icing. Her mother's cakes were from scratch. Mary Grace, on the other hand, favoured Duncan Hines. But similar to her mother, Mary Grace made cake practically once a week. Cake was a diet staple for the Falcones. Her father loved chocolate cake, and her mother baked what she had long ago named Anytime Cake often to please him. There was so much her father did to please her mother, too. But the stuff he did was quiet. Covert, even. Like just doing what she said. "Lou, you have to flip the mattress over," her mother would say. Her father nearly always complied.

He taught Mary Grace the same approach to Angela's happiness. But he was dead now. Dead for so long that the Anytime Cake Mary Grace shared with him was no more than a distant memory. It was akin to a fantasy. A fantasy she loved to recall, but one she wasn't entirely sure existed. *Like a childhood picture. Do I remember the event from which the picture was taken, or do I only remember it because there is a picture to confirm it happened?* Sometimes Mary Grace wished there was a picture of her and her father eating cake. A picture to confirm it really happened, and wasn't purely some mythological experience. *Of course it happened. I was there for God's sake.*

Three bites into her cake and Mary Grace knew what she was going to do.

CHAPTER SIX

"Your good friend has just taken a piece of cake out of the garbage and eaten it. You will probably need this information when you check me into the Betty Crocker Clinic." MIRANDA – SEX AND THE CITY

Monday night's air was heavy and thick. Mary Grace could see waves of heat rising off the black parking lot pavement as she circled the mall, looking for a parking space. She eyed a group of women exiting the mall and continued to stare as the trio slogged through the humidity on the way to their car. She tried to catch their attention. *Where are you parked?* But the women, too engrossed in some conversation, didn't notice her. Instead, Mary Grace prayed her mother's parking lot prayer, repeating it, just like her mother, over and over again.

She remembered being a teenager, laughing at her mother and the stupid prayer, and yet, here she was, a grown woman, replicating the behaviour, her mother inside of her, part of her, always and forever. She smiled at the irony and prayed out loud, "Hail Mary, full of grace, help me find a parking space."

Mary Grace thought the thick air was a good sign, one indicating the stars were in perfect alignment, the gods were in her favour, and her decisions were correct. She interpreted the weather to be some sort of transference action, where the thickness of her head, once heavy with questions and now light with answers, was released and reloaded into the earth's atmosphere. Perhaps a mass of rationalization, but it worked for Mary Grace, who suddenly found a parking spot right in front of the mall's entrance. Her transference theory was happily confirmed and her mother's prayer worked. She blessed herself, the fingers of her right hand lightly tapping first her forehead, then her chest, then her left shoulder, and finally, her right shoulder.

At peace with her decisions, Mary Grace paced outside the mall, waiting for Jayde and Annie. No, she didn't regret her decisions. Nor did she regret leaving the phone messages last night, calling for an emergency meeting of her friends, not at MexTexas, but the mall. What she did regret was having to leave the messages. *What if they didn't get them? What if they didn't check their machines, or look at their cells? What if they didn't show up?* She glanced at her watch again: 7:45 p.m. They were fifteen minutes late. *This doesn't bode well for me.* She wiped the sweat from her forehead, then ran her fingers through her frizzy curls, which, like everything else in Mary Grace's universe, were feeling the effects of the severe humidity.

Answering the calls of her grumbling stomach, Mary Grace bent down and buried her head into her big brown bag, looking for candy, gum, or anything that could alleviate her sudden hunger. While her hand was in her bag, her cell rang. She pulled the phone out and checked the number, wondering if it was Jayde or Annie. *Mom.* She thought about not answering, but decided against it. Her mother would just call back. Again and again. *It's not worth it. Best to get the call over with now.*

"Mom?"

"Mary Grace, where are you? I tried you at home. It's Monday night. Why aren't you home?"

"Mom. Relax."

"They say we're expecting a thunderstorm, you know. All this humidity means a big storm is on the horizon. Do you have your raincoat, Mary Grace? And an umbrella? And if there is lightening, do you know not to put your umbrella up? You could get struck and die."

"Please. Stop. Which question do you want me to answer first? I'm shopping."

"Alone? At the mall. That's not safe. Why do you make your mother worry so?"

"Annie and Jayde are meeting me."

"So you're alone now?"

"Yes. But not for long. Why are you calling?"

"Why am I calling? I don't know why I'm calling. Oh that's right. Mrs. Lunt's daughter needs an answer."

"What a surprise. You actually heard me say 'no'?"

"Of course I heard you, Mary Grace. I would never put you in a position you didn't want to be in. I was just giving you some time to think about it. I know how smart you are. I knew you would make the right decision, if given some time."

"So it is my decision?" Mary Grace was still fumbling in her purse for a mint. A piece of chocolate. Anything.

"Of course it is, dear."

"And whatever I say goes?" She found a mint, popped it out of its cellophane wrapper, and flipped it in her mouth. The fresh taste was a relief.

"Stop playing games. Tess Lunt needs to know if you and Ralph will be a part of the show. They begin taping next week. I promised her an answer. And just think; if you marry Ralph I won't have to worry about you alone at a mall anymore. You don't want your mother to worry, do you?"

"Why is it that my life is always about you, Mom? And here's another question. Why have you never asked, not even once, if I love Ralph?"

"I love him, Mary Grace. What's not to love?"

"I didn't ask if *you* love him. How come you never asked me if *I* love him?"

"Oh stop it. I heard you. Listen to me. You are not a young woman anymore. This is your first and only marriage proposal. You don't want to die alone, do you? I want what's best for you, but face it, the men aren't racing cars to the finish line to see who gets to marry you first."

Mary Grace gasped, nearly choking on her mint. She gagged, then coughed, almost grateful for the incident because at least choking prevented her from crying, the pain of her mother's words hurting her heart. Like a shot from a stun gun, Mary Grace was left motionless. *She doesn't really mean it*, Mary Grace reminded herself. *Just do what Angela says and everyone's happy, right, Dad?* Mary Grace glanced up toward heaven, where she was certain Lou had earned a spot. Thinking of Lou helped Mary Grace regain her composure. It was better than losing it.

"What are you really trying to say, Mom?"

"What I'm saying is sometimes you take what you can get. And just be happy with it."

"This isn't some sweater, Mom. This is a life-altering decision."

"Oh, Gracie, always so dramatic."

"Me? Me? You should change your name to kettle. Or pot. Or I don't know. You have me so flustered I don't even know what I'm talking about anymore. I can't believe I'm even asking this, but do you swear you're not setting me up? Tess Lunt wants me and Ralph?"

"On your father's grave. God rest his soul," Angela answered, blessing herself.

"I'm probably going to regret this but, yes. I'll do the show. And yes, I'm marrying Ralph. Are you happy? I'm hanging up now, Mother."

"Oh Gracie, I am so happy. And you won't be sorry. I promise. I'll call Mrs. Lunt right now. And if those friends of yours don't show up soon, please go home. I can't bear to think of you alone at the mall with a thunderstorm on its way. So dangerous, Mary Grace. What were you thinking?"

Mary Grace melted into the sidewalk in front of the mall. Was it the heat? Was it her mother? Or was it the toxic combination of the two? It didn't matter because the results were the same and Mary Grace looked ridiculous. She knew it, but she didn't care. She hugged her knees to her chest and buried her head into her body, contorting herself into what could only be described as some sort of yoga position. *Inward Dog. Let everyone think I'm nuts. I just don't care. Let me eat cake.* She allowed herself to smile at her old, stale Marie Antoinette joke, wondering how long she would allow herself to remain a boil on the sidewalk of the mall.

"Oh my God! Are you okay? What's the matter?" Annie rushed up to the freak show she immediately recognized as her friend, she and Jayde having arrived at the mall only minutes earlier.

"Gracie? What the hell is going on?" Jayde was jogging right behind Annie.

"Be soft, Jayde. Try to be a bit soft. Something is wrong," Annie scolded Jayde, albeit breathlessly.

"Hi," Mary Grace said, peeking her head from out of her knees, raising her eyebrows nearly to her hairline, while allowing herself the tiniest of smiles.

"Hi?" Annie asked. "Hi?" she repeated, even louder. "You have us scared to death and all you can come up with is hi? What's wrong with you?" Annie was now nearly shouting.

"You told me to be soft?" Jayde shot Annie a glare before taking Mary Grace by the arm and lifting her off the ground, leading her to the bench in front of the mall. "What's up, buttercup?" Jayde gently sat Mary Grace down on the bench and took the seat right next to her, motioning for Annie to get on the other side.

"Why are you guys so late?" Mary Grace said, without looking up. "My mother called. If you weren't late, I wouldn't have talked to her. And you wouldn't have found me in that yoga-in-front-of-the-mall position."

"And you answered the phone because?" Jayde asked.

"Because if I didn't she would just call and call and call and…"

"Call," Jayde interrupted. "We get the picture. We've been getting the picture for a long time now."

"And the best thing about best friends is, when everything goes wrong, you can just blame it on us." Annie patted Mary Grace's knee using a gentle, maternal touch while firing Jayde a small, apologetic look for the earlier breech of calm.

"And we were late because—" Jayde nodded at Annie, both accepting her apology and silently telling her to reveal the surprise.

"Ta da." From a shopping bag, Annie pulled out a bakery box, complete with the red string bow. "In this box is the main staple of any Mary Grace emergency meeting." Annie tugged on the bow, opening the box and revealing a chocolate frosted cake.

"Cake? For me?" Mary Grace's eyes lit up. "How did you know?"

"We know," Jayde said, digging her nail into the plastic that covered the cake plates and ripping the package open. She then gave each girl a plate and a plastic fork she pulled from her purse.

Annie cut the cake and passed hunks to Mary Grace and Jayde, giving herself a smaller slice. There was silence as the women savoured their first two bites. Finally, Mary Grace spoke.

"I'm marrying Ralph."

"Oh my God! Congratulations!" Annie couldn't contain her excitement. "I am so happy for you."

"Why?" Jayde made that tiny, three-letter word sound like the longest word in the dictionary.

"Jayde Anderson, that's no way to respond," Annie said.

"You respond your way and I'll respond mine. Why did you say yes?" Jayde looked directly at Mary Grace, whose head was hung low.

"It's complicated." Mary Grace refused to meet Jayde's stare and instead concentrated on another bite of cake.

"So is life," Jayde said.

"He loves me so much. He really does," Mary Grace mumbled, her mouth full.

"I know," Annie agreed. "You're lucky."

"But that isn't the question," Jayde felt obliged to remind her friends. "The real question is, do you love him?"

"My mother is crazy about him." Mary Grace lifted her head the tiniest bit.

"Your mother is just plain crazy," Jayde said. "Do you love him?"

"I don't know. I guess I just don't know. I mean, what is love? I love you guys. If I were a lesbian, I'd marry either of you. Or both of you. A lesbian bigamist. Now there's a television show."

"If you're not sure, Gracie…" Jayde started to say before being interrupted.

"Then why say yes?" Mary Grace read her friend's mind. "I'll tell you why. I don't want to be alone. He is so good to me. And until Ralph came along, no man had ever paid any attention to me. Notwithstanding a few one-night-stands, with no return phone calls, a couple of bad dates, with no return phone calls, and a handful of phone numbers given on request, with no return phone calls, my dating life has been dry."

"Honey, those losers are no reflection on you. You're the winner. The prize. They're the losers. You were just meeting the wrong men." Annie tossed her cake in the trashcan next to the bench, and then reached for Mary Grace's hand.

"Wearing the rock will cure your dating woes." Jayde stretched her hand in front of her face, staring at her naked ring finger.

"Just stop it, Jayde," Annie said.

"I'm serious. I once did this experiment where I bought this huge CZ off QVC and wore it out every night. And let me tell you, I got more dates with the ring than without. Men love a woman who is already taken. It's that no commitment thing."

"Jayde, can you just, for once, stop giving advice on dating. We're working with Mary Grace now. We can work on you next."

Jayde threw her head back and laughed. "I'm just saying, Mary Grace, if you are looking for phone numbers, the ring begets the ring. But if you are looking to spend the rest of your life with someone, you've got…"

"Ralph," Mary Grace interrupted Jayde, blurting the name out like it was something she couldn't forget on her grocery list. *Apples. Cereal. Ralph.*

"Ralph, the Virgin," Jayde added.

"He's not a virgin anymore," Annie felt obliged to remind Jayde. "And their sex life is good."

"You can't have good sex with a man named Ralph Ichy. It's just so, well, icky." Jayde made a face like she had just taken a huge whiff of curdled, sour milk.

"That's ridiculous, Jayde. Good sex has nothing to do with a person's name. And wipe that look off your face. Who are you? One of Mary Grace's third graders?"

"What do you know about good sex?" Jayde quipped. "You've been married for the last decade."

"Are you implying single sex is better than married sex?"

"I'm not implying. I'm saying."

"You are so wrong. You pretend to be such a know-it-all, but in this case not only are you wrong, but you're not even eligible to answer the question. I am the only one married here, so I am the only one who can report on married sex. And I report, even after two kids, it is fantastic. At least when we have time to do it." Annie watched as Jayde took one deep breath, but before Jayde had the opportunity to speak, Annie continued. "And sex with a married man doesn't count as married sex."

"Oh." Once again, Jayde stared at her naked ring finger.

"Guys," Mary Grace said. "This is not about sex. It's about…"

"Love," Annie said. "It's about love. Ralph loves you. You say he loves you, right, Mary Grace?"

"Yes."

"I rest my case. Congratulations. You're a lucky woman. I call Maid of Honour." Annie shot her right arm up in the air.

"You can't call that," Jayde said. "If Mary Grace is actually marrying the CEO of Antiseptic Hands, she gets to pick her Maid of Honour. And she's known me longer."

"Actually, I don't get to pick." Mary Grace's voice was nothing more than a whisper.

"What the hell are you talking about?" Jayde demanded. "Of course you get to pick."

"I agreed to something bad." Mary Grace put her cake aside and buried her face in her hands.

"Bad?" Annie said.

"Very bad. My mother's best friend's daughter is the producer of *I Do*."

"That stupid wedding reality show?" Jayde said.

"Yep, that one. I told my mother to tell her friend's daughter Ralph and I would go on the show."

"Live television? That's so exciting," Annie said. "I've always wanted to go on one of those shows."

"Have you lost your mind, Gracie? Cut this girl another piece of cake," Jayde said.

"No more cake," Mary Grace replied. "I called this meeting to go shopping. I need the right clothes for my first television appearance."

"And Ralph agreed to this?" Jayde inquired.

"Not really," Mary Grace said.

"What do you mean, 'not really'?" Jayde asked.

"He doesn't know yet. In fact, he doesn't even know I'm saying yes to his proposal. I thought I'd make it all one big surprise. I'm telling him tomorrow morning."

"Forget the cake for you. I need another piece." Jayde sliced herself an additional sliver. "You *are* losing your mind."

"She's not the one wearing an engagement ring to get dates, Jayde," Annie reminded her cynical friend.

"You didn't find me in a ball in front of the mall." Jayde gave a sideways scowl to Annie. "This is not good, Gracie. Not good."

"I know," Mary Grace whispered. "I'm in pretty deep. And I don't know how to dig out."

"Okay, people. Everyone just needs to take a step back." Annie used her old teacher's voice in an attempt to grab hold of the situation. "This is all good. You're getting married, Mary Grace. You're going to be on television. You've got us. You're in deep, all right. Deep into everything that's good."

"Do you really think so?" Mary Grace's eyes were wide with wonder.

"I don't just think so, I know so," Annie said. "Ralph loves you. You love Ralph. And you're getting married."

"For the record, I'm not happy about any of this," Jayde said. "I don't like Ralph, and committing to him on national television sounds absurd. But if you're going to be stubborn about it, you are going to need the right clothes."

"So let's shop," Annie said.

"Let's shop," Jayde agreed.

Mary Grace just nodded while Jayde tossed both of their remaining slices of cake into the trash and boxed up the leftovers, returning them to the shopping bag. The three women stood up, interlocked arms, and marched their way into the mall. As they did, a huge shudder of thunder echoed through the sky. Mary Grace, who was already feeling skittish, jumped at the sound. *My mother was right. A storm is coming.*

CHAPTER SEVEN

"All the world is birthday cake, so take a piece, but not too much." GEORGE HARRISON

When the alarm sounded off at four thirty Tuesday morning, Mary Grace was startled awake. She thought she had been in the middle of some sort of semi-erotic dream but couldn't, for the life of her, remember the details. The man was faceless. *Was it Ralph? Impossible.* The faceless man of her dream had a model's body, chiselled with six-pack abs and the guns to match. Ralph, despite being in excellent cardio shape, favoured the skinny, less chiselled side. But she reminded herself this was a dream and her lover had no face, so he could have been Ralph. She wanted him to be Ralph, because if he wasn't Ralph, who was he? And what would that say about her?

"Just put your feet on the floor and get going," she said out loud, tired of thinking about her senseless dream. "No thinking, just doing," she continued, knowing herself all too well. If she allowed herself even one more minute of sleep, one minute to close her eyes and try to reenter her dream, the moment would be lost and the next time she opened her eyes it would be 7:10—too late for the gym. She needed to talk to Ralph and she needed a hard workout.

Feet on the floor, Mary Grace made her way to her dresser where she pulled out grey nylon shorts, a white T-shirt, and a sports bra. As she stepped into the shorts, they felt cool against her hot skin. It was almost invigorating for this ungodly hour, and she could use all the stimulation she could get. And positive thinking, too. *I am going to the gym. I am talking to Ralph. I am going to be happy.* She exited her bedroom, grabbed her purse and keys, and trotted down her apartment steps.

As she made her way to the car, Mary Grace remembered why she joined her gym in the first place. It was some two or three years ago. Jayde, honest to a fault, had told her she was putting on weight.

"You're eating too much cake, Mary Grace. And you're not a teenager anymore. Your body can't burn calories the way it used to," Jayde said. "Even mine can't," she added, giving herself the once over, allowing a little smile to cross her lips, pleased with what she saw.

"Telling me not to eat cake is like telling me not to breathe." Mary Grace remembered being dramatic, but cake *was* her life force. "You might as well kill me."

"I'm not telling you not to eat cake. I'm telling you, you need to work out."

"Work out?"

"Um, exercise. Burn the fat. Treadmills. Stairmasters. Ellipticals. Weights. You need to join my gym."

And so, Mary Grace did. It wasn't easy at first, and it took a bit more persuading from Jayde, but Mary Grace joined the local Y and became a regular exerciser.

Mary Grace and Jayde started working out together in the evenings, but Mary Grace discovered nights weren't the best time for her. Evening workouts left her too revved up and unable to sleep. As hard as it was to drag herself out of bed, she preferred a morning workout, and getting the whole thing over before the day began. And so it happened that Jayde and Mary Grace never saw each other at the gym, despite both being "regulars."

She didn't have Jayde in the mornings, but she did have a new workout partner. Ralph. She met Ralph not long after beginning her new routine. He held the door for her one early morning and she smiled and said thank you. They ran on side-by-side treadmills, and through deep breaths and sweaty armpits, blurted out a couple of simple questions and answers. Names. Jobs.

Those sorts of things. Mary Grace worked hard to coincidentally bump into Ralph again, arriving at the exact same time on the exact same day. There was something about him—she couldn't put her finger on it—that made her want to see him again. And, as Ralph confided early into their relationship, he tried hard to force the coincidence, too. Things progressed slowly, until finally, Ralph asked if she would like to meet him for a cup of coffee after work one day. Their first date.

When Mary Grace related the "how they met" story to other people, she liked to tell them she met Ralph in the wee hours of the morning, neglecting the part about the health club. It sounded more adventurous. Like they were club-hopping celebrities, whose fates were sealed as the sun was rising after a night of parties and paparazzi. When truly, they met at the gym. And three years later, they still met at the gym. Monday through Friday.

Mary Grace arrived extra early this Tuesday morning, needing an hour to herself. She would spend it in the weight room, doing sit-ups on the stability ball, and working her arms with the ten-pounders. She needed the time to really think and get her endorphins pumping before Ralph came. She needed time to prepare herself, psyche herself up even, to tell Ralph of her decisions.

As Mary Grace stood facing the mirror, ten-pound weights in hand, she noticed the man to her left. He was wearing a black singlet and tight white shorts that exposed his muscular thighs. Mary Grace took in a quick gasp of air. *Was he the faceless man in my dream? It was his body, all right, all cut and buff. But I didn't even know I knew him. Maybe he's buried somewhere in my subconscious.* She stared at him, and never once did he meet her gaze. He just concentrated on his workout, and his repetitions on the Life-Flex machine were fast and heavy. He was in excellent condition.

Her eyes wandered to a woman on her right. *Probably early forties.* She was wearing a huge engagement ring and an additional diamond band. She was chubby, but okay looking. Mary Grace wondered about these folks, speculating if they were happy. Was the woman married? Did she have kids? A dog? A job? Did buff man have a girlfriend? A wife? Were they happy?

Am I happy? She didn't know anymore. She could barely remember what the word meant.

Before Ralph asked her to marry him, she would have answered yes to that question. Yes, she was happy. But since the proposal, her life had become all-consumed by it, twenty-four seven. She could barely think of anything else. That sort of one-track thinking was bound to get on anyone's nerves.

Am I happy? she wondered again. *What is happy?* Between bicep curls she stared at herself in the mirror and thought about the word. *Happy. Happiness. Happiful. Okay, happiful is not a real word.*

Am I happy? she wondered once again. *I don't know. My mother is. No, my mother is more than happy. She is on cloud nine. Ralph's proposal didn't make me content. It didn't make me glad. It didn't make me cheerful or delighted or feel like I'm up there lounging on cloud nine. It just made me confused. But it put my mother on cloud nine.*

Now, working her triceps, Mary Grace thought harder. Even though Ralph's proposal didn't make her happy, their relationship made her content; perhaps even glad. *Oh, why did the idiot have to go and ruin everything by proposing?*

And why did I agree to go on that stupid show I Do? *What was I thinking? Oh, the lengths I go to, just to keep my mother happy. Daddy, do you see me down here? I'm still trying to keep Mom happy.*

Now, well into sit-ups on the stability ball, Mary Grace was startled by Ralph's arrival.

"You're here early. I would have met you if you told me."

"Oh, hi," she said between breaths. "I know. But I didn't do it on purpose," she lied. "I couldn't sleep. Wait a minute. Forty-seven, forty-eight, forty-nine, fifty," she counted, before finishing her sit-ups, and then standing up to give Ralph a quick kiss on the cheek.

"Ready for the treadmill?" he asked.

"Not really," she said, surprising herself even as the words came out of her mouth. "Can we go sit in your car? We need to talk," she said.

"Oh?" Ralph took a step back. "Okay," he blurted, typically amenable to her suggestions.

They opened the car windows, but even so, the June heat was suffocating. There wouldn't be enough air in the car for any sort of lengthy conversation.

"I will." Mary Grace pushed the words out before taking a deep breath of stale air.

"What?" Ralph cocked his head, trying to make sense of his girlfriend's odd morning behaviour.

"Let's try this again." Mary Grace detected Ralph's confusion and tried to make herself as clear as possible. "Ask me to marry you. Please. The way you did the first time."

"You're kidding?"

"No joke. Ask me. Please?"

Ralph just stared into her begging eyes, trying to gauge her mood and figure out what had changed. The silence was as thick as the air, until finally, he spoke.

"Mary Grace Falcone, you make me so happy. My hope is I do the same for you. I have never felt as secure, safe, and happy as I do when I am with you. I know I want to spend the rest of my life with you by my side. Will you do me the honour of becoming my wife? My partner in life? Mary Grace, will you marry me?"

"I will." Tears filled her eyes. And finally, she was certain they were tears of happiful happiness. Mary Grace stretched over the console and threw her arms around Ralph. His arms returned the hug. But he was certain he felt her tense up. He pushed her away and looked his fiancée in the eyes.

"Are you certain, Mary Grace?"

He paused, desperately wanting the answer to be yes.

She bit her lower lip while nodding her head yes. "Positive," she said, unable to convince either Ralph or herself.

"What's wrong? I know you, MG; something is wrong."

Mary Grace wiped her forehead. Was the car's heat getting to her? Or was it the next piece of news she had to tell Ralph?

"Are you pregnant?"

"No. No." She was unable to look Ralph in the eye, her head bent down in prayer that this moment would pass. She didn't want to. Or mean to. But somehow she channelled her mother, and a new prayer popped into her head. *Hail Mary, full of grace, help speed up, this moment's pace.*

Ralph reached his hand to Mary Grace's chin, tilted her head slightly up, and looked directly into her eyes. "Listen, I would have been thrilled if you were pregnant. You know, my guys can swim sort of thing," he said, trying to lighten the heavy mood. "Try me, Mary Grace. Together we can handle anything. Just blurt it out."

"I told my mother we would go on the show *I Do.*"

"What?" Ralph snorted.

"The reality show, *I Do.*"

"Back up," he said. "What are you talking about?"

"*I Do,*" Mary Grace repeated with a sense of urgency, hoping Ralph would catch up without her having to explain a thing.

"The one where America plans the wedding?" Ralph asked.

"Yes," she whispered.

"And…"

"And my mother's friend's daughter is the show's producer. And I promised her something. Actually, Ralph, I promised her us."

"Us?"

"Yes. My mother says she really needs us."

"For what?"

"For the ratings on her show. She needs us to boost ratings."

"We'll boost ratings?" Ralph gave himself a onceover.

Mary Grace looked at him with eyes that said, "I'm telling the truth."

"Mary Grace, that's just about the funniest thing I've ever heard." Ralph roared with laughter. "With that look on your face I thought you were about to tell me you had two weeks left to live. This? This is funny."

"It is?" she asked.

"Compared to death. I know the difference."

"I know you do." Mary Grace was still unable to let her eyes meet his.

"Can't you tell your mother no?"

"Do you want to rethink that question?"

"You're right. I take it back. Nobody tells your mother no."

"Even when I tell her no, things turn into yes."

"But do you want to do the show?" Ralph asked, surprised they were even discussing its possibility.

"Not really. Although Annie thinks it will be fun."

"Annie knows?" Ralph tensed up, surprised he wasn't the first to hear the news.

"And Jayde, too. I'm sorry. I told them."

Ralph paused, taking a rational moment to absorb the idea of Jayde and Annie hearing such vital information before him.

"Well—"

"It's okay," Ralph interrupted, raising his hand and making a stop motion. "They're like sisters to you. Go on."

Mary Grace sighed, Ralph's approval offering a sense of relief she hadn't expected to feel.

"Jayde thinks it's ridiculous."

"Of course she does." Ralph nodded. "Anything that's not about Jayde is ridiculous. What do you think?"

"It could be fun?" Mary Grace said, working hard to convince herself. "Besides, if we do the show, everything is free. Our wedding. Flowers. Dress. Food. *Everything.* And our honeymoon. All free."

Ralph noticed an excitement boiling up in Mary Grace as she talked.

"Then let's do it," he said. "It'll be a great story for our kids. Our fifteen minutes of fame."

"What will your mother say?" Mary Grace asked.

"My mother?" Ralph was pleased Mary Grace was concerned about her. "She'll be thrilled her little boy is on television. She'll love it. Each and every time I tell her, she'll love it."

Mary Grace smiled.

"C'mon. If we're going to be on television we are going to have to hit the treadmill. Let's go, MG."

"Ralph?" she said, not ready for the moment to end.

He raised his eyebrows and looked directly at Mary Grace, his heart filled with love, commitment, and gratitude.

She whispered three words she thought she was certain she meant.

"I love you."

CHAPTER EIGHT

"You know you are getting old when the candles cost more than the cake." BOB HOPE

Ralph sat at his desk in his classroom at Minot High School, his leg pulsing up and down, almost of its own volition, as he tried to read through his students' Symbol Analyses of *The Catcher in the Rye*. It was nearly four in the afternoon and the buzz in the cavernous, echoing hallways had long since died down. There were still kids in school, but they were mainly in the gymnasium, in the locker rooms, or on the fields. His area of the building was fairly quiet. Peaceful, even. That is, it would have been if he were at peace with himself. When he glanced outside he could see the varsity baseball team practising. He was never any good at baseball, or sports in general, preferring instead to spend his time reading. He noticed Grant Dwyer up at bat; at least he thought it was Grant—it was hard to tell from this far away. *What a coincidence.* Ralph shrugged as he stared at the analysis Grant had written. He tried to read the words Grant had laboriously put to paper, but Ralph was having difficulty concentrating. "The symbol I found most interesting in this book was Holden's wish to be the catcher in the rye." Ralph nodded his head, figuring if he tried to appear interested, he could actually trick himself into becoming interested. It didn't work. His leg continued to pulse, and after re-reading Grant's first sentence some twenty times, he gave up.

Ralph let his mind wander through Salinger's book, a book he had read every summer since he was sixteen. *The Museum of Natural History.*

The Lunt Theater. Holden's red hunting hat. Offensive words written in subways. He, like Grant, was quite interested in *The Catcher in the Rye.* Holden's dream job was to protect children playing in a field of rye. Protect them from the fate of falling off a cliff. But who and what was Holden really protecting? *The children? Their innocence? Himself?* Ralph could discuss the intricate themes and symbols of this book forever.

In certain ways, where Mary Grace was concerned, he equated himself with Holden Caufield. Ralph, plagued by a youthful innocence that was snapped from his grasp at too tender an age, and little previous knowledge of things sexual, was the catcher in the rye, trying to save Mary Grace from falling off the cliff. Save her from her fear of being alone for the rest of her life. He loved her; that was certain. But did he love her enough for the both of them? And can one person's deep, genuine love sustain a two-person relationship? Mary Grace had finally said yes to his proposal, but did she mean it, or was she just saving herself from falling off the cliff of loneliness? Or, perhaps he was saving himself from falling off that exact same cliff. Can a catcher in the rye save himself?

Ralph tugged at the collar of his yellow plaid, short sleeved, button down shirt. He was starting to perspire, and could feel the beads of sweat forming on the back of his neck and trickling down his shirt. He wiped his forehead and scratched his shoulders before letting out a huge sigh. His leg was still pulsing.

His mind continued to roam. The room was hot, but despite being a factor contributing to his profuse sweating, it wasn't the genuine cause of his nervousness. He had agreed to go on national television, but that wasn't it either. *Is it because Mary Grace finally agreed to marry me? Possibly.* Ralph didn't believe a one-sided love was the way to begin a marriage, but he loved Mary Grace with all his heart and her saying yes was the greatest joy he had ever known. But really, deep down, Ralph knew the cause of his current anxiety. *Jayde.*

Jayde had called him on his cell early that morning, and requested time alone with him after school. More than requested—she demanded.

"I'll be at your school at four o'clock today," she said. "We need to talk." She spoke for another minute, mentioning she was concerned and didn't want Mary Grace to know about their meeting. Ralph was stunned, and when he tried to respond, she shut him down. "No excuses. Just be there." She hung up the phone, without even allowing the possibility of a goodbye.

Ralph was uneasy with both Jayde's abruptness and request. Their morning conversation had left him agitated and unable to concentrate the whole day. And now he was a sweaty, wet mess.

He couldn't shower so he did the next best thing. He squirted a big blob of Purell in his hands from the bottle that sat on his desk. He rubbed his palms together and then drew them to his face, covering his nose. He took a deep breath, allowing the scent to fill his lungs. The clean, antiseptic aroma was soothing. He looked down and noticed his leg had stopped pulsing. He let all his air out. For one brief moment he felt calm. Then, the knock. The noise, and knowing who was behind the door, caused Ralph to jump from his seat.

"Come in," Ralph said as he trotted over to the door to greet Jayde. "Come on in." He tried to sound calm but failed miserably. He noticed the squeak in his own voice.

"I haven't been in a high school in practically forever," Jayde said with a little smile that Ralph took as a nice icebreaker. She was wearing a tight white tank top with spaghetti straps, dark skinny jeans, and flip flops. Her long hair hung straight down her back, and Ralph could only imagine the looks she had received from the teenage boys, and the high it had given her.

"God, all high schools must be the same." Jayde flipped her hair to one side. "This room is the exact replica of my high school classrooms. The boys haven't changed, either. I think I saw Mike Nuggio, captain of our football team, in the hallway."

"It's all pretty much the same, I guess."

"Hey, *Catcher in the Rye*." Jayde picked the book up off Ralph's desk, thumbing through the pages. "I was supposed to read this book in what? Tenth grade? I never got around to it. Any good?"

"Some people think so," Ralph said. "I'm one of them. I must have read it at least a dozen times."

"You're kidding. You've read the same book more than once?"

"You haven't?"

"No. First time round most books bore me. After that I'd need to poke needles in my eyes to stay awake." Jayde chuckled, but when she glanced up at Ralph, she noticed the look of horror in his English-teaching eyes. Since the conversation was going nowhere, she needed to turn it around. Fast.

"Um, do you like teaching teenagers?" She tried to sound genuinely interested. "I remember being so gross and awful at that age."

"Actually, I do," Ralph said. But what he thought was, *Jayde Anderson, you're still gross and awful.* "It's a good age. It's a challenge to motivate them, though." Ralph pulled a student's chair across from his desk and motioned for Jayde to sit down.

"Yeah." Jayde played with a strand of her hair, then took one more look around the room before sitting down. Ralph didn't sit on his desk, so much as lean on it, stretching his legs out before him and trying, casually, to air out his sweaty underarms.

"You have a lot on your mind, Jayde," he said with as much ease as he could. "Why don't you just dive right in?"

"Thanks. Thanks for letting me talk to you."

Ralph tilted his head in confusion, wondering what part of their earlier phone conversation he had missed. As he was about to speak, once again, Jayde cut him off.

"I didn't give you much choice, did I?" She raised her questioning eyebrows.

Ralph shook his head and mouthed the word "no."

"Well then, thanks for trying to make this easy," Jayde said. "I want it to be easy, but I'm afraid it is going to be hard. It's just I'm so worried about Mary Grace. You know she's like a sister to me. I've known her since we were six. I saved her the first day I found her on the playground."

"I've heard. Apparently you're still trying to save her."

"Not save so much as, just, I don't know. I just don't want her making any wrong decisions."

"Wrong?" Ralph repeated, his eyes as big as Frisbees.

"All right. This isn't going well."

"Dive in. Like I told you." Ralph could feel more sweat trickle down his back.

"Are you gay?" Jayde whispered, leaning in to Ralph. She never believed either Annie or Mary Grace when it came to the subject of Ralph's sexuality, and was entirely aware of the inappropriateness of discussing all this at Minot High School.

"What the hell are you talking about?" Ralph was visibly flustered and unable to control his leg from pulsing again.

"It doesn't matter, you know. It's okay to be gay."

"The Rainbow Coalition's new banner: *It's Okay to be Gay.* There'll be a little registered trademark at the bottom. Courtesy of Jayde Anderson."

"You don't have to get nasty."

Ralph just shook his head. "I just asked Mary Grace to marry me. I'm not gay."

"Are you sure you just haven't come out yet? Like you're still trying to figure it out? Let me see your underwear."

"No. You cannot see my underwear. And what does that have to do with anything, anyway?"

Jayde shrugged her shoulders and paused before blurting out the next words.

"Why were you a virgin when Gracie met you?"

"I should have guessed that was coming next. I really don't have to go through this with you, do I?"

"No, you don't. But then I don't have to be happy about this marriage thing, do I?"

"What are you saying? You'll convince MG it's the wrong decision?"

Jayde let out a long, deep breath of air, almost as if she were exhaling smoke from a cigarette.

"Something like that."

"You're not just jaded, Jayde. You're evil. I didn't see that in you."

"Not evil. Just concerned."

"Okay, so I'll say this one time. And never again. I always thought a relationship should be more than just physical stuff. I wanted to connect with a girl. I wanted to be able to talk to her. So I never wanted to just get laid and get it over with. I thought it should be more important than that. But I was young and it never happened that way. And then time sort of went by and it still never happened. And then more time went by and by the time I was ready to concede and just allow it to be sex for sex, it was too late," Ralph said, stopping to take a deep breath. He was exhausted and uncertain he could continue.

"Go on." Jayde's voice was a whisper as she listened with great interest.

"I became too self-conscious," Ralph said, taking one more deep breath. "I never wanted to tell anyone it was the first time, and if I didn't tell the girl I thought for sure she would know and think I was a freak. So it never happened. More time went by. The next thing I know, I'm a grown man who never had sex. And then? I meet Mary Grace. What I wanted to happen when I was eighteen, instead happened when I was thirty-two. It finally happened."

Jayde raised her eyebrows, begging Ralph to continue.

"I fell in love," he said, a huge smile spreading across his face. "I connected with MG. It was more than just physical. It was physical and passionate and we didn't have sex, we made love. It was amazing. And here's the crazy thing. I'm glad it happened this way. I wouldn't change a thing because I wouldn't be where I am now."

"Wow."

"Wow good or wow bad?"

"Just wow. I didn't think guys like you existed." Jayde shook her head to get ahold of herself. She couldn't lose her grip now. She had more questions to ask.

"So why do you still live with your mother?"

"It's a long story."

"I have time." Jayde glanced at the watch on her wrist.

I'm doing this for Mary Grace, Ralph told himself before beginning. With her picture in his head, he plodded on. "When my mother was widowed I didn't like the thought of her living alone. She had already been through so much."

"Like?" Jayde inquired, her curiosity heightened.

"I don't know." Ralph paused to wipe the sweat off his forehead, buying more time as he decided just how much he would, or could, tell Jayde. He clearly understood that Mary Grace, who shared everything with Jayde, hadn't indulged her best friend in his personal history. A tiny smile formed on Ralph's face.

"My mother has had a tough life, and in certain slight and unintentional ways, she took it out on me. But here's the deal. I didn't want to leave her alone. Without my father, I mean. In that big house. It made me sad. So I decided to stay with her. It wasn't going to be forever, just until I felt she had a routine down, and felt at ease in it. Only then would I be comfortable leaving her. Well, about the time I got comfortable, she showed signs of the onset of Alzheimer's. Now, I won't leave her alone. She deserves better than that."

"And what about…"

"Listen, Jayde. Before we keep going on with this, let me just say, I am not perfect. Far from it. I've got a clean thing. I'm somewhat of a germaphobe, I guess." Ralph nodded his head at the bottle of Purell that sat on his desk.

"But I've got my reasons. And anyway, so is Howie Mandel, and it never held him back. I err on the side of sensitive, but it doesn't make me a bad person. Just sensitive. But I am better with Mary Grace. A better person. Please don't come between us. Don't split us up. I need her and I'm pretty sure she needs me, too."

"Who else could handle her mother?" Jayde laughed.

"Not many," Ralph agreed. "At least not the people I know."

"Is her mother the reason you're doing that stupid show?"

"MG is doing it for her mother. I'm doing it for MG. So basically, yes. Her mother is the driving force behind *I Do*."

"That's impressive." Jayde pretended to brush some non-existent lint off her tanned shoulder.

"Enough already. I'm tired of Twenty Questions. Do I get Jayde's Seal of Approval?"

"For now. But don't fuck up."

"I'll keep that in mind," he said with a half laugh, half snort.

Ralph walked Jayde to the door and watched as she strutted down the high school halls. He cringed when he saw two puberty-struck boys gawk as Jayde passed. *It must have been tough to have Jayde as a best friend. Tough and safe all at the same time.* He wondered how Mary Grace dealt with it as he pulled his sweaty shirt away from his body and blew some air down the neck hole to help cool off.

CHAPTER NINE

"The most dangerous food is wedding cake." JAMES THURBER

Jayde walked through the high school parking lot toward her car. She couldn't stop thinking about her meeting with Ralph, replaying their conversation in her head. *He's not gay. Mary Grace and Annie said it. Ralph confirmed it. All right. So he's straight. But he's spineless. Why did he let me grill him like that? A real man would have cut me off before I started.* She opened the door to her BMW and sat down. The black leather seats were so hot they seared the underside of her thighs, right through her jeans. She jumped up and winced, more from surprise than pain. She rocked herself from side to side until her thighs acclimated to the temperature. When they did, her gaze became transfixed on the rolling, brick building and circular driveway that filled up her windshield. She noticed the flagpole on the little patch of green. It was front and centre. *Just like my old school.*

Where the hell was Ralph when I went to high school? Jayde wondered in somewhat of an angry trance. *Did he actually say he wanted sex to be meaningful?* The fifteen-year-old boys she had encountered didn't even know what the word "meaningful" meant. Come to think of it, most of the thirty-year-olds didn't, either. And the fifty-year-olds? *That's a laugh.*

She continued to stare at the school, and noticed the Mike Nuggio look-alike exit the building. He was the spitting image of her first boyfriend, the football captain. And the way he walked, with a side-to-side swagger, aped Mike as well. For a brief moment, Jayde wondered if this teenager could possibly be Mike's son. "Nah," she said out loud. "Impossible," she laughed. Mike would have had to have him at, like, fifteen, she thought. Then she thought again. It was *totally* possible. She was having sex with Mike at fifteen. *He's not Mike's kid*, she convinced herself, and yet she couldn't get her mind off him.

When she lost her virginity to Mike, he was completely and totally crazy about her, professing his unwavering devotion and stringing words together into sentences that left Jayde confused about both love and life. "Sex will deepen our relationship," was perhaps his favourite go-to phrase.

Mary Grace had endured hours and hours of endless conversations with Jayde regarding the topic of "doing it." *Will it deepen what we already have?* Jayde wondered. *What if I get pregnant? What if I suck? What if he wants me to suck? What if he thinks my naked body is gross. My boobs are too small. My thighs are too big. I'm too scared. I don't want to look like I've never done it before.*

With no boyfriends of her own to talk about, Mary Grace just listened to Jayde go on and on. It never occurred to Jayde that Mary Grace would want to discuss something else; at least, Mary Grace never indicated otherwise.

When Jayde and Mike finally "did it," in his twin bed, in his parents' house, while his folks were out at a movie, she felt nothing. No pleasure. No pain. No remorse. Nothing. Mike, on the other hand, went crazy; moaning and screaming and having, what sounded to Jayde, like the most sensational experience of his life. Honestly, Jayde didn't understand it. But after doing it once, sex was *all* Mike was interested in. Jayde, who was not as keen on having sex, became very intrigued by the power sex had over men. She broke it off with Mike soon after, and for the next thirteen years was never without at least one boyfriend, and sometimes two, dangling her sexuality before men like the carrot to the bunny.

"You are so lucky," Mary Grace would say. "The boys are all crazy about you." Now, Jayde couldn't remember the names of at least half her boyfriends. *Real lucky.* She fumbled in her purse for a cigarette, put it between her lips, and lit it up with the matches she found in her console. She took a long drag and blew the smoke out her window. *What's wrong with me?* When she looked up, she didn't see Mike Nuggio's look-alike anymore; the speck of his varsity jacket had finally disappeared.

Ralph, whom she pictured sitting in that high school classroom, reading through boring papers written about a boring book, wearing a fashion don't of a shirt sticking to his sweaty body, was one of the good ones. He answered all her Twenty Questions and passed her test. Jayde was okay with Mary Grace marrying him. If she wanted to, that is. *So what is wrong with me? I should be happy. I'm the successful one here. I bought the big house in the artistic suburban community for tax purposes only. I'm the one paying sexy, shirtless contractors to restore my home to its natural grace and beauty, while adding all the modern, expensive conveniences. I'm the freelance fashion writer with the great clothes and good body. I get to go on exotic assignments. My best friend is engaged to marry a good one, yet, I feel depressed.* Jayde took another drag of her cigarette, then reached for her cell to call Mary Grace at home, mostly because Jayde knew she wouldn't be there.

"Mary Grace. It's me. No movie tonight. I'm not feeling well. Must be coming down with something. I'll check in with you tomorrow," she said before hitting the end button. A knock on the window startled Jayde. She looked up and it was Ralph.

"You're still here?" he asked, wondering if she was planning on following him or something. *Jayde the stalker; now that's a twist.*

"Business," she lied, holding up her cell phone as proof. "I'm leaving now," she said. Ralph nodded, then walked to his car, listening for Jayde's ignition. He didn't hear it for what felt like an eternity.

As Jayde watched Ralph get into his dented, ancient car—what she, or anyone else for that matter, considered to be a pathetic mode of transportation for someone his age—it hit her. She, Jayde Anderson, was jealous. For the first time in the twenty years she'd been best friends with Gracie, she was jealous of her. Gracie got the guy. The good guy, no less. Ralph the Virgin, the nerd with a car Jayde would rather die than been seen in, turned out to be a good one. And Mary Grace got him. That was the position reserved for Jayde. She was the one who was supposed to land on top, get married, and live happily ever after. Not Mary Grace. At least not Mary Grace first. She took a final drag of her cigarette and let the smoke sink deep into her lungs. She flicked the butt out the window and started the car, a sound that did not go unnoticed by Ralph. She didn't feel good. On the contrary, she felt sad and ashamed all at the same time. The combination was nearly lethal. She lit another cigarette and sped away.

CHAPTER TEN

"Someone left the cake out in the rain." JIMMY WEBB

B ut for a plastic palm tree, a floor lamp, and two chairs, the room
was next to empty. Jayde noticed the palm tree. For the first time,
she studied it. It was covered in a layer of dust so thick you could write
your name on one of the leaves, or perhaps some secret message just
waiting to be found by someone, anyone, who would finally dust it.
"I love you." "I'm sorry." Or "Fuck you." *Wouldn't someone be surprised to
find that message?*

Annie would be horrified. Neat as a pin, clean Annie, whose kids never
left the house looking anything less than impeccable, would certainly
frown at a dusty palm tree. If this were Annie's therapist, she might
even make a note to bring a dust wipe and clean the tree on her next
visit. *"Clean me" would be the message Annie would write in dust,* Jayde thought.
But Annie would never be here. Annie didn't need a therapist. Annie
had a husband, two kids, and a perfectly clean house, no therapy needed
there. *I'm the one in therapy. Me. How the hell did I wind up being the screwed
up one?*

Jayde sat in the big comfy chair and her therapist occupied the sturdy
armchair. She didn't want to talk this week. Dr. Upadya was familiar with
the silent treatment from Jayde. And so she waited. Nearly twenty minutes
of their fifty-minute session passed in silence. Silence that did not even
include a hello from Jayde. Dr. Upadya said hello, of course. But Jayde said

nothing. She just took her seat in the big comfy chair. Dr. Upadya remained calm, and said whenever she was ready Jayde could talk. Jayde's plan was to remain silent the whole time.

The last time she didn't feel like talking she only lasted fifteen minutes before opening her mouth.

"I hate therapy, you know," she had said. "It's a waste of time."

"Why is that, Jayde?" Dr. Upadya had said.

"Oh shit. Now you'll want some sort of story from me. Can't I just hate it because I hate it? You know, sometimes I just have nothing to say to you and I drive here thinking about what stories I can tell you."

"Jayde, you can, and must, have feelings. And you can hate anything you want, but sometimes figuring out the whys of feelings isn't fun. I understand hating therapy," Dr. Upadya had said.

Her therapist's even temper and complete understanding pissed Jayde off even more.

"Great."

"What story were you thinking of telling me on your drive here today?" Dr. Upadya had asked in her even, unwavering voice.

"You really want to know?"

"Only if you want to tell me."

"I don't."

"Okay."

Silence.

Jayde thought about the story instead, pretending she was confessing to Dr. Upadya. *I was an oops baby; you know, the kind that comes when both your brothers are teenagers. And I was a brat, too. I squealed on my brother when I caught him smoking. He yelled at me. "You should have been an abortion," he said. I laughed, having no clue what he, or that word, meant. Then, ten years later, I remembered what my brother said. It came to me in some sort of a dream. This time, I knew what the word meant. I should have been an abortion.*

Jayde's heart felt tight with the pain of her memory. Forgetting was so much easier. At the twenty-minute mark of her current therapy session, she uttered her first words.

"Shit. I'm afraid to tell you what's on my mind." Jayde folded her torso over her thighs and buried her head in her hands, unable to look at Dr. Upadya.

"Why?"

Jayde heard the question but took a moment before answering. "Because you'll think I'm an awful person," Jayde said, whispering her answer.

"It's scary, I know, but sometimes when you put something out there, just get it out, it becomes less of an albatross," Dr. Upadya said. "Can you look at me, Jayde?" she added in earnest.

Jayde lifted only her chin, opening her eyes to see the seriousness in Dr. Upadya's face.

"Sometimes, what we keep to ourselves hurts the most."

Jayde nodded but remained skeptical. "When I finally do put it out there, I can't get it back. It confirms I'm a selfish, sick person. You'll know it."

"What if I don't think you're a selfish, sick person?" Dr. Upadya countered.

Jayde, still hunched over, looked at her doctor with tear-filled eyes. Eyes that said, *What if you do?*

"Let's play this from a different angle," Dr. Upadya said, shifting in her seat. "What if I do think you are a selfish and sick person already?"

"I am not." Jayde sat straight up in her chair, her voice filled with indignation.

"No. You're not."

Jayde snorted.

"I get it. So you want to know what's on my mind?"

"Only if you want to tell me," Dr. Upadya said.

Dr. Upadya's words made Jayde feel like she was back at square one, but she was too tired to keep her revelation a secret anymore.

"I'm jealous of Mary Grace," she said. "I'm prettier than her. I've always had more boyfriends. Cuter boyfriends. I'm skinnier. She is my best friend in the whole entire world. The girl I've known since I was six. And then she gets engaged. Engaged to a guy who could've replaced Steve Carell in *The Forty Year Old Virgin*."

"So why do you think you're jealous?" Dr. Upadya asked.

"Because it turns out he's a great guy." Jayde was serious.

"How did you arrive at this conclusion?"

"I requested a meeting with him. Without Mary Grace's knowledge, I went to see him at his school. I was worried about my friend. Worried she was marrying him for the wrong reasons. So I decided to get to the bottom of the whole thing. You know, Jayde to the rescue sort of thing."

"And what happened?"

"Like I said, it turns out he's not crazy. He is sweet and thoughtful, and deep and sincere, and just perfect for Mary Grace. And instead of being head over heels happy for her, I discover I'm jealous. Can I have a cigarette? I really need a cigarette." Jayde reached for her purse.

"No."

"I know. I can't believe I said that out loud," Jayde said, bringing an unlit cigarette to her lips, just for the oral satisfaction. "Not the cigarette part. The jealous part. I am a horrible person. I don't deserve a friend like Mary Grace." Jayde's eyes welled with tears.

"Here," Dr. Upadya said, handing the box of tissues to Jayde. "Do you see what you're doing here, Jayde? You're drawing that line again. That definite line. Being jealous of Mary Grace, and saying it out loud, doesn't make you a horrible person. Nor would being exceedingly happy for her make you a wonderful person. Life is rarely that clear cut."

"So you're saying I'm not evil?"

"I don't believe you're evil, no. I don't think you allow yourself to feel any sort of range of emotions. Any emotion that is foreign to you becomes immediately bad."

"So what do I do?"

"What do you want to do?" Dr. Upadya responded.

"I don't want to feel this awful," Jayde answered. "I want to be happy for Mary Grace. I want to be so happy for her and Ralph. My whole life I've always gotten the guys. I've had boyfriends and dates and men pledging their love to me. I've been the pretty, popular one. And not Mary Grace.

She's always lived in my shadow of boyfriends. If I hadn't fixed her up, she wouldn't have dated at all."

"Jayde to the rescue?"

"Exactly," Jayde said, giving a quick fist pump to her chest. "And now this really terrific thing happens to her."

"This terrific thing that you didn't do for her?" Dr. Upadya said, speaking the unspoken.

"I suppose." Jayde nodded her head. "And instead of being happy for her, I'm pissed and jealous and I almost ruined it for her by making Ralph meet with me."

"Jayde, I want you to try something," Dr. Upadya said, making a quick note on her pad. "Instead of forcing yourself to feel something you don't, why don't you embrace the feelings you have?"

"I don't get it."

"Instead of trying to bury your jealousy under the carpet, I want you to face it. Feel it. Look at it. Maybe it won't be so scary after you've lived with it. And maybe after you've lived with it, you can decide you don't like it. But if you never allow yourself to feel it, it will remain a scary demon."

Jayde stared at Dr. Upadya with curious eyes. "Should I tell Mary Grace?"

"That is entirely up to you. I'm afraid we're out of time. Live with it this week. If you need to call me, you know my number," Dr. Upadya said, handing Jayde one of her cards, just in case. "Otherwise I will see you next week and we can discuss this further."

"But if I'm living with it, what do I do about Mary Grace?"

"We'll talk about it next time."

CHAPTER ELEVEN

"Nothing seems to please a fly so much as to be taken for a currant, and if it can be baked in a cake and palmed off on the unwary, it dies happy." MARK TWAIN

Mary Grace paced back and forth on the train platform, waiting for Ralph and the train to New York. *Both should be here soon,* she thought, *and hopefully in the correct order.* The day was certain to be another scorcher, as it was eighty degrees and only five after eight in the morning. A handful of commuters were waiting on the platform, and they were fanning themselves with their newspapers. The smarter folks favoured the inside office where the tickets were sold, and the air was cool with air-conditioning.

That morning, Mary Grace had doubled up on her deodorant, just to be certain. Discreetly she raised her right shoulder and nuzzled her nose to her armpit, pretending to scratch an itch. She took a quiet whiff, and was relieved to discover her deodorant was working. But despite her hard-working deodorant, the heat still annoyed Mary Grace because of her hair. Her curls were beginning to frizz, and the pins she had tried to insert that morning, replicating the style Annie had created the night before, were popping out all over.

Mary Grace didn't want to meet Tess Lunt with a frizzy mop of pin crazy hair. *I'd like to make a good first impression just once in my life. Is that too much to ask?* Mary Grace straightened out her blouse and looked up toward the cloudless sky. *How does Jayde manage to make a good impression every single place she goes?* She turned on the heel of her black ballet flat to pace in the other direction. *Me? If it weren't for Annie and Jayde and our shopping spree, I would never be wearing this hip outfit. I didn't even know ballet slippers were in. Fashion writer Jayde knows. Even stay-at-home-mom Annie knows. Me? I never even threw away my penny loafers.*

With her mind still on Jayde, Mary Grace wondered why her friend hadn't returned any of her phone calls. No movies. No lunches. No hour-long conversations solving all the world's problems. Basically, no Jayde. Jayde knew she was going to *I Do* today. Jayde knew she would need her fashion advice, and yet Annie was the only one to show up at her apartment last night. The one who helped decide which of the outfits from their shopping extravaganza was the best for the first day of *I Do*. Annie insisted on the black casual capris with the lacey white top and black ballet flats, because black and white is always in and always a fashion-do.

"We don't need Jayde to tell us that," Annie said, knowing how severely Mary Grace missed Jayde's presence. "And here, take my diamond earrings," she added, unscrewing the backs. "These will look so classy and sophisticated."

"I can't." Mary Grace only mildly protested, because they would, in fact, look perfect. "They were an anniversary present from John."

"So what? I'll enjoy seeing them on television. The little darlings need an exciting night out, and lord knows John and I aren't going anywhere that doesn't serve nuggets and fries."

"I'll baby sit. How about tomorrow?" Mary Grace offered, smiling at her own attempt at avoidance. "Seriously, I know it must be hard to get out." Mary Grace slipped into her old penny loafers and stuck her right foot out for Annie's approval.

"Not in a million years. Get those old, disgusting shoes off your feet right now! And baby sitters aren't the problem." Annie put the earrings into Mary Grace's ears, then spent some time fussing with her curls. "You should pull your hair off your face a bit. Do you have any bobby pins?"

Mary Grace made a quick dash to the junk drawer of her night table, pulled it open, and fished around for a handful of bobby pins.

"Ta da." She passed them to Annie, who immediately kept one in her hand and shoved the others in her mouth, leaving them to dangle out like tiny black cigarettes.

Annie started playing with a couple of curls here and there, pinning and tugging. She tilted her head to the left, trying to decide if she liked what she was doing. She began talking through the pins in her mouth.

"You don't have to sit, just because you are borrowing my earrings, either. My mother is almost always available. It's more an issue of time. Ooh, this curl is being stubborn. Stop popping up," Annie laughed, as if talking to the curl would make it listen. "We just can't seem to get the time. John is working long hours and by the time he gets home, he's too exhausted to go out. What do you think?" Annie asked, holding the handle of the square mirror in front of Mary Grace's face.

"I like it." Mary Grace tilted her head to the left and then to the right. "I really like it. Just that little hair pulled back really shows off the earrings. But you need to get out."

"We will. Soon. This whole ensemble looks so good on you. You are ready for prime time, baby."

"Annie?" Mary Grace asked, her voice soft, her legs dangling off the edge of her bed.

"Yes?"

"Do you ever regret getting married?"

"No," Annie said without hesitation.

"You're always happy?"

"Of course I'm not always happy." Annie took a seat next to Mary Grace. "I have a husband and two kids—three people pulling me mentally and physically in millions of different directions each day. But that doesn't mean I regret getting married," she added, taking Mary Grace's hand in hers.

"What's the real question?"

"How do I know I am making the right decision?" Mary Grace squeezed Annie's hand. "Jayde never thought I should say yes to Ralph in the first place."

"I don't think Jayde should be your go-to gal on advice about men, Mary Grace. But honestly, I don't think I should, either. I mean, I'll talk to you all night if you want. You know that. But the final decision has to come from here." Annie extricated her hands from Mary Grace's grip and placed one of them over her heart.

Mary Grace laughed.

"That sounded sappier than I intended."

"Like a Hallmark movie," Mary Grace said.

"Just listen to your heart, okay?"

"But what if my heart doesn't answer?"

"It will, Mary Grace. It will. Now get up and look at yourself." Annie shut the bedroom door, revealing the mirror that hung on the back.

Mary Grace stared at her reflection and allowed herself the tiniest of smiles. Then Annie began a sort of roll call, the kind they used to do when they were preparing for a project with their kids in school.

"Shoes?" Annie asked.

"Check," Mary Grace replied.

"Capris?"

"Check."

"Blouse?"

"Check."

"Hair?"

"Check."

"Earrings?"

"Perfect," Mary Grace said, and Annie shot her a look that screamed, "wrong answer."

"I mean check."

"Okay, you're good to go. Call me if you need to talk some more. But I mean it, Mary Grace; listen to your heart. I need to get home and see what disasters my husband and kids left for me." Annie kissed Mary Grace on the cheek. "No need to walk me out. Just get those clothes off and hang them up before they wrinkle. Put on a big T-shirt, relax, and see what Chef Guruli has going tonight." Annie checked her watch. "He should be coming on soon," she said before blowing one last kiss to Mary Grace and leaving her room, shutting the bedroom door behind her so Mary Grace could linger on her look.

"Thank you," Mary Grace shouted at Annie, who was walking out. "I mean, really. Thank you," she repeated, still staring at herself. Annie was right about everything. The earrings looked terrific. The shoes. The blouse. The hair. Mary Grace clutched both hands to her heart. Mostly she hoped Annie was right about listening to her heart. Oh, and Jayde. They really *didn't* need her.

Mary Grace couldn't remember the last time she had gone a whole week without taking to Jayde. Not even the time when they were ten years old and Jayde killed Mary Grace's fish, while trying to dress it in a Jayde Anderson original blouse, made especially for fish. Even then Mary Grace only lasted a day. And that was an idea Jayde was certain would make them both rich, not kill her fish. It just wasn't natural, she thought as she turned again on the train's platform to pace in the other direction. When she spun around and lifted her head, she spotted Ralph on the train platform. An uneasy grin spread across her face as she picked up her pace and trotted toward him.

"Ralph, I can't believe we're doing this," she said.

"You look fantastic," Ralph said. "Really fantastic."

"Oh, my hair is a big frizz ball. It looked so much better last night."

"I didn't see it last night and I think it looks just perfect right now."

"Annie had it looking so good, with these little pins that showed off the earrings. Oh, what do you think of these earrings? Annie lent them to me."

"Don't lose them."

"Don't say that! You'll put a curse on me."

"I'm kidding…"

"Ralph?" Mary Grace interrupted, not letting him finish. "Are we really going to do this? Are we really going to go through with this?" Mary Grace asked as a loud horn tooted, signalling the train to New York was only seconds away. With a big gust of wind and the loud screech of the wheels stopping, the train pulled into the station.

"It's now or never," Ralph said, grabbing Mary Grace's hand and leading her to the steps. Together they climbed four steep steps and entered the train. They looked around for two seats together, and when Mary Grace spotted them, Ralph took out a wet nap from the pack in his pocket and wiped them down before sitting.

"I can't believe we are actually on the train to New York to go on *I Do*. Is this crazy or what?" Mary Grace said.

"It is a bit crazy, but it could be fun. Let's let it be fun," Ralph said.

"We don't have to do it, you know."

"Now you tell me?" Ralph said, giving himself the onceover. "I bought this new suit. I showered. I shaved. Twenty times I told my mother I'd be on television, and now is when you choose to tell me we don't have to do it?" There was a glimmer in his eyes.

"Let's turn around. We can take the train right home and not step one foot into Manhattan."

"Nobody says no to Angela Falcone. Besides, they need a couple like us for the show: mature, self-sufficient, ready for marriage. America will have fun planning a wedding for us."

"But we would have fun planning a wedding for us."

"Mary Grace, stop. Try to enjoy this. Please. We've made the decision. We're helping your mother, who is helping her friend, who is helping her daughter." Ralph cocked his head to the left, a little smile on his lips. "Did you follow that?"

"I'm confused, not stupid."

"I know."

"I'll try. Promise."

"Good."

Mary Grace pulled out a celebrity magazine from her bag and began pouring page by page through the pictures. Ralph opened the newspaper. Both pretended to read as they sat through the twelve train stops to Manhattan.

CHAPTER TWELVE

"A bad review is like baking a cake with all the best ingredients and having someone sit on it." DANIELLE STEEL

M ary Grace couldn't concentrate on her magazine. She idly stared at its glossy pages, licked her pointer finger, and then used it to flip from advertisement to advertisement. Between page turns, she glanced at Ralph. He sat across from her on the train, arms folded over his chest, reading the paper, which sat on his lap, neatly creased in fourths. Ralph read every article on the front page, refusing to open the newspaper until the entire front page was done. Feeling her stare, he glanced up and smiled. She offered a tiny grin in return, but shuddered when she spotted the small bottle of Purell that shared his lap with the newspaper.

"You okay?" Ralph asked, arms still folded, as he looked up from his paper.

"Yeah, fine." Her eyes darted from Ralph back to her magazine. Ralph shrugged and went back to his paper. Mary Grace tried not to think about Ralph's idiosyncrasies, but more than that, she tried to forget her current life.

She let the chug of the train lull her into some sort of self-induced trance. With each three hundred and sixty degree turn of the wheels, she went further back in time, meeting Annie, college, high school, her father, Jayde, being a little girl, staying home with her mother. She hung on to that memory for a moment, remembering how she hadn't even gone to nursery school. Angela preferred her daughter's company at home. Mary Grace was another person in an otherwise quiet house, a person to whom Angela could talk. While other mothers were working on their children's colours, numbers, and ABCs, Angela was busy cultivating her daughter's knowledge of television game shows, and ultimately, knowledge of everything worthless.

Mary Grace remembered an endless string of game shows. *The Newlywed Game* was always her mother's favourite, and Angela revolved her day of laundry, cleaning, and errands around the time it aired. Angela started each show the same way, picking her favourite couple, and then she sat, impatiently, as the show unfolded, often times sending a prayer up to God that her chosen couple would get the right answer.

"Mary Grace, they better get this answer correct. We need these points. They have got to be smarter than that, Gracie," Angela would shout at the television.

Even at the age of five, Mary Grace knew her mother had a crush on the show's host, Bob Eubanks. Angela Falcone, the first of the celebrity stalkers.

"Look at that man's smile," Angela said practically every day the show was on. "That man's smile lights up the day. And he is so funny, too."

"Daddy's smile is much nicer than his."

"Oh, Mary Grace, Daddy's smile is nice, too. But Bob Eubanks, he's a celebrity. You can't compare Daddy to Mr. Eubanks," she would say. Mary Grace was never certain why her mother used such formality with the host of a television show whom she didn't even really know. "Just watch the show, Mary Grace. Couple number three is today's winner. I can tell just by looking at them; they really know each other. They are in love. Watch."

Often times, long after Mary Grace was supposed to be sleeping, she could hear her parents talking. Mary Grace would sneak out of her bed and curl up in her door jam, stretching her ears to listen. Her mother would ask her father Bob Eubanks' questions from the day's show.

"What is the first meal I cooked for you? What is my favourite colour? Would I rather wear a pant suit or dress to an evening party?"

Her father typically went fifty-fifty on these sorts of questions, and Mary Grace could tell her mother wasn't happy when he got the answers wrong. She would sigh and moan. He would wind up saying things like, "I love you, Angela. Just because I don't remember our first date doesn't mean I don't love you. You watch too much television. It's not real."

"I'll decide what is real," she would shoot back, often storming out of the kitchen. Mary Grace would hop back into her bed, neither parent the wiser for what she had overheard.

Despite remembering those evenings like they had occurred last week, Mary Grace couldn't remember how often they happened. Was it once? Twice? Or every night? *It's funny*, she thought, *when you are in the thick of something, you feel as though it is a moment, or string of moments, you will remember, in exact detail, forever. And then years go by and what was once crystal clear becomes clogged and fogged by the addition of new situations and new memories, and you don't even remember it happening.*

"Penn Station," the overhead voice resonated, shaking Mary Grace from her thoughts.

"This is us; let's go," Ralph said, using one hand to reach for Mary Grace's, and the other to pat his pocket, to make sure his Purell and antiseptic pads were where he put them. Mary Grace reached back and held on tightly as they maneuvered through crowds of people, making their way up escalators and staircases to the streets of New York City. Ralph took one huge deep breath; a breath, Mary Grace was certain, which would have to hold him until they were safely in the *I Do* building. *Forget high school teacher,* Mary Grace thought. *Ralph ought to figure out how to make a living holding his breath.*

CHAPTER THIRTEEN

"I tried to commit suicide by sticking my head in the oven, but there was a cake in it." LESLEY BOONE

R alph let out his first noticeable breath when the building where *I Do* was filmed came into view. With its large windows and tall sleek lines reaching high into the heat of the summer sky, as if daring the sky to start something, the building was a quiet relief. Ralph allowed his pent-up oxygen to escape through his mouth in a slow, steady stream of wind. It felt so good that he shut his eyes, grateful that his twenty-block walk through the dirty streets of New York was nearly over. They walked, because despite the distance, Ralph refused to take a cab. Of course, during the walk, Ralph had taken a scared breath or two. He had to, because even with his fear of breathing air that smelled of body odour, rising steam, burnt pretzels, and swine flu, the consequences of not taking in air would have been death. And Ralph was not willing to die for his phobias. He refused to let his mother bury two sons.

Ralph was only seventeen years old when the same words he had been repeating to his mother for as long as he could remember finally caged him in. They were shopping for college supplies, a chore he wished his mother had cared for alone; alone, like every other mother he knew. His friends' moms all came home with bags of stuff—coffee makers, blankets, buckets of toiletries—and all his friends were required to do was unload the car. But not Ralph's mother. Agnes insisted he accompany her, so she could make the right decisions. *It's just blankets and shampoo and stuff; how could the decisions possibly be wrong?* But as always, he obliged. It was just his nature, and so the two ventured out to a bed and bath store, where predictably, a debate ensued.

"Get this blanket," his mother said. "It's heavier and it will keep you much warmer during those cold winter nights at college. You know I'm not even sure there will be enough heat in those dorms," she said, rubbing her eyes with her bony fingers. "Those cinder block walls appeared pretty chilly. Feel the thickness?" she asked, moving her hands from her eyes to the blanket, allowing her frail touch to bask in the softness of the nubby blanket.

"I am not going to college with a horse mural on my blanket. It's college, Mom, not kindergarten," Ralph said, refusing to give in this time.

"But it's thick, Ralph. Feel how thick it is," she said, grabbing his hand and forcing it to the blanket with as much gusto as she could muster. "See?"

"This blue one will be just fine, Mother."

"Too thin, Ralph. It is way too thin. You will freeze with a threadbare blanket like that. Please? Get this one? For me?"

"No. I don't want to start college looking like an idiot whose—" Agnes didn't let him finish his thought before interrupting him to make her point.

"But I want to make sure you're warm."

"Mom," Ralph said, a bit louder than was appropriate in public. His mother just looked at him, daring him to say the next words. "I'm not going to die like Walter did!"

Silence.

There. I said it. He hated to resort to Walter, but it was the only phrase that could reel his mother in from insanity. They remained quiet for a few moments until his mother broke the silence.

"Walter, I'm sorry."

"I'm Ralph, Mom," he said, guiding his mother to one of the pre-made beds and sitting her down on the edge before taking a seat next to her. "I'm Ralph," he repeated.

"I was pregnant with you when Walter died."

"I know, Mom. I'm sorry," Ralph said. And he was. He was sorry for his mother. And he was sorry for himself. So often he was sorry for himself. He had missed out on knowing Walter. Walter, whom he had never met, was permanently eight. Eight-year-old Walter. Brazen Walter, taking his fishing pole and walking down to the park by himself.

"When the baby is born, I'm going to teach him to fish," Walter told his mother.

"What if the baby is a girl?" his mother said with a smile.

"I'll teach her to fish, then. It doesn't matter. We'll be fishing buddies."

Off Walter marched, with the messy brown hair he never bothered to comb, and the trademark dirt under his fingernails, carrying his pole, off to the town pond to fish for coy. To fish for fun. To practise how he would teach his new brother or sister to fish. But Walter never made it to the park. He was killed in a car accident. One week later Agnes was back at the hospital in which Walter had died, giving birth to Ralph.

Ralph would have loved to have had Walter as a real, live older brother, and not just a figment of everyone else's memories. Memories Ralph used to paint his own picture of the brother he never knew. For a long time Ralph even played with his imaginary brother Walter, talking to him at night while trying to fall asleep, saving some dinner for him, or the best, homemade chocolate chip cookies. But Ralph stopped pretending when he turned nine. He stopped when he himself became the older brother. And now Walter, the brother whom Ralph had never even met, was used like a stop sign, a traffic light, a brake. He was used purely to make Agnes stop.

"I'm sorry, Mom," Ralph said again, putting his arm around his mother's shoulder. "But I'm not going to die like Walter." And this time, when Ralph said it, something different happened. He didn't feel strong and indestructible. He didn't feel as if he was comforting his mother. Mostly, he didn't feel like he was telling the truth. After saying the same words he said to his mother every time he needed to rein her in from some heightened anxiety trip, he no longer believed them. He doubted himself. What if he did die like Walter? What if his mother lost two sons?

Ralph lost something that day. He lost his innocence and became trapped by the words he had been saying for as long as he could remember.

The truth was, he could die like Walter had. And the truth hurt. At seventeen, he became an old man. He didn't buy the blanket. The thick one with the horse mural, or the thin blue one, either. He didn't buy any blanket because he didn't go away to college. He lived at home and commuted to the local school. He lost his innocence and, simultaneously, made his mother happy. But what started as a fear of dying morphed into a fear of living. Don't touch escalator handles. Money is dirty. Water fountains breed disease. Germs live on sponges. Bathroom doors spread viruses. It was a difficult way to live, but Ralph had slowly gotten used to it. *It doesn't stop me from doing things*, he reminded himself on occasion, *like venturing out into New York City.*

But when the *I Do* building came into view and the long walk through the dirty streets of New York was nearly over, Ralph felt something that could only be called relief. Pure relief.

"There's the building, Ralph," Mary Grace said, using the voice she reserved for her students, linking her arm through Ralph's. "We did it."

Ralph nodded.

CHAPTER FOURTEEN

"A compromise is the art of dividing a cake in such a way that everyone believes that he has got the biggest piece." PAUL GAUGIN

When they got off the elevator there was a cardboard sign on an easel with the words "*I DO*," all in caps, and an arrow pointing left. Following the sign's instructions, Mary Grace and Ralph walked in unison, feet falling out in army perfection. Left. Left. Left. Right. Left. They followed the sign for what felt like a mile, down a long, narrow hall. At the end of the hall was a glass door with *I Do* painted on it in gold. Ralph pulled open the door, allowing Mary Grace to enter first. What she saw startled her. There was a crowd of people milling about the room. Maybe even more than two hundred.

"What are all these people doing here?" Mary Grace asked.

Ralph shrugged his shoulders, and then reached for his Purell, well overdue for a shot of the antiseptic cleanser.

"Must be production people. Sure takes a lot for one lousy reality show," she said before bumping into a petite girl with short black hair.

"Sorry," the girl said, looking at Mary Grace before returning her gaze to her clipboard. "I-wasn't-paying-attention-there's-some-food-over-there," the girl added, stringing the words together, turning nine into one with the ease of an auctioneer. Before Mary Grace could say no thank you, the girl flitted off to another location.

"I wonder if that's my mother's friend's daughter," Mary Grace mused. "She looks pretty important with that clipboard. And so New York with that spiky hair," she added with a laugh. She thought for a brief moment before speaking again.

"You know what, Ralph?" she said, not waiting for an answer to her rhetorical question. "That girl is androgynous, sexy, and beautiful all at the same time. She's an ASB girl. I could never pull off that look. My face is too fat."

"Your face is just fine."

"I wanted to ask her what all these people are here for, but she left too fast. Hey! Check out the table ASB Girl pointed to. I see cake."

"You would know, MG. Let's get some."

"Nothing like cake to soothe my frazzled New York nerves," Mary Grace said, grabbing a plate from the start of the buffet and loading it with cookies and a piece of cake.

"You guys here to interview for the show?" a tall, sickly, skinny girl asked Mary Grace without even the tiniest sign of a smile, a fact Mary Grace neglected to register.

"Oh, hi. What's your name?" Mary Grace inquired, reaching her right hand out to greet her new acquaintance.

"Rhonda. And remember it, because you'll be seeing me on television. A lot. And you didn't answer my question," Rhonda said.

"What question?" Mary Grace asked, so caught up with Rhonda's nerve that she truly did forget the question.

"Are you here to interview for the show?" Rhonda repeated.

"Oh, no," Mary Grace said, laughing at the thought. Interview. *Ralph and I would never interview for something like this.* "We're not interviewing. We're doing Tess Lunt a favour. Our mothers are friends, so we agreed to do this show. Apparently they were looking for a couple like us," Mary Grace continued.

"I don't know who blew so much smoke up your high-waisted pants legs, but this is all about the interviews."

"What are you talking about?" Mary Grace said, feeling less confident with each passing second.

"No," Ralph said, jumping into the conversation. "She's right. We're not interviewing. In a minute the producer will come out and bring us to some other room, I'm sure. We're doing a favour for her."

"Do us all a favour," Rhonda said. "Leave."

"Listen, I don't know what we did to make you so mad," Mary Grace said, using her best teacher voice. "But your behaviour is rude."

"This world is rude. And nobody is getting *my* spot on *this* show. So watch your backs," she said, grabbing a handful of carrot sticks. "And you might want to think about pushing away from the table every now and then."

"Listen up, gang," the petite girl with the short black hair called before Mary Grace had a chance to react to the sting she felt. "My name is Gabriella. I'm Miss Lunt's assistant. Help yourselves to the buffet, and Miss Lunt will be out in a minute to go over the interview process with you. Just relax. If you're tired, eat chocolate and drink coffee. If you're edgy, have some herbal tea. We've got it all. Make yourselves at home, and most importantly, remember, we want you to just be yourselves."

Mary Grace shot Ralph a confused look. "My mother swore. She swore on my father's grave that we were doing a favour for her friend's daughter."

Ralph didn't speak. He just threw his hands in the air.

Mary Grace trotted after Gabriella, shouting her name. "Gabriella? Gabriella? Excuse me, can I ask a question?"

"A quick one."

"Privately?"

"I suppose," Gabriella said with a nod.

"Miss Lunt is my mother's friend's daughter."

"I'll make sure she knows you're here," Gabriella said; her voice sounded ready to dismiss Mary Grace.

"No. That's not what I mean. Miss Lunt wants us on the show."

"I don't know what you are implying, Miss…?"

"Falcone. Mary Grace Falcone."

"Okay. Miss Falcone, this process is totally fair and above board. No special treatment here. If Miss Lunt gave special treatment to everybody's mother's sister's friend's cousin's daughter, there would be no show."

"No, you don't understand," Mary Grace said. She couldn't stop herself from pleading and sounding insecure. "We're doing *her* the favour. Apparently she needs a couple like us."

"Apparently, you're gullible. She'll be out soon."

"I'm getting my mother on the phone. Now," Mary Grace said, her voice loud and crackly.

Ralph put his arm around Mary Grace.

"What did she do to me? To us?" Mary Grace wondered.

When she looked up at Ralph, he noticed tears were pooling in her eyes. He drew her into him and kissed the top of her head.

"What?" she said, staring into his eyes.

He reminded her of the first conversation she and Angela had about *I Do*, the one in her kitchen. Mary Grace remembered the conversation, but remained confused.

"You didn't even know what we were talking about."

"I didn't then. But I do now. I can put the pieces together. I'm not stupid, Mary Grace," he said, his voice soft and gentle. "And neither are you."

"Are you saying I knew she was setting me up?" Mary Grace demanded, pulling out her cell, ready to speed dial Angela, tears now spilling down her face. She wiped them away with the back of her hand, painfully aware of what she had allowed her mother to do to her. Again.

Ralph raised his eyebrows, pulled her tighter, and kissed her again.

"So, you two are beginning to see the light, huh?" tall, skinny Rhonda said with a laugh and a grin. "This show is mine."

"Where did you come from? You were across the room a second ago," Ralph said, pushing away from Mary Grace and turning his head left and then right.

"It doesn't matter where I came from. The question is, where did you two come from? Bumfuck City? Don't mess with my big chance here."

"Mom?" Mary Grace said. "Mom, pick up. It's me. Mom, pick up. Mom! We're here at the show. Mom," Mary Grace repeated, shaking her head and rolling her eyes. Ralph could tell Angela Falcone was not picking up the phone.

"Mom. It's me," Mary Grace said, grateful her mom had finally answered.

"Yes. I get it. Very clever, Mom. I know what it feels like now. I'll try to remember the next time I don't answer the phone. Yes. Okay. We're here at the address you gave us, and there seems to be some mistake. A mistake, Mom. They think we're here to interview. They don't know we're the couple Tess Lunt wants. Tess? She's somewhere. Haven't seen her yet. Some girl named Gabriella told us Tess would be out soon. But there's over fifty couples here. No, Mom, not couples over fifty years old. There are more than fifty couples. Over one hundred people, Mom. And some are nasty," Mary Grace said, looking at the tall skinny girl.

"You swore on Daddy's grave. What? What detail did you leave out? Daddy told you to do it? Oh, for God's sake. This isn't some sweater *I* should wear because *you* are cold. This is my life, Mom."

"She hung up on me," Mary Grace said.

"What did she say?" Ralph asked. "Before hanging up on you, that is."

"She lied."

"She said she lied?"

"No, I say she lied. I'm done with her."

"She's your mother, Mary Grace."

"I don't care. I'm done," Mary Grace said. There was an edge to her voice that made Ralph truly believe she was ready to cut Angela out of her life. "Let's get the hell out of here."

"That's what I told you," Rhonda said. "Get the hell out of here. This show is mine."

"You can have it," Mary Grace said. "You can have my mother, too."

"Good morning, everybody. Welcome to the *I Do* interviews," a statuesque woman said, flipping her hair behind her back with Cher-like style. "My name is Tess Lunt and I am the show's producer."

"Oh God, we can't leave now," Mary Grace said, panic entering her voice. "Tess it at the door. We'll make too big of a scene."

"What do you want to do, MG?"

"Wait until she's done talking."

Ralph nodded in agreement, then looked up as Tess began her speech.

"I trust you've all met my assistant, Gabriella. And I trust you've all helped yourself to our buffet. We want nothing more than for you to be relaxed."

Mary Grace looked at her cake. *It was good cake*, she thought. She raised her head to take in a full view of the room. The way the sun streamed through the window bank, illuminating the food table, made the buffet look like a scene from a Martha Stewart cookbook. It was almost as if a set designer had planned the sun to be that bright. The way it glistened off the donuts was breathtaking. Damn, the sun even made the carrots look good. And the people, too. The sun made everything look radiant. Or maybe it was the buzz of the coffee. Or the adrenaline rush of being this close to a live television show. But the people looked good and eager. Even skinny Rhonda looked good. *If that bitch didn't open her mouth*, Mary Grace thought, *she would be a winner*. Ralph even looked good. Certainly nobody would mistake Ralph for George Clooney or Brad Pitt. Perhaps Pee-wee Herman, she thought with a chuckle. But we do make a good couple. A good, average American couple. People would love to plan our wedding. *We wouldn't be a threat to anyone. Nobody would necessarily wish they were us. Die to be us. They could spend all their time just being happy for us. This show does need us. Ralph and I are the keys to this season's success. An average American couple.*

What am I saying? Mary Grace thought. *I don't want to be on this show. My mother lied to me. Again. As soon as the time is right, Ralph and I are gone.*

"Let me break down the morning for you," Tess said. "After we're done here, the majority of you will be moved to another waiting area filled with televisions, video games, books, newspapers, ping pong and pool tables, decks of cards, and more. Attached is a smaller, quiet room, with light music and a waterfall, for those of you who prefer peaceful solitude. While the majority of you are there, two couples will go out for interviews. You will each have a turn interviewing with me and the show's host, Nick Charmin. These interviews could be as short as two minutes, but will never take longer than one hour. When you are through with your interviews, you must return to the holding room and check out with Gabriella, and then you are free to leave. We will call you with next steps. Any questions?"

"Does a short interview indicate non-interest?" asked a plumpish woman in a red dress.

"Not necessarily," Tess answered. "And neither does a long one mean you are a shoe-in. Try not to focus on that. Try to just have fun with it and show us your real selves. Believe me, if you are putting on an act, we'll see right through it. We've been doing this a long time."

"How long before we hear from you?"

"No more than two weeks. Enough questions for now. The rest you'll get as we go along. Think of it like a board game you've never played before. Okay, I'm looking for the Mary Grace Falcone/Ralph Ichy and Sindy Wasserman/Brandon Scott couples. Gabriella, will you please escort one couple to Nick's office and one to mine in, say, ten minutes? The rest of you, please follow Jake to your hanging room." Out of nowhere, a man—presumably Jake—appeared to herd people to what Tess Lunt had called "the hanging room." Mary Grace and Ralph stared at each other, each giving the other a tiny shoulder shrug. *What are we going to do now?* they said without even talking.

Sindy and Brandon moved next to Mary Grace and Ralph. Together they silently waited with Gabriella for what felt like an hour until it was time.

CHAPTER FIFTEEN

"You can't have your cake and eat it too." PROVERB

The first interview room in *I Do*'s midtown office building was uncharacteristically bright. The floor to ceiling windows ensured a heavy supply of natural light streamed in, bouncing off of the blue and white striped wallpaper. The two glowing wicker floor lamps that made their homes on either end of an overstuffed love seat were used more for atmosphere than light. And the hooked rug in front of the couch added just the right nautical touch, as it was a scene of the Barnegat Lighthouse. The room screamed "nautical" and magically smelled like the ocean. It was home. It was cozy. It was Tess Lunt's interview room.

As Gabriella led Mary Grace and Ralph into the room, the two potential contestants were trying to send each other cryptic hand signals to determine exactly what they would say to Tess Lunt. The problem was, neither Mary Grace nor Ralph knew what the other was trying to say. Mary Grace shrugged her shoulders in a sign of defeat.

"Welcome," Tess Lunt said from the comfort of the wicker chair. She had an ease about her that didn't go unnoticed and a professionalism that was no doubt mastered by years in the business. She motioned for Mary Grace and Ralph to take their places on the love seat. "That will be all, Gabriella; thank you," she said with one great big wave of her hand. "Tea, anyone?" Tess asked, pouring herself a mug. "I can't get comfortable without a piping hot cup of tea."

"No, thank you," Mary Grace said. "The cake was enough for me." Ralph just shook his head to indicate no, unable to believe the circumstances of their current situation. Mary Grace had allowed her mother to dupe her. Again. And he, Ralph, was the willing accomplice. If Mary Grace was unable to get them out of this predicament, he would have to jump in.

"No tea, Ralph? That's okay." Tess kicked off her shoes and curled her long legs under her body. "You don't have to have tea," she added, cupping the mug between both hands, pretending to feel the chill off the ocean.

"Now tell me, what brings you two to *I Do?*"

"We're not supposed to be doing this," Ralph blurted out, before allowing Mary Grace the chance to back out herself.

Mary Grace shot Ralph a sideways glance that said, "Please don't offend this totally with-it, sort of famous, really cool woman."

"I'm just going to tell the truth, MG," he said. "Don't worry."

"Truth?" Tess asked. "Of course I want the truth."

"Mary Grace's mother duped us into being here."

"Oh?" said Tess, her left eyebrow rising like a slow moon.

"If her all time favourite fantasy is to be on a game show, then her all time second favourite fantasy is to get her daughter on a game show."

"This is not a game show." Tess' voice suddenly became hard, her eyes steely.

"You try arguing with Angela Falcone."

"Angela Falcone? Your mother is Mrs. Angela Falcone?"

"The one and only," Mary Grace said, her face lighting up. "You know her?"

"Not personally. But my mother talks about her all the time. Mom asked me if you could interview for my show. She said it would be a great favour to your mom. Oh my God, this is nuts," Tess said. At the mention of Angela's name, Tess' aura had changed from austere television producer to gal-pal friend. "Seriously. This is funny."

"No. Here's what's funny," Ralph said, with more animosity in his voice than he had intended. "Angela told us showing up here, on your show, would be doing *you* an enormous favour. She told us your career was on the skids and you needed a couple like us to pull it back. She lied. She wanted us on television and she lied to get us here. And the thing is, we don't want to be here. It was one thing when I thought we were helping—" Ralph said, before being interrupted by Tess.

"Is this true?" Tess asked, looking into Mary Grace's eyes.

Mary Grace hesitated just long enough to make the quick decision to spill the truth. "Every word."

Tess laughed. Not a giggle. Not a smile. But a deep, hearty, from-the-belly laugh. "That is the funniest thing I ever heard."

"Why?" Ralph said.

"Why are you laughing?" Mary Grace chimed in.

"Because it's no wonder they're friends, your mother and mine. My mother would have done the exact same thing. Well, not to get me on a show, per se, but to get me a man. She is so bothered by singleness. I have told her a million times, I like being single. Right now, anyway. I love my job. I love my life. But she can't hear me. Her ears are shut to the truth. She thinks my being single is a bad reflection on her, so on more than one occasion she has invited me to dinner and, poof, sitting at the table is a 'nice young man' she wanted me to meet. Now that I think about it, I bet our mothers concoct these crazy schemes together."

"So why do we go along?"

"It's like you said before—you can't argue with them. And—"

"They're our mothers," Tess and Mary Grace said at the exact same time.

"So what do we do now?" Mary Grace asked.

"Leave?" Ralph suggested.

"No way," Tess said. "I'm not letting you two out of my sight. In her own weird way, your mother probably did do me a huge favour."

Mary Grace just stared at Tess Lunt, eager to hear what she was about to say.

"I've got a good eye for this sort of thing. That's how I got to be here," Tess said with one grand sweep of her arm. "You might as well let me interview you. Okay, Mary Grace?"

"Okay," she said, looking to Ralph for confirmation. He just shrugged his shoulders.

"Okay, Ralph?" Tess prompted.

"I suppose. If you think we might really be what you want."

"That I do," Tess said. "Let's get on with this, shall we?" Tess took one huge gulp of tea, then swallowed it ever so slowly. "Mary Grace, why are you marrying Ralph?"

Mary Grace coughed, the first question taking her quite by surprise, although she didn't know why. She wanted to answer but no words would come. Her head started spinning, trying to come up with something cute, clever, or just truthful to say. *Answer. Answer. Why am I marrying Ralph?* she said to herself once more. "Why am I marrying Ralph? Oh my, did I just say that out loud? I thought I was still thinking," Mary Grace said with a nervous little laugh. "Just give me a minute. Just a minute and I'll be ready to answer."

"Take your time." Tess Lunt took another, considerably smaller, sip of her tea.

Ralph turned to Mary Grace and gave her a look that begged her to answer soon. *Answer, Mary Grace. Answer.* He was channelling those exact words to Mary Grace. It took a long few minutes but Mary Grace finally answered. And Tess smiled as she did, eating Mary Grace's words up like a piece of Anytime Cake. Upon hearing Mary Grace speak, Tess knew she wanted Mary Grace and Ralph to be *I Do*'s next couple.

Thanks to the blackout shades and a sleep mask, Mary Grace's bedroom was the opposite of Tess Lunt's interview room. Pitch black. She was tucked beneath her down comforter, curled up on her left side, but she didn't last long there. She pushed and moved and rolled to her right, picking up her pillow and punching it to life. Her new sleep position lasted but a minute before she repeated the procedure, winding up on her back. It was times like these Mary Grace wished for more sleeping positions. *There are only four ways to sleep: front, back, side, side*, she thought. *There ought to be more for nights when sleep won't come. I'll sleep sitting up*, she thought, arranging her pillows and comforter and body in a new way. Mary Grace prayed sleep would come. It didn't, and she harrumphed her way back to position one. Fetal left.

"Why are you marrying Ralph?" Tess had asked, all curled up in her cozy chair. She asked it like it was the most normal thing in the world. Like she wasn't a mega television producer. Like she was Mary Grace's best friend, on par with Annie or Jayde, even. They were simply chatting, maybe catching up after having been separated by one or the other's cross-country move. *Why are you marrying Ralph?* Was Tess psychic? Did she know how many weeks Mary Grace spent not answering Ralph's question? *Why are you marrying Ralph? Remember me?* Mary Grace wanted to ask her old chum. *I'm the girl who made out with the high school jock at some football party after having gulped down four shots of scotch. Liquid courage. Ha! I'm the one who got stood up for a date at the diner. The diner. Who stands someone up at the diner? And if I wasn't stood up, my first dates were quick, the boys heading home faster than you can blow dandelion dust. Loser.*

Why are you marrying Ralph? *Because I'm me. Mary Grace Falcone. The girl no sober boys were interested in. The girl with the overprotective mother. The girl who could never dance the right way or make the right joke. The girl who was always there but never it. And then Ralph entered my life, stage left. He's no prize, but I'm not, either.*

"Why are you marrying Ralph?" Tess asked. Mary Grace wanted to be able to say something charming like, "Because he swept me off my feet." Or something witty like, "Cantaloupe, I'm already married." Instead, when she finally opened her mouth she said something practical: "Because we love each other."

But deep down, the answer she was afraid of, the one that kept pounding at her brain, was, "He's the only one who asked." *There. I said it*, Mary Grace thought. *Happy now?* She tossed and turned to position two, fetal right, and yet she was keenly aware that sleep wouldn't take her in for hours.

Her mind was on a treadmill. *If my body could get as much exercise as my brain, I'd be a size two*, she thought, remembering her interview with Nick

Charmin, the actual host of *I Do*. After Tess asked her final question, she made it perfectly clear she wanted them on her show. "You're the ones that I want," were her exact words. Ralph agreed to continue with the process, as long as Mary Grace wanted to. Caught up in the thrill of live television, Mary Grace said she did. It was now host Nick Charmin's turn to interview.

Gabriella escorted Mary Grace and Ralph from Tess Lunt's office to Nick Charmin's. Where Tess' office was warm and homey, Nick's screamed New York modern with metallic grey walls and black wood blinds covering the floor-to-ceiling windows. Nick sat on a sleek black sofa, his head buried in some book, allowing his thick black hair to make the first impression on his guests. The way the daylight bounced off the wave of his black hair highlighted certain sections until they looked nearly blue, almost like Veronica's from the *Archie* comic books. Somehow, though, on Charmin blue hair looked sexy and intriguing, not cartoon-like at all.

"Mr. Charmin, may I present Mary Grace Falcone and her fiancé, Ralph Ichy," Gabriella said, walking toward him to hand over the folder Tess had begun. Charmin put his book down and took the folder without either looking up or saying a word. Mystery seemed to surround his every move. To Mary Grace, it seemed Charmin waited a calculated amount of time before lifting his head and lighting up a room already soaked in daylight with his hundred-watt smile. Mary Grace immediately felt the warming effects of his grin, and was fascinated by his blue eyes. She allowed herself an internal chuckle when she saw his fashionable stubble, thinking how much her mother would hate it. Through all these subtle gestures, Nick Charmin had yet to utter one word. The silence made Ralph a bit uncomfortable, and he gave Mary Grace the tiniest of shrugs.

"Please, sit down," Gabriella said, talking for her boss. "Mr. Charmin will take a few minutes to review Miss Lunt's notes and then he will be right with you. Can I get you anything while you wait?" she asked.

"No, thank you," Mary Grace said, while Ralph shook his head no. They both sat down on the sofa and fidgeted a bit to get comfortable. Gabriella left the room, shutting the door silently, and leaving in its wake an even quieter hush. Nobody moved. Charmin didn't even flip the pages.

Neither Ralph nor Mary Grace was certain he was reading them. It looked more like he was just trying to absorb them in some sort of Zen fashion.

He sure is handsome, Mary Grace thought. *My mother would flip out in his presence and Bob Eubanks would be forced to take a back seat.* But she'd want him to shave. *She'd tell him, too,* Mary Grace thought. "Nick Charmin, you don't impress me with that dirty-looking half-beard. Now go clean up," she would say, and Mary Grace let herself smile at the thought. Mary Grace wondered for how long Mr. Charmin would give them the silent treatment before letting them hear his voice. And the more she waited, the more curious she became. *Will he sound as deep and velvety as he does on television, or is that his* acting *voice?* she wondered. The suspense was nearly killing her, and the awkward silence was doing a number on Ralph as well, who checked his pits before giving Mary Grace another one of his tiny shrugs, as if to say, "What the hell is going on here?"

Finally, Nick Charmin turned a page from the notes Gabriella had given him. And something—Mary Grace could only wonder what— caused him to smile his broad grin, the one Mary Grace recognized from television. His smile exuded warmth. He nodded his head and continued to smile. For both Mary Grace and Ralph, it became obvious he was reading, not just absorbing, the information set before him.

"Tess seems impressed," Charmin said, still grinning and now looking directly into Mary Grace's eyes. His look was so singular that it made her feel as if she was in the room alone with Charmin. "Tess is pretty good at this interview stuff. In the three years we've been doing the show, we've always hit it with the *right* couple." When Charmin said the word "right," he made air quotes. Mary Grace, who typically found air-quoters annoying, thought Charmin's were sort of charming. "And it's a good thing, too, because without the right couple the show would bomb. I'm not that great. But here's the deal. Mary Grace and Ralph. May I call you that?" he asked, still looking only at Mary Grace.

"Of course," she said, answering quickly, and noticing that when she did, her stomach fluttered.

"Good. The challenge, with each passing season, gets harder and harder. The *right* couple must surpass the previous year's *right* couple, with that certain something that will get America buzzing. Last year America fell in love with Jake and Shawna because America loves a good comeback story. And Jake was all about the comeback, wooing Shawna for an entire year after she broke up with him, citing irreconcilable differences. Flowers. Candy. Three-foot cards. You name it, and that guy did it," Charmin said, leaning back in his chair.

"There was a similar *Mary Tyler Moore* episode," Ralph said, using the pause as an invitation to add to the conversation. "The guy even put up a billboard professing his love for Mary."

"And he handcuffed himself to Mary's desk, too," Mary Grace said with a laugh as she remembered the exact episode to which Ralph was referring, pleased she could add something to the conversation.

"Mary Tyler Moore? Who is she?" Nick Charmin asked. "Scratch that. I don't want to know."

When Charmin spoke, Ralph shot Mary Grace a sheepish grin, and Mary Grace felt her stomach drop like it had been left behind in the turbulence of some horrific plane ride.

"But I do know about Shawna and Jake," Charmin continued. "In some circles, they call Jake's behaviour 'stalking.' I think the guy could have been arrested. But Shawna, after a year, saw it not as stalking, but rather as devotion. She agreed to spend the rest of her life with Jake, and more importantly, to begin the rest of their life on our show. We played up that underdog angle for all it was worth. And it worked. America treated Shawna and Jake like royalty. Dare I conjure up images of Princess Diana in her heyday? Yes, Shawna and Jake; they were the *right* couple with that *it* factor." This time, Charmin made the air quotes twice. "But each year, *it* gets harder, no pun intended. And, of course, the *it* factor changes." Nick Charmin was still looking only at Mary Grace. She felt like he was dissecting her very being with his piercing stare. She could melt under his heat, she thought, wondering if her schoolgirl flush was noticeable.

"So tell me, why are you right for my show? What is the *it* factor you bring me?"

Mary Grace cleared her throat, trying to think of something, anything to say, thinking how their little Mary Tyler Moore reference had bombed. She was coming up dry, though. And Nick Charmin, still looking deep into Mary Grace's eyes, said, "Ralph, you go first."

The only one the move startled was Mary Grace. Ralph was perfectly ready with an answer. "I don't know if we are right for your show," Ralph said. And with those words, Mary Grace's heart froze. "We don't have any *it* factor. The only thing we have going for us right now is Tess Lunt's love and, perhaps, knowledge of *Mary Tyler Moore* trivia. It was a television show, by the way. The rest is pretty boring," he said, going on to explain the messy events and the one and only Angela Falcone, who had gotten them to this point in the first place.

A bottle of Purell later, Ralph and Mary Grace were riding the train back to New Jersey. Ralph accused her of drooling over Nick Charmin. "So squeezably soft he's irresistible, huh, MG?"

"The toilet paper commercial, Ralph? You can do better than that," Mary Grace said, feeling tired and irritable. And a tad annoyed, because his comment had pulled her out of a daydream where Nick Charmin was by her side, smiling that wonderful smile. "Besides, that is so not true," she said, perhaps protesting just a bit too much. "He is just another celebrity type who is madly in love with one thing. Himself. And he happens to be the host of a game show."

"Not a game show," Ralph corrected. "Did you not learn anything from our experience? This is no game show. This is reality television, baby," he said, using his best radio announcer voice. "But we're not getting picked so you can call it—"

"What do you mean, not getting picked?" Mary Grace interrupted, the pitch of her voice heightened. "Tess loves us, remember? We're the ones she wants. She used those exact words, too. I heard her with my own ears."

"I know, but once Charmin gets ahold of her, it's over. There is no way he'll want us on the show. Not after what I told him. We have no *it* factor," Ralph said. "Now we can plan our own perfect wedding, MG. The way it should be." Ralph reached for her hand. She pulled away.

Mary Grace leaned her head back against the seat of the train, more disappointed than she wanted to admit.

Mary Grace rotated to position two, fetal left, and begged for sleep to come, calculating the number of hours she would get if she fell asleep at this exact second. Four and change. "Ugh," she screamed out loud to nobody. If she were speaking to Jayde, she would have called her and complained of insomnia. Complained about Ralph and how he had blown their chance to be on television. Complained about her mother and how she had lied. Admitted something she wouldn't admit to anybody else: feeling flushed when Charmin smiled at her. *Horrible person.*

Even in the wee hours of the morning, Mary Grace and Jayde called each other when they needed to talk. "Hotline," Jayde would answer, her voice groggy with sleep. But they still weren't talking and Mary Grace didn't know why. All she knew was that, for now anyway, she had stopped trying. She was no mind reader. If Jayde wanted to tell her what was wrong, she would have to call. Or at least return one of the many phone calls Mary Grace had placed.

And Annie, she could never call her at this hour. Never. Annie had a husband. Annie had kids. Annie needed her sleep in a different way from either Mary Grace or Jayde. Mary Grace had nobody to talk to. And the thing was, she wasn't entirely sure she knew what she wanted to talk about. She just knew sleep wouldn't take her in, and now, with dawn looming on the horizon, she'd be forced to face the new day, and her mother, exhausted and with dark circles under her eyes. *Damn, why did I tell Angela I would come over today? I'm done with her anyway. I'll just cancel.*

Nobody cancels on Angela Falcone.

CHAPTER SIXTEEN

"Life for me has been exactly what I thought it would be, a cake which I have eaten and had too." MARGARET ANDERSON

Only hours after waking up from a restless night, Mary Grace found herself hot with anger, stuck in her mother's non-air conditioned kitchen, on a most humid day. She could have called her mother and feigned sickness, or used the truth of her anger as an excuse for her absence. She was, after all, *done with Angela*. But she knew, deep in her soul, she could never truly be *done* with her mother. They would have to meet eventually. Better to get it over with.

Angela Falcone's harvest gold kitchen was small, with just enough room for a half circle table for two. The double hung window was open, but there was no hint of a breeze, leaving the white lace curtains to stand still and Mary Grace and her mother to dab at their perspiring foreheads with the cheap napkins that sat in a pile on the table.

Mary Grace was happy she was wearing a sleeveless dress despite her mother's disapproval. What had her mother called it? A muumuu.

"This is not a muumuu, Mom," Mary Grace said. "It is a little summer dress, perfect for unbearable heat." To which her mother responded that she looked like a shapeless blob before commenting on the raccoon bags around her eyes.

"You look terrible," Angela Falcone told her daughter. Mary Grace's father had been dead ten years, and yet she still felt his absence deeply, most particularly in her parents' house, where his presence would have reigned in the ever out-of-control Angela.

"So tell me, Mary Grace, how did it go yesterday?" Angela asked, as if everything were normal.

"Don't be all cute and interested with me," Mary Grace said. "The only reason I am here today is because I promised. I'm still mad at you. Really mad. You lied, Mom."

"It's not a lie if it's in the best interest of your child," Angela said, her look high and mighty, as if no person in the entire world would disagree with her. Mary Grace stared at her mother as if she had lost her mind.

"But you wouldn't understand," Angela added. "You don't have kids."

Mary Grace shivered at her mother's words. Mean and stupid. Her mother had been making these kinds of comments for years. And for years, Mary Grace let her. She was going to fix that right here and right now.

"You said they *needed* me and Ralph. You said without us, Tess Lunt was a goner. You said—"

"Oh, stop telling me what I said."

"You really don't care, do you?" When would she learn her mother was never, ever going to change?

"Of course I care. I'm asking you to tell me about your day, aren't I?"

Mary Grace shook her head. "It's all about you, isn't it, Mom?" Mary Grace didn't even know why she bothered with the dig. Her mother didn't recognize it anyway.

"Mary Grace, you have always needed me to help you make the right decisions and steer you in the right direction. This is no different. This show could be the best thing that ever happened to you. But I knew you wouldn't have agreed to do it, so I had to bend the truth a bit."

"Bend the truth? You lied. Look the word up in the dictionary."

"You're so touchy, dear. Are you expecting a visit from your little friend? Please. Tell me about your day. What does the *I Do* set look like? How many people were there? Did you get to meet Nick Charmin? Is he as handsome in real life as he is on television?"

It was no use. Arguing with Angela was simply no use. If the whole thing weren't so damn sad, Mary Grace might have broken out in intense laugher. Instead she concentrated on her mother's last question. Is Nick Charmin as handsome in real life as he is on television? *Yes. He was very handsome. Butterfly in the stomach, handsome. Make a girl blush with his smile, handsome.* But there was no way Mary Grace would share that with her mom.

"He's okay," she said instead. As she was thinking about what she would share with her mother, the doorbell rang, startling her a bit. "Who else are you expecting?" Mary Grace asked. "Perhaps Mrs. Lunt? Or the needy Tess herself?"

"No. I'm not expecting anyone. This is odd," Angela said, exiting the kitchen and walking toward her front door. She peeked through the tiny window at the top of the door. "Gracie, it's Jayde!"

"Jayde? My Jayde? What is *she* doing here?" Mary Grace began picking at her curls. "Could this day get any better?" she whispered under her breath, rolling her eyes for nobody's benefit but her own.

"Hello darling Jayde; to what do we owe this pleasure?" Angela said upon opening the door, winking her left eye frantically and talking two decibels too loudly.

"You asked me to come, Mrs. Falcone. Remember?" Jayde said. Her face scrunched with confusion.

"Oh, you and your crazy ideas. And you say it's the old ladies who don't remember anything. You kids today have too much going on in your lives, you can't even remember the simple details of a phone conversation."

"Whatever," Jayde said, still standing in the entrance. "Is Mary Grace even here yet?"

"I'm here," Mary Grace said, startling Jayde as she seemed to appear at the front door from out of nowhere.

"Hello?" Jayde said with a tentative whisper, her eyes glistening with tiny pools of tears.

"Jayde, you haven't—?" Mary Grace said, not sure where to begin, or even what was happening. "Why are you here?"

"Come, girls. Let's get out of the hall," Angela Falcone said, grabbing Jayde by the hand. "Come to the dining room where we can all sit together. Don't argue, Gracie. And stop making that face. With your luck, it will freeze that way. Just come and Jayde will tell you why she is here."

"Fine, Mom. But before I get comfortable, just tell me, do we have any other unexpected visitors I should be prepared for?"

"Now listen to yourself, dear. How can you be prepared for an unexpected visitor? Even your old mother knows you can't prepare for the unexpected."

"Oh my God, I'm getting a headache. What is this all about?"

"Tell her, Jayde," Angela prompted, sitting at the head of her dining room table while orchestrating for the young ladies to sit one on her right and one on her left. "Tell Mary Grace why you are here."

Before Jayde had a chance to open her mouth, Angela continued. "Gracie, I was concerned. I am your mother and I was concerned Jayde was brainwashing you like those cults I see on television. Y'know, those poor victims don't stand a chance. And next thing you know, they are all running around naked in San Francisco just because some cult leader told them to."

Mary Grace looked at Jayde, who appeared utterly helpless and sincerely sorry.

"Mom, we live in New Jersey," Mary Grace said.

"There are cults in New Jersey, too. I know about these things, Gracie. I am hop," Angela said.

"What?"

"Hop. I'm hop," Angela repeated

"You mean hip?" Mary Grace said, laughing despite her anger.

"Hip. Hop. Whatever. But I'm it. I know these things. And I was afraid you were being brainwashed."

"To run naked in Princeton?"

"Don't be fresh, young lady. I am still your mother. I was afraid Jayde was brainwashing you against Ralph. I know she doesn't want you to marry hip. I mean him. So I had to nip her negativity in the bud. I had to call that friend of yours and set her straight."

"She called you?" Mary Grace said, looking at Jayde, and using only her eyes to apologize for her mother's crazy behaviour.

Jayde nodded, not opening her mouth.

"So I told Jayde she had better be happy for you, or else. And then I told her to meet us here today so we could eat cake and agree that we are all happy about your wedding. And then you could tell us both about *I Do*," Angela said. "So, Jayde, tell Mary Grace this is the right decision and you are happy for her."

"Yes, Mrs. Falcone," Jayde said, nodding her head like a puppet.

"I mean, say it. Say those exact words," Angela said.

"Mary Grace, you made the right decision and I am happy for you," Jayde said.

"Good girl. Now let me get the cake. But give me a few minutes because I have to ice it. I'll be right back," Angela said, satisfied with the way her little meeting went.

Jayde and Mary Grace waited until Angela was gone before breaking into silent hysterics, almost—but not quite—forgetting they hadn't talked in weeks.

"I am so sorry," Mary Grace said, leaning into the dining room table.

"No, Gracie, I'm the one who is sorry." Jayde grabbed her friend's hands. "Because in this totally weird sort of way, your mother was right."

"What do you mean?"

"I really wasn't happy for you. At first, anyway. I totally thought you were making the wrong decision."

"I know—"

"Let me finish. You see—I went to talk to Ralph."

"You did?" Mary Grace pulled her hands away and leaned back. "He didn't tell me."

"I'm not surprised. He's a good guy, Gracie. I laid it all out for him. Told him my concerns. I even asked him if he's gay."

"Jayde!"

"He's not."

"I know. I told you."

"You told me. But I didn't trust you. Or him. Here's the thing; he didn't kick me out. He listened like I had some right to be there, or something, and he answered all of my borderline-rude questions. And guess what? He's terrific."

Mary Grace just stared at Jayde, a tiny smile on her face.

"It gets worse." Jayde lowered her eyes, avoiding her friend's gaze.

"Worse than all the people I love meeting behind my back? What could be worse? Jayde, I expect this kind of behaviour from my mother, not from you."

"Don't go all commando teacher on me, Gracie. Just let me get through this."

Mary Grace nodded, prompting Jayde to continue.

"So after I figure out Ralph's all decent and shit, I am more pissed. I use an entire therapy session on it. More like half the session. I couldn't even talk for the first half. And what do I discover? I'm jealous. I, Jayde Anderson, am jealous of you, Mary Grace Falcone."

"You're jealous of me? And that's why you haven't been returning my phone calls?"

"I guess."

"Impossible."

"I thought so too at first, but it's true. I am jealous of you. You got the good one, Gracie. I've had more men than you'll ever know in your entire lifetime, but none of it means a hill of beans, because you got the one good one. But here's the thing. When I say it out loud, it sort of goes away. I'm not so crazy jealous as I am happy for you. More like a little jealous and a lot happy. Does that make sense?"

"Totally. It's the way I've lived my entire life as your best friend. A little jealous and a lot happy. I just never knew to put it quite that way. I think a little jealousy is okay, though. So long as it doesn't ever come between us."

"Nothing could ever come between us, Gracie. And I'm sorry I waited so long to talk to you. I've missed you," Jayde said, tapping her fist to her chest.

"You have no idea how much I missed you too, Jayde. But I'm confused. If you came to this epiphany that you are only a little jealous, and a lot happy, why are you sitting here in my mother's dining room? Couldn't you have just told her you were happy for me and Ralph and you really do like him?"

"Tell your mother something when her mind is already made up? She had more fun believing I was the evil cult leader of an underground 'I Hate Ralph' group, and my sole mission in life was to brainwash you, her precious daughter, to our sinister way of thinking."

"Sorry. I forgot."

"Besides, I figured today would be as good a time as any to apologize. I am sorry, Gracie."

"No need to apologize." Mary Grace reached her hands across the table, clasping hold of Jayde's. "Friends?"

"Best. Now spill. How was *I Do*? What did you wear? Was it the outfit we picked out?"

"Forget the outfit. Charmin is hot," Mary Grace whispered, craning her neck to make sure she was still out of earshot of Angela.

Jayde shot her a wicked look, one that begged for more.

"Chocolate cake, girls." Angela pushed through the swinging door to the dining room holding a serving platter with a dark, rich cake, forks, napkins, and plates before Mary Grace had a chance to breathe another word about the dreamy Nick Charmin. "To die for," she would have said. She smiled as she recalled Charmin, and the phrase she and Jayde were fond of in high school. But there was no time.

"There is no problem in life that can't be solved with a good piece of cake. Right, girls?" Angela glanced from her daughter to Jayde, certain she had just broken up a moment of which she would have loved to be a part.

CHAPTER SEVENTEEN

"I don't exactly know what it means to be ready. A cake when the oven timer goes off? Am I fully baked or only half-baked?" JESSICA SAVITCH

It was Monday, the first full day of summer vacation for Mary Grace, and still no relief from the oppressive weather had appeared. The weather folks on television were fond of calling this hot streak the "Haze Craze." For Mary Grace, heat or not, the start of summer vacation was a day she filled with mindless errands, all necessary, but performed in back-to-back fashion so as to keep her mind off life, marriage, television, Ralph, and *I Do*. There was the bank, the office supply store, the dry cleaners, the shoe repair, Home Depot, and finally the grocery store. Each time she entered a store, she appreciated the ultra-cold blast of overused air conditioner units.

After carrying her laundry, paper, ink cartridges, markers, binders, and assorted gardening supplies from her car to the stoop of her apartment, there was only one more package to go. The last one to lug from the car to the steps was a brown paper grocery bag filled with cake mix, icing, eggs, and milk. It was just heavy enough to make Mary Grace sweat. Here it was, nearly five thirty in the evening, and yet the temperature remained just shy of ninety degrees with the humidity at one hundred percent. Mary Grace pictured the weather girl on television—her apologetic face. "Add another one to the Haze Craze," she would say. *It's a craze, all right*, Mary Grace thought. And the torrential rain that had poured and stopped while Mary

Grace had shopped for her cake supplies did nothing to cool off the air. Instead, it left in its wake the distinct smell of steamy water on hot blacktop. It was an odour that made Mary Grace long for the warm smell of cake baking in the oven.

Despite her sweaty upper lip, she picked up her pace because she couldn't wait to pour the chocolate cake mix in a bowl, add oil, eggs, and water, and beat with her electric hand mixer for four straight minutes. *In under ten minutes I'll have this cake in the oven*, she thought, before wiping her forehead with the back of her hand, and jogging just a touch faster to her front steps. Staring at all the packages she had to haul upstairs, she balanced the grocery bag on her right hip, dug for her keys, and then, finally, after nearly seven hours, she let herself back into her apartment.

The hot, thick air she walked into was nearly suffocating. Before even dropping the bag of groceries on the kitchen table, she walked to her two air conditioner units and blasted them to high, thinking how she should have let them hum all day while she was running around so she could have walked into a cool and comfortable apartment. Instead, as always, she chose to save on her electric bill, thinking about what her father always said when Mary Grace asked for frivolous things like Bonnie Bell lip gloss or the Pet Rock.

"When you work hard for your money, you won't want to waste it."

A disregard for money was the only thing that could get her father visibly mad. He put up with a lot from Angela. And in doing so, he never had a cross word for her. He wore the clothes she asked him to. Visited the relatives she told him to. Played bridge with the couples she liked. And before it was popular for dads to help out around the house, he willingly did all the grocery shopping and at least half of the laundry. And he never complained. But Mary Grace remembered the day her world changed.

The Price is Right was on television in the bedroom, the kitchen, and the living room, so Angela could move seamlessly among the rooms, doing her chores, without missing one moment of hospitable host, Bob Barker. Every light was on, too, and Angela had left the freezer door hanging wide open, as she was in the midst of pulling out frozen meat when she got distracted by one or another of the games Bob Barker was discussing with his contestants.

In the middle of Angela's egregious waste of electricity, Mary Grace's dad came home unexpectedly for lunch, and a fight ensued, scaring five-year-old Mary Grace half to death. Her father screamed at her mother for wasting money, his face red and puffy with anger. Lou paced around the house, turning off every television and every light. For the coup de grâce, he pulled hamburger meat out of the open freezer and flung it across the kitchen, watching it slam against the wall and bounce to the floor. For her part, Angela screamed right back. But Mary Grace couldn't help but detect a trace of fear in her mother's eyes, and that's what scared her the most.

When he was gone, Angela turned every light and every television back on. Such a blatant disregard for her father and his tirade sent a shiver of panic deep into the heart of Mary Grace. She never wanted to witness such a scene again, and though she did, she never did grow comfortable with them.

I don't want to waste my money, she thought to herself, feeling as if she were betraying her father by even thinking about keeping her air conditioner units on when she wasn't home. *But I'm a grown woman,* she reminded herself. *Dying of heat stroke isn't practical either.*

Finally, she put the grocery bag down on her kitchen table and unloaded the contents, putting only the eggs and milk away, so they wouldn't spoil, because she needed to haul up her other packages and she wanted to let the place cool off a bit before adding the heat of the oven to her apartment. When everything was unloaded and where it should be, she walked to her bedroom to change out of her sweat-sodden clothes, and the phone rang.

"Hello?" she said, taking the cordless with her on her way to the bedroom.

"What's up?" Ralph asked.

"Just got home. I've been running around the whole day."

"I know. I've been trying to reach you."

"Listen, Ralph, can I call you back? It's an oven in here and I have to get out of these clothes."

"Oooh. What are you getting into?"

"Not now, Ralph. I'm too hot."

"I like hot."

"Not sexy hot. I've got to call you back."

"Wait. Have you heard from Nick Charmin?" Ralph asked, stalling for time.

"No. Not at all. Why? Why would I hear from him?" Mary Grace said.

"I don't know. Didn't mean to make you jumpy. If not Nick, how about Tess or anyone from *I Do*? Do they want us or not?" Ralph asked, trying to pretend he hadn't heard the awkwardness in Mary Grace's voice at the mention of Nick Charmin.

"Not a word. It's been a week. Probably not interested."

"Are you disappointed?"

"No," she lied. "Ralph, I really have to go," she said, pulling shorts and a T-shirt from her drawer. "If I don't change out of these clothes I might die of heat prostration."

Ralph sighed. Heavy and deep. "Wait. Don't hang up. You never want to talk anymore. You've always got something to do or something to read, or somewhere to be that doesn't include me."

"You're just being paranoid," she said. "Today was my first day not going to school. I just had some stuff to do."

"You have that much to do? That much to keep you occupied? We can't even have lunch?"

"It was my first day, Ralph. Give me a break. Listen," she said, her mind on Nick Charmin, wondering if he kept his air conditioner units on all day. Of course he did. He probably had his central air on some touch screen, temperature moderated setting. But before he was the famous Nick Charmin, Mary Grace wondered what he did with his air units. Keep them on all day or save on the electric bill? Mary Grace had to do something. *Throw Ralph a bone.*

"I know what Jayde did to you," Mary Grace said. "She told me."

"She did?"

"Yes. You're a good man to put up with her," she said, meaning it. *And your crazy fiancée*, she thought, but didn't say.

"It seemed important to her. And since she's important to you, I figured what the hell."

"If it means anything to you, Jayde was impressed. Impressed with you taking the meeting. Impressed with what you had to say. And amazed you never even mentioned it to me."

"Honestly, Mary Grace, what Jayde thinks doesn't mean as much to me as what you think."

Mary Grace knew she had to stop Ralph's paranoia. She had to give him more than conversation. She had to give him time. "I'm just about to put a cake in the oven. Want to come over for dessert? Say, one hour?"

"I'll be there."

"Ralph?" Mary Grace said, before he hung up the receiver. "When we're married, do you think we'll be happy?"

"I'll be there in less than an hour," he said, pretending not to hear her question, acting as if there were no inner demons Mary Grace was battling, because being blind was easier than being hurt.

CHAPTER EIGHTEEN

"When someone asks if you'd like cake or pie, why not say you want cake and pie?" LISA LOEB

Annie was driving her car, a black BMW John wanted her to have. She glanced at the clock. *It's not too early to call Mary Grace,* she thought. *She'll be up.* Nodding her head, agreeing with herself, Annie touched the hands-free button on her steering wheel, called out the digits to Mary Grace's number, and within seconds was connected.

"Annie? What's the matter? Why are you calling so early?" Mary Grace demanded, looking up at her own alarm clock. She was sitting on the floor, cell phone next to her, along with piles of socks, underwear, stockings, bras, and assorted random papers, too. Her empty underwear drawer was in front of her.

"Nothing's wrong. I didn't wake you, did I?" Annie asked, a sound of panic in her voice.

"God, no! I'm cleaning out my drawers. You know, stuff I've been meaning to get to since September. I think I have bras in here from high school." Mary Grace held up a dingy, grey bra that was missing one of its two under wires. She chucked it into the throw-away pile. "What are you doing? Where are the boys?"

"John is taking them to day camp. I'm heading to my mother's. She's redecorating."

"Again?"

"You know her. She no sooner finishes the last room in the house before starting all over again. It gives her something to do. My decorator gave me a bunch of fabric samples for her to check out. Last time Mom wanted city chic. Now she wants country casual."

"Ha! Your mother's project is her house. My mother's is me," Mary Grace said, holding up a pair of fuzzy socks her mother had given her. She put them on; they were soft on her feet, but her mother was so hard on her heart.

"Speaking of you—"

"Nice segue," Mary Grace said with a laugh, pulling the socks off, balling them up, and placing them in her sock pile.

"Yeah, not really. But what'd you hear from the show? It's been two weeks."

"I know. I'm counting. Ralph and I were just talking about it." She spoke the name Ralph, but her mind wandered to thoughts of Nick Charmin, thoughts she knew she needed to suppress. She didn't want to share her thoughts with Annie, her friend of the perfect marriage. It would make her seem so… horrible. She was about to marry Ralph. She shouldn't be thinking about anyone but Ralph. Why, then, was Nick Charmin constantly popping up in her brain? She had only met him once, but he was hard to forget. His smile. The way he made her stomach flip flop. *Snap out of it,* she told herself.

Mary Grace opened a letter from the pile of papers that sat before her. She had tucked it in her underwear drawer, along with a dozen others from Ralph. It had been written after their first date. *I am thrilled I met you,* the letter said. Mary Grace felt a warmth envelope her heart. Ralph was an open book, and the words he shared always made Mary Grace feel like a queen. Most times. She smiled at the thought.

"Mary Grace? You still there? You got quiet," Annie said.

"Still here." Mary Grace put the letter down gently in the save pile. "Just got distracted for a second. Multitasking."

Annie laughed. "I am the King of Multitasking," she said. "It's John's nickname for me. You have to be, y'know? There aren't enough hours in the day otherwise. Before showing my mother these samples," she continued, reaching to the passenger seat to pull out one of the samples from the bag for a quick peek, "I have to stop at the dry-cleaner, bank, and pharmacy." She couldn't find her sample bag. She glanced over and still didn't see it. She quickly twisted her neck around and checked the back seat. She saw the dry cleaning bag but no samples. "Shoot!" she exclaimed with disgust in her voice.

"What's the matter?"

"I think I left the samples for my mother at home. I'm losing it, Mary Grace. Seriously. I'm helping her redecorate and I forget the samples."

"That sucks. Where are you?"

"Almost at the bank. I'll stop here first. Check the car once more. If they're not here I'll swing back."

"What if you left them on top of the car and they're strewn all over town?" Mary Grace said with a laugh.

"That's not funny. I better go. I need to get my head fixed on right. Keep me posted about the show, okay? I mean it. I want to know everything." With the emphasis Annie put on the word "everything," Mary Grace couldn't help but wonder if Jayde had told her how hot she found Charmin, but Annie hung up before Mary Grace had a chance to respond.

Mary Grace opened up another letter from Ralph and read it, the smile never leaving her lips.

I'm such an idiot, Annie thought as she realized that forgetting the fabric samples was wasting a good hour of her day. *An hour I can't spare to lose. I might even have to call John to pick the kids up from camp,* she thought as she calculated each minute of the rest of her day.

After the bank, and a thorough examination of a sample-free car, Annie decided to finish up with her other errands. Then she placed a quick call to her mother to let her know she was running late.

"Like always," her mother said, not trying to hide her disappointment.

Annie felt incompetent, and was becoming increasingly angry with herself and all the time she was wasting. She took a deep breath and released it slowly, trying hard to squelch her feelings of inadequacy. She pulled up to her house and spotted John's car in the driveway. Her personal anger shifted to panic. Fast. *What's the matter with the boys? Why didn't he bring them to camp? Are they sick? Is he sick? Why didn't he call?* She parked the car as fast as she could and raced into the house, afraid of what she would find.

"John? Boys?" she called as she raced up the stairs. "What's the matter? Who is sick?" Annie could feel her heart racing. "Where are you guys?" She could hear the fear in her own voice. *Oh, I should never have agreed to go to Mom's,* she thought, beating herself up. Again. She entered the boys' room and couldn't find them.

She entered her bedroom, and was shaken to depths she hadn't even known existed. She was speechless. For a moment. And then,

"What the fuck?"

John shot up, stared at his wife, and then froze. He remained like a statue for what felt like an eternity.

Annie's eyes were as wide as saucers. She was unable to blink. Or swallow. But she felt the saliva building up in her mouth. *I'm going to throw up.* She turned her back on the sight that was her husband in bed with another woman and wretched. She wiped her mouth with the back of her hand, took a deep breath, and then turned back around. John hadn't moved.

"It's not what you think," he said, his voice only vaguely familiar to Annie.

She took a moment to let both the sight and his words sink in. Finally, like a loose trigger finger, she let it rip.

"What are you talking about? Not what I think? I trusted you, you big fuck. You know why? You know why I trusted you? Because you never gave me reason not to. But now? Now? I will NEVER trust you again."

John still didn't move.

"Say something," Annie screamed. "Wait. No. Don't. Just fuck you and your little whore." She plunged her hand into her pocketbook and pulled out her fat, heavy wallet. She hurled it at John, nailing him right in the nose. John screamed with pain.

"Shit. I'm glad I got you, you fuck-head," Annie seethed.

"Annie… you don't curse," John said. There it was again; the vaguely familiar voice of someone she used to know. The blow to his nose unfroze John's stony self, and a little blood dripped from his left nostril. He wiped it with the sheet.

"I do now. And I'm going to start doing a lot of things I've never done before if you two don't get the fuck out of here. Things with knives and shit. So just go," Annie said, her face so red she could feel the fever glowing.

"Annie, please," John pleaded, trying to get his pants on and stand up, all at the same time. He failed and fell back on the bed.

"Don't. Say. Another. Word," Annie said. "Just leave. Now. Wait," she added, checking out John's partner, who had finally rolled over, covering herself with as much sheet as possible. "What the fuck is that? You can't weigh more than one hundred and ten pounds. Who is that skinny?"

The woman didn't utter a word. Her eyes were filled with fear, regret, and panic.

"Oh. Wait. You didn't have TWINS! Did you? This is the body you get after two humans grow inside you. At the same time," Annie said, pointing at herself with dramatic emphasis. "Now get your skinny ass out of my house. John! Our bedroom? Across from MY boys? You weren't being nice this morning. You were getting rid of me. Now I'm getting rid of you. Go," she said, pointing toward the bedroom door.

"Annie?"

"Don't 'Annie' me. Just go. Now."

Annie made a beeline for the boys' room, shut and locked the door, and leaned against it before sliding down into a heap of pathetic. She wretched again, but this time nothing came up. She couldn't cry. She couldn't breathe. She couldn't move. She just listened for the sounds of John and his whore leaving the house; feet tramping down the stairs, doors closing, car ignition igniting. When she was certain they were gone she began sobbing and shaking uncontrollably, her life over.

CHAPTER NINETEEN

"Let them eat cake." MARIE ANTOINETTE

Mary Grace was looking forward to an evening at MexTexas with the girls. Annie had called a meeting that morning, and Mary Grace easily obliged, looking forward to getting out and getting her mind off being engaged, *I Do*, and Nick Charmin. After a long cardio workout, she would indulge herself in some highly caloric dinner, margaritas, cake, and the company of her best friends.

"Annie called a meeting," Jayde said on the phone that morning, right after Mary Grace hung up with Annie and right before Mary Grace left for the gym. "Annie never calls a meeting."

"I know," Mary Grace said. "She faithfully attends each and every meeting, but she never calls one. Must be big."

"What do you think it is?" Jayde pushed her hand out before her eyes, inspecting her manicure.

"I bet she's pregnant," Mary Grace guessed.

"I bet she's moving," Jayde said. "I bet John got some big promotion and they are moving to California."

"Did she tell you that?" Mary Grace felt panicked by the thought of one of her two best friends moving clear across the country.

"No. But we had lunch the other day and she told me John's crazy busy at work. He stays late every night to talk to the folks in Cali. I vote promotion."

"Wait. You had lunch with Annie? Without me?"

"Don't get all whiny. We had to talk about you. You've got some big shit going on, Gracie. We couldn't really talk about you in front of you."

"Well that makes me feel better." Mary Grace coughed with sarcasm.

"Oh stop. You know we love you."

Mary Grace nodded to herself, allowing a half smile to form.

"This is about Annie," Jayde continued. "And I think it's a promotion."

"Did you press her?" Mary Grace asked, resigned to the fact that her friends did in fact love her and were only trying to make sure she was okay.

"Of course I pressed her. Annie said we've got to wait until tonight." Jayde, still checking out her manicure, noticed two nails were chipped. *I'll take care of my nails over lunch*, she thought. "What's up with *I Do* and the lovely Nick Charmin?"

"Nothing. But I am so sick of thinking about myself. I can't wait to go out tonight and concentrate on someone else."

"I'm sick of thinking about you, too," Jayde said with a laugh. "We'll talk tonight. About Annie. I've got to hop. I need to listen to an hour's worth of the interview I recorded with fashion designer JAYTEE, then write my blog. If I don't get working I'll be in bad shape. Hey," Jayde shouted, almost as an afterthought. "Care to make a little wager? California or baby?"

"Shut up, Jayde. I am not wagering on Annie's life. See you tonight," Mary Grace said, pushing the end button on her phone.

Driving to MexTexas, Mary Grace thought about the easy money she could have won from Jayde, had she been so inclined to bet. There was no way Annie was moving to California. John would never leave Jersey. And even if he wanted to, Annie wouldn't let him. Pregnant. Annie was definitely pregnant. Mary Grace thought about what she would say when Annie told her the news. After Annie's difficult time with the twins, she always said she didn't want more children. Two were enough for her and John. But

Dane and Drew were five now, and in all-day kindergarten. Perhaps she had changed her mind. Or perhaps it was an oops. It would be up to Jayde and Mary Grace to convince Annie oops babies were the best. Jayde was an oops baby, born when her mother was forty-three years old and her brothers were both in high school. Oops, Jayde is here. And where would Mary Grace and Annie be without Jayde?

After fifteen minutes of driving, her mind occupied with something other than herself for the first time in weeks, Mary Grace found herself parking her car in the MexTexas parking lot. She spotted Jayde's car right away and pulled into the available spot next to it. She flipped down the mirror hidden in the visor and applied some lip gloss. "Oops babies are the best," she whispered under her breath, ready to use the phrase that night.

Mary Grace spotted Annie and Jayde immediately. They were already seated with drinks in hand. *Drink in hand*, Mary Grace thought. *That's not good. Pregnant women aren't supposed to drink. Maybe it's a virgin drink.*

"Hey, ladies." Mary Grace slid into the vacant seat.

Maria, their favourite waitress, was on Mary Grace's heals. "Don't want you to be behind your gal pals." Maria plopped a margarita down in front of Mary Grace.

"Thanks, Maria," Jayde said, trying to speed things up so they could get to the news.

"Cheers." Annie raised her glass. "Here's to the best friends a girl could ever have. Please, don't leave me now," she said, her eyes brimming with tears.

"Cheers?" Jayde and Mary Grace mimicked. The three women gulped from their drinks.

"Nobody's leaving anybody," Mary Grace said after swallowing. "Having a baby is a wonderful thing. We wouldn't ditch you just because you're having another baby. Was it an oops, honey?"

"Having a baby? What are you talking about? Who told her I'm pregnant?" Annie shot Jayde a curious look.

"Nobody," Mary Grace said. "I just assumed—"

"You assumed wrong. This isn't about me being pregnant—"

"You're moving to California?" Jayde interjected.

"No," Annie said.

Jayde looked disappointed, and fired Mary Grace a look that said, "What now, then?"

"Who told her I'm moving to California?" Annie asked, giving a nod to Mary Grace.

Mary Grace just offered a little shrug of apology.

And then there was silence. Annie waited a solid twenty seconds before speaking. "John is having an affair." Annie leaned her entire body into the table and spoke so low it was nearly impossible to understand her.

"No way." Mary Grace shrugged off the thought of John cheating. "He adores you, like nothing I've ever seen before in my life. He wouldn't cheat on you. Why do you think he's cheating on you?"

"Gracie's right," Jayde said. "This time she's right. What makes you so suspicious?"

"I'm not suspicious. I said he's having an affair. And you want to know how I know? I caught him. In my bed. With another woman. Turns out all the times he said he was too tired, he was just too tired for me."

"Holy shit." Jayde reached for Annie's hands. "I'll kill him. Where are the kids?"

"My mother is babysitting."

"Where's John?" Mary Grace asked.

"At this exact moment, I don't know. But in general, he's staying at some hotel. I told the kids he's on a business trip, just till I figure out what to really say or do."

"Good. Now back up. Start from the beginning and tell us everything," Jayde said, polishing off her drink and waving her hand in the air in the hopes Maria would soon provide another round.

"It's ugly." Annie reached her left thumb to her ring finger to play with the diamond wedding band that was no longer there. Its absence made her shudder. After a deep breath, Annie proceeded to tell her best friends every last sordid detail.

"You threatened them with a knife?" Jayde said. "I didn't think you had it in you."

"Where did all those f-bombs come from, Annie? I don't think I've heard you utter that word in the ten years I've known you," Mary Grace added.

"I didn't know I was capable of any of that either. I think I was in some sort of shock. That asshole even gave me a fifty that morning. 'Treat your mom to lunch,' he said. What a guy," Annie said, followed by a sarcastic, throaty laugh. She stopped talking for a minute, reached for the napkin on her lap, and wiped her tears. Nobody said a word as she regained her composure.

"What an idiot I am. An idiot," she said, louder than she meant to. The couple at the table next to them turned around. "I'm sorry," Annie said, using a whisper. She continued with the story in a low voice.

"He's a bastard," Jayde announced. "I will kill him. Mary Grace will help. Right?" Jayde looked at Mary Grace, who nodded her confirmation.

"No. My children need a father. And I need his money."

"*This isn't what it looks like.* I can't believe he copped the worst line in history to use on you," Jayde said.

"What'd you do with the kids?" Mary Grace asked. "That day, I mean?"

"I couldn't very well pick them up myself. I was comatose. I couldn't tell my mother. I'm already her biggest disappointment. John? Ha. I wasn't ready to tell you guys," Annie said with a sorry look on her face. "So, I called their friend's mom and lied. Told her I had the stomach flu. Asked her to take them home with her and keep them all day."

"And?" Jayde asked.

"She did. And I stayed in their room, in my coma, all day."

"What can we do?" Mary Grace inquired, her heart beating excessively fast as she reached for a huge gulp of her drink. There was a ringing in her ears that drowned out the conversation for a moment. In some sort of crazy way, at that exact moment, she felt she was doing to Ralph exactly what John had done to Annie. Hers, she conceded, was mental cheating. But just the thought made her nauseous. It took steady concentration for

Mary Grace to return to the conversation, and when she did, she heard the distinct throaty voice of Jayde.

"I know an excellent divorce lawyer. Remember Robert Altmann? We dated for a while. He's the best there is. That's why I never married him. Ha! Too tight a pre-nup," she said with a smile.

"Don't go ape-shit on me, Jayde, when I say what I'm about to say."

"Promise. This is about you, right now. And your feelings."

Annie swallowed long and hard before spitting the words out.

"I'm not sure I'm filing for divorce."

"What the hell are you talking about? You catch your husband in bed with another woman and you're not filing for divorce? Annie, there are no alternatives here."

"I said don't go ape-shit." Annie raised her left hand like a stop sign. "It's just not that easy."

"Yes," Jayde said, rummaging through her wallet for Robert Altmann's card. "It is that easy. This isn't some show like *I Do*," she said, glancing at Mary Grace. "Or *The Marriage Games*."

"More like *The Hunger Games*," Annie said with a chortle. "Last one standing kind of shit."

Mary Grace just looked at Annie, begging her to continue.

Annie hesitated and then went on. "Ten years ago, before I had been in this marriage for twelve years, before I had two kids, I would have agreed with you, Jayde. No alternatives. Divorce. But in reality, there is so much more I need to know before throwing my entire way of life down the drain and two kids into complete turmoil. It's not just about me."

"It is about you. You can't stay with him. I won't let you," Jayde argued.

Annie banged her fist on the table. "I hate him," she said louder than expected, causing more stares. "And I hate what he did to my family," she added, lowering her voice to an acceptable volume. "But it's not that simple." Her voice was down to a whisper.

"You're crazy," Jayde said.

"Don't be so quick to judge," Mary Grace interjected. "Obviously she thought this through. You thought this through, right, Annie?"

"That's all I've been doing, and here's what I figured out. The only person I can change is me. I can't change John. Or my mother."

Annie looked directly into Mary Grace's eyes and paused before speaking. "Mary Grace," she said, her voice firm and assertive, "you can't change Angela."

Mary Grace sat up straight, feeling the sting of Annie's words.

"Nobody can," Jayde added with a wave of her hand.

"And Jayde," Annie said, taking a huge gulp of her margarita.

Jayde stared back, eyebrows arched in anticipation.

"You can't change Mary Grace. Or me."

Jayde shot Mary Grace a look.

"So now what?" Jayde said, confident she was speaking for both herself and Mary Grace.

"I didn't know. Until now. Just this second. Here's what we're going to do." Annie dug a hand deep into her purse.

Jayde covered her face with her arms and ducked. "You're not going to hurl your wallet at me, are you?"

Annie laughed, allowing her buzz to let her be light-hearted for a moment.

"No. Here." She shoved a pen in front of Mary Grace, then one in front of Jayde. "We are going to have a ceremony." Her words were a bit slurred from the drinks.

"Maria?" Annie waved her hand to get their waitress' attention. When Maria glanced her way, Annie shouted, "Three shots of tequila, please." She held three fingers up to make certain Maria understood.

"Okay ladies, on the napkin in front of you, you must write down what you believe about yourself. What you want to believe about yourself. Or, and this is huge, what you would like to change about yourself."

Mary Grace and Jayde looked at each other with curious stares.

"I'm not kidding. And don't show them to anyone. Ever. This is about you," Annie added.

Maria put the three shots on the table, one in front of each woman.

"I don't know what to write," Jayde said, staring at her blank napkin.

"Stop whining. And just do it," Annie demanded.

The women thought for a moment and then began to jot down their thoughts, neither willing to disagree with a drunk Annie, especially at such a vulnerable time.

"Okay, are we done?" Annie asked, looking down at her own napkin and then over to Jayde and Mary Grace.

Jayde and Mary Grace nodded.

"Shots on the count of three. Then put your napkins in the centre, upside down, and your shot glasses on top. When we are done we will remember how empowered we are because WE ARE THE CHANGE. One. Two. Three," Annie said.

Shots downed, napkins in the centre, shot glasses on top, the girls laughed.

"That felt pretty good," Jayde confessed. "I think I got more out of this than any therapy session with Dr. Upadya."

Annie just smiled, feeling drunk and more powerful than she had in a while. They paid the bill and exited MexTexas, a bit loopy from the margaritas and shots.

"I have to pee," Mary Grace said. "Wait for me."

Mary Grace backtracked to the bathroom, making a quick stop at their table. She noticed Maria was already bussing the dishes, but the napkins they had written on were still in the centre of the table. She grabbed the napkins, winked at Maria, and shoved them deep into her purse. She promised herself never to read them, but wanted to keep them forever as proof that this night of empowerment had really happened.

When she returned to her friends they were in front of the restaurant, arms linked. Mary Grace easily linked her arm with Jayde's. "What now?" Mary Grace asked.

"Let's buy a pack of cigarettes and smoke them all," Jayde said.

"Yeah—" Annie said.

"No," Mary Grace finished. "Seriously, Annie. What now?"

"Let's walk off the drunk," she said, still arm-in-arm with her best friends. So they began walking around town, window-shopping, talking about their newfound power, and not saying one more word about John's affair. Mary Grace was incredulous, sad, and drunk. She took a mental picture of the three of them, arm-in-arm.

More proof.

CHAPTER TWENTY

"Someone left the cake out in the rain." RICHARD HARRIS

Mary Grace was back in her car, and as Annie had suggested, they had walked off the drunk. She was no longer buzzed, but remained unable to process the events of the night. Annie had caught John in bed with another woman. She couldn't even imagine what it would feel like in real life. Your house. Your bed. Your husband. It's a violation of everything you take for granted. Like nothing is sacred. Nothing is true or real. *How could John do that to Annie? To the kids? To us? Doesn't he realize an act like this is no standalone thing?* The trickle down effect is enormous. That shit is only supposed to happen in the movies. An affair like that is the stuff you see on television, read about in the papers, overhear at the gym. It isn't supposed to be the thing that happens to your best friend. *How could Annie be so strong and so calm? How could she not want to kill him? Or divorce him? Or take him for every penny he is worth?*

Mary Grace couldn't help but replay Annie's words. *There is so much more I need to know before throwing my entire way of life down the drain and two kids into complete turmoil. It's not just about me.* Jayde had countered with the fact that Annie wasn't the one doing the throwing; it was John. *It matters, but it doesn't,* Annie had said. *Maybe if he is doing the throwing, I need to do the catching.*

I Do. That's a laugh, Mary Grace thought. *It's more like I Don't. And I never will.*

Mary Grace let the car retrace her route back home, but practically without her control, it stopped at the diner. It was early, only nine thirty, since Annie had to get home for her mother. Mary Grace didn't feel much like going home. She dug for her cell and dialled Ralph.

"I'm at the diner," she said. "You sleeping?"

"A little bit," he answered, reaching for the lamp on his nightstand. He clicked on the light, which was too bright for his sleepy eyes. He turned it off again. "How are the gals?"

"Ralph, can you meet me here for cake?"

"Now? I can't meet you now. I'm getting up for the gym tomorrow."

"Yeah, so you can get to the equipment before anyone else touches it for the day."

"Did you drink mean drinks, Mary Grace?"

There was silence on Ralph's end of the phone. Then he heard what he thought was a sniffle.

"It's bad, Ralph," Mary Grace whispered. "Can you please meet me?" Her voice was soft and pleading.

"I'll be right there. The diner by the gym?"

"Yup. Make it fast. I need you."

Ralph hung up the phone and dashed across the hall of his mother's house to the bathroom. He ran the faucet to heat the water before jumping into the shower-over-tub. Starting with his feet and working up, he soaped himself with the white bar of Ivory. He used the same soap for his hair and allowed the hot water to wash the residue away. The whole procedure took less than five minutes. He towelled dry, wrapped a fresh towel around his waist, and went back to his room where he pulled a clean pair of pressed jeans from his drawer. He put them on, making sure the creases were just so. From his closet he drew a pressed blue T-shirt from its matching blue plastic hanger. Socks and sneakers, and he was ready to go. He trotted down the stairs and called to his mother in her first floor bedroom.

"Mom, I'm going to meet Mary Grace at the diner."

"At this hour?" she asked. "It's late and you have work tomorrow."

"It's summer, Mom. There's no work," Ralph said.

"If it's summer, then why am I watching new shows on the television?"

"They're not new, Mom; you just don't remember seeing them."

"Don't lie," she said. "I would remember an episode if I saw it. I'm telling you, these shows are new."

"It's probably some new network schedule then. All the new shows are aired in the summer," Ralph said.

"You're right. I like it. None of this re-run business. Now you get a good night's sleep, Ralph."

"I'm going out, Mom."

"Have a nice time, dear. Where are you going?"

"Just to the diner," Ralph repeated without flinching. "Can I bring you back something?"

"I never ate dinner," she said. "How about a roast chicken?"

"Okay," Ralph agreed, with no intention of bringing home a dinner she wouldn't remember asking for anyway. Especially since she had eaten every ounce of the steak he had grilled earlier. "Sleep well, Mom."

"You showered?" Mary Grace quizzed upon seeing Ralph walk up to her booth, his hair still wet and gleaming.

"You know I can't go out unless I've showered and put on clean clothes. It took less than five minutes."

"But this is an emergency." She played with her final bites of cake.

"I'm here, aren't I? I'll have whatever she ordered," Ralph said to the waitress before she even got the chance to spit out the question. "What is so awful, MG? Tell me."

"Can two people really spend a lifetime together? Maybe it's just not practical."

"Are you talking about us?" Ralph asked, puzzled by the emergent question.

"I think we should enter into some sort of ten-year marriage contract," Mary Grace said, not having even heard Ralph's previous question. Without taking a breath, she kept on talking. "Or perhaps a five-year one. It could be renewable, of course, upon completion. That is, if both parties are amenable to the idea."

"Mary Grace. Stop," Ralph said, atypically raising his voice.

Mary Grace stared at him and cocked her head, not at all accustomed to hearing that tone. She didn't open her mouth, but appeared to have so much to say. They remained like that, quiet for a moment, until Ralph reached across the table for her hands. She let him. With his thumbs, he gently rubbed the backs of her hands and watched as her eyes filled with tears.

"Things just aren't what they seem," Mary Grace whispered.

Ralph didn't reply. He just raised his eyebrows, begging Mary Grace to continue.

"Did I ever tell you about my five grandmothers?" she asked, reclaiming her hands so her left one could twist her curls.

Ralph shook his head no.

"My father had three spinster sisters: Sophie, Isabelle, and Trudy," Mary Grace continued, her voice slow and deliberate. "They lived together in my Grandmother's house. My whole young life I just assumed they were my grandmothers."

"I can see that," Ralph said, nodding his head in agreement.

"So one day, I'm eight, and I go bragging to Debbie Korner about how lucky I am to have five grandmothers, one on my mother's side and four on my father's. Debbie gets all high and mighty and says, 'impossible.' So I say, 'possible.' I have five grandmothers. And she gets real serious and tells me to stop lying. And if I keep on lying she won't be my friend anymore and, worse, she'll start telling everyone in school I'm a liar. So I run home crying." Mary Grace could feel her eyes welling with tears, as if Debbie were calling her a liar all over again. She became silent.

"Go on," Ralph said, prodding her to continue. After a moment, she did.

"I tell my mother about the five-grandmother thing. And she laughs. Angela Falcone just laughs. So I cry harder. And she laughs harder. And then she says, 'Mary Grace, whatever would possess you to go around telling people you have five grandmothers?' So I tell her about how I thought Sophie, Isabelle, and Trudy were my grandmothers. And now she is laughing so hard she can hardly speak. Between gasps of air she tells me they are my aunts, not my grandmothers. How could I possibly confuse that?"

"What did you say?" Ralph asked.

"I say, 'Because they are all old, fat, have big boobs, and squeeze my cheeks whenever I see them.' It made sense to me at the time."

"I can see that," Ralph repeated, agreeing with Mary Grace's memory. "What'd your mother say?"

"Between laughing and gasping for air she tells me they are your old, fat, big-breasted aunts who squeeze your cheeks. But they are not all your grandmothers. And little one, if you don't stop lying to your friends like that, you're going to wind up alone like those aunts of yours with nobody to marry."

"Nobody to marry." Ralph repeated the words under his breath. *Angela Falcone has been beating up on this poor kid her whole life*, he thought, tears now pooling in his eyes. "What does it all mean, MG? To you?"

"Don't you get it? Things aren't what they seem. For the first eight years of my life I thought I had five grandmothers. I thought I was something special. And then I found out the truth."

"And the truth hurts?"

"Sometimes," Mary Grace said, stabbing her fork into one of her last two pieces of cake.

"Mary Grace, what is hurting you so bad right now?"

Mary Grace told Ralph about Annie. Every last detail. "And John's affair is no stand-alone act. It's not like he can do that sort of thing in a vacuum. His inability to keep his thing in his pants has the potential to break Annie's ability to trust, ruin the kids' self esteem, crush the in-laws, kill the friends. And take out a few neighbours on the way. It is not just about him, and he did it anyway. Their marriage was a lie. It wasn't what I thought it was and he isn't the person I thought he was," she said.

"And the truth hurts?" he asked again.

"So bad, Ralph. It hurts so bad."

"I would never do that to you, Mary Grace. I'm not John."

"I know you're not John. But I'm me. And things happen, Ralph. Bad things," Mary Grace said, thinking about just how much time, in the last two weeks, she had spent daydreaming about Nick Charmin. Just the daydreaming was filling her with guilt. "I can't go on *I Do*, Ralph. Even if they call, I can't do it. And I can't marry you. Please don't hate me. My mother will hate me enough."

"I could never hate you, Mary Grace. But listen, MG, they called."

"What?"

"Tess Lunt called me. Left you a message too, she said. She apologized it took so long. But they want us. Tomorrow. She called it a preliminary taping."

"What'd you say?"

"Okay. But that was before I knew about you. About Annie. About this. I'll call her back. We don't have to do it. But please, MG," Ralph begged. "Don't call off the wedding. I want to get married, just you and me. And some Justice of the Peace. All I care about is you and me."

"I'm so confused, Ralph. I'm tired of being so confused. I thought what Annie and John had *was* the real thing. If not them, then who?"

"Us," Ralph said, his voice strong and determined.

"Us?" Mary Grace repeated, turning the word over in her mouth like a marble. "Is that possible?"

"Anything is possible. Anything *you* want is possible. And *I* want us to be married. And live together for the rest of our lives."

"You are so good to me, Ralph. Are you really what you seem? Or is this going to be my five grandmothers all over again? Or worse, Annie and John?"

"I have no crystal ball, MG. But I trust you and I trust me. So let's take the ride, okay?"

"The train ride to Manhattan? For tomorrow's show?" Mary Grace said.

"I didn't mean the literal ride. I meant—"

"I know what you meant. I was trying to be funny. Or ironic. Or something. I don't know. But I suppose we should do it. Let's do the preliminaries, anyway. And mostly, Ralph, let's get married."

"You mean it?"

"As much as I can mean anything in my state."

"I love you, Mary Grace."

"Eat your cake, Ralph," she said, nodding toward the plate in front of Ralph. Ralph looked down and saw his cake. He hadn't even noticed the waitress had put it there.

"And don't go out with a wet head again. You'll get sick," Mary Grace continued, keenly aware she sounded like her mother. Or Ralph's mother. *Maybe, sometimes things are what they seem*, she thought, allowing herself a tiny, toothless smile.

CHAPTER TWENTY-ONE

"If I Knew You Were Comin' I'd've Baked a Cake." AL HOFFMAN, BOB MERRILL, AND CLEM WATTS

I t was early. Wee hours of the morning early, but Nick Charmin couldn't sleep. Instead of fighting his restlessness, he gave in and got up. He maneuvered himself out of the bed quietly so as not to disturb his latest girlfriend, Tanjia. She stirred, but only for a brief second. Charmin was relieved. He didn't feel like answering any of her questions or pretending to be grateful Tanjia was concerned about him. He also didn't feel like having sex. With Tanjia. He wanted a scotch and he wanted to be alone. He pulled on the shorts and T-shirt he had thrown on the chair only a few hours earlier and walked ever so quietly out of the bedroom. He let out a huge sigh after shutting the bedroom door, relieved that in moments he would be alone, sipping scotch.

He poured two fingers, neat, into a tumbler, sat down in his living room club chair, put his feet up on the ottoman, and finally allowed himself to take a sip, letting himself feel the warmth travel through his body. He closed his eyes, enjoying the sensation. He glanced around the living room, letting his eyes settle on his Emmy. He had won it the first year *I Do* was on the air. He was a lucky son-of-a-bitch. He wasn't particularly smart, barely making it through college; something he wouldn't have accomplished at all without the help of a few lovely girls. He hadn't been particularly dedicated, flopping from major to major, girl to girl, project to project. And he hadn't always been good looking, either; the majority of his adolescence had been spent as a chubby, acned, self-proclaimed loser.

But somehow, what he had always been was optimistic; born with a feeling, a sense, an idea that things could be different. The summer between high school and college, Charmin reinvented himself. Nobody told him he could. In fact, his father suggested he not even go to college. "Learn a trade," he had said. "Like television repair. One thing we can count on is television. And there will always be a need for someone to fix it. You don't want to drive a truck, like me. But you don't need college, either; you'll be saddling yourself with all those loans. It's just not worth it."

Charmin didn't exactly disagree with his dad. Television would always be there. And college probably wasn't necessary. But their reasons were different. So that summer, the one between high school and college, he devised a plan. With no money to join a gym, he started running every day. Small distances at first; barely a half mile. But he worked himself up to five miles a day, and the more he ran, the more the weight fell off his chunky frame. He became, dare he even say it, lean.

He poured through celebrity magazines like *People* and *Us* and examined what the men wore, how they cut their hair, how they posed for pictures; studied it like it was his job. By the time he started college that fall, he looked like he had popped off the page of one of his textbook magazines. Charmin's attention to detail paid off. He transformed himself into a guy girls swarmed. He noticed the difference, because he became the one from whom girls asked information: *Do you have a pen I could borrow? What did the professor say? Can you help me move my desk?* But he also felt the difference.

The way the ladies looked at him felt different. They weren't really interested in the pen, what the professor said, or the desk. They were interested in him. His experiment in self-transformation was a success. But what the glossy pages of his magazine didn't teach him was how to act. That he was forced to make up on his own. He opted for bastard-bad-guy, useful for short-term flings with a long line of women waiting in the wings.

He was lucky. Just after graduation, he was working in a high-end clothing store when someone from a modelling agency spotted him, offering him a chance at a print ad. He took the chance, got the job, and earned several more after that. His print ad success morphed into a job as the newsreader for a local New York news station, which in turn morphed into dating a few B list celebrities, landing him on Page Six on more than one occasion. He became a pseudo-celebrity in his own right, netting him the hosting responsibilities of *I Do*, which earned him the Emmy and the chance to sit in the club chair in his swanky New York apartment, with a gorgeous, vapid girl named Tanjia in his bed.

So why couldn't he stop thinking about Mary Grace and Ralph? Ralph was the man he would have become had he not transformed himself that fateful summer. He would have been a bit paunchy. A bit nerdy. A bit quirky. And Mary Grace was the woman with whom he was supposed to be. He had a very soft spot in his heart for Ralph, and an even softer one for Mary Grace. He wanted her. He was the guy with whom she should have ended up. He swore to himself right then and there, sitting in his club chair, sipping his scotch, that he would do anything—ANYTHING—to get her. But having only minimally developed his personality that same summer, he only knew one way to come on. Strong. He forced his hand, every time. Having never been in one, he didn't know how real relationships progressed. He didn't know how to let life unfold or how to just be.

CHAPTER TWENTY-TWO

"I can say I'm going to stay home, cut flowers, bake a cake, and tomorrow I'm going to go back to the evil empire." SANDRA BULLOCK

Mary Grace wanted, with all her heart, to just be. *Just be*, she told herself, like Crash Davis told Annie Savoy at the end of *Bull Durham*. But Mary Grace couldn't listen to Crash. *He's not real. That might work in the movies, but not in real life. To just be is just tough.* Annie's news— Annie, wife to John, mother to Dane and Drew, not Susan Sarandon as Annie Savoy—that Annie and her news had rocked the entire institution of marriage. An institution based on a lifetime agreement into which she herself had recently agreed to enter with Ralph. *How could she just be?* If Annie's marriage was a lie then her engagement to Ralph, filled with unwelcomed thoughts about Nick Charmin, must be a lie, too. And now, she found herself getting ready for a preliminary taping of *I Do*, a test episode, bringing her lie, and the lies of the entire institution of marriage, to all of America, thank-you-very-much. *It is just a test*, she reminded herself. But could life get any crazier? At this stage of the game, Mary Grace wouldn't be surprised to find Clark Kent in a phone booth, turning into the man-in-tights before her very eyes. Like Ralph said, anything is possible.

Just be. That's a laugh. Just be crazy is more like it, she thought as she sat in one of two rotating salon chairs that were cemented before a twenty-foot mirrored wall. She was getting primed for television in what could only be described as a museum to makeup and hair care. In front of Mary Grace was nothing but mirror, and behind her stood wall to wall shelving fitted with hundreds of matching wicker baskets, labelled and filed alphabetically. The baskets were filled with applicator brushes, hairbrushes, elixirs, fixers, gels, glosses, liners, mascaras, powders, shadows, shimmers, shiners, and sprays. For someone interested in those sorts of products, it was makeover heaven.

The morning sun cut a path between the variegated New York buildings and peeked through the side window of the *I Do* salon, refracting off the twenty-foot mirror and leaving a tiny prism rainbow on the hardwood floor. All that makeup, and the only thing Mary Grace could focus on was the prism. *Red is for Ralph. Orange is for OMG I'm marrying Ralph. Yellow is for the coward I am. Green is for Jayde's envy. Blue matches my mood. And purple is the passion I feel when I think of Nick*, she thought, staring infinitely at the colours.

"You have perfect cheekbones," Janelle said, using a soft brush the size of an orange with a twelve-inch handle to apply some sort of powder to Mary Grace's cheeks. "Just perfect. You're not too skinny so your face has a shape. I love a face with a shape, not all hollowed out and scary. It's those hollow faces that are impossible to make up. I have to create flesh with powder. Like blood from a stone. Your structure is a dream to work with."

"Thank you?" Mary Grace said, trying to process Janelle's words.

"Oh, and what Maxine did with your hair? Perfect. Just that little trim gave your curls the lift they needed. And the blonde highlights frame your face. You are going to look great on television."

Janelle sprayed Mary Grace's face with a setting spray that nearly looked like hair spray.

"Ta da," Janelle said. "What do you think?"

Mary Grace looked at herself in the mirror. *My mother will love this look*, she thought. *My students, too. They will love the glamorous side of Miss Falcone. Me? I'm not so sure.* But Mary Grace didn't want to make Janelle feel bad, so instead of sounding unsure or disappointed she blurted out, "I like it. I like it a lot," with a forced grin spread across her face. "Thank you, Janelle."

"Someone from wardrobe will be up shortly to take you to the Palace of the Clothes. Can I get you anything before I leave?"

"A piece of cake?" Mary Grace said with a laugh. Janelle looked puzzled. "Just kidding. Nothing. I need nothing. I'll be fine, Janelle. Thanks again." Mary Grace watched as Janelle left the salon.

Mary Grace was alone with her rainbow. She pictured Ralph in a similar room and wondered if he had a similar rainbow. *All this work for a preliminary shoot*, she thought as she watched her rainbow changing shape. Time passes. Suns rise. Prisms come and go. Had she been alone in her apartment she might have broken out into the chorus of "Sunrise, Sunset." The thought made her smile.

"Hello, Miss Falcone. We meet again." The recognizable voice of Nick Charmin startled Mary Grace. She looked up from her prism and saw him and his electric smile and thick head of black hair. Her heart fluttered. She had been dreaming about this meeting for two weeks straight, and now that it was no longer a dream but an instant reality, she had no clue what to say. She was afraid to speak; afraid her words would come out sounding jumbled like the grownups in all the *Charlie Brown* specials. "Wah wah wah wah."

"Hello, Mr. Charmin," Mary Grace said, forcing out the words, sounding tense and nervous.

"Call me Nick," he said in his engaging and easy way, lowering his body into the empty salon chair next to Mary Grace.

"Forgive me," he said. "But you look utterly hot. Janelle is the best in the business," he added. Strong. It was the only way Nick Charmin knew how to come on.

"She is?" Mary Grace asked.

"Indeed. I only work with the best," Nick said. "That's why I wanted you on my show. Remember when I told you I would know in two minutes if you were right for my show?"

Mary Grace nodded.

"With you, I knew in one minute. You're a natural woman," he said.

"I am?"

"Most certainly. Naturally, you will appeal to the men. But you'll appeal to the women, too."

"I will?"

"Without a doubt. The women will want to be you without being entirely too jealous of you. And that, my love, is your magic *it* factor."

Are you flirting with me? Mary Grace wanted to scream, but didn't. *He was, wasn't he? How is it possible I'm not certain?* Mary Grace wondered. She tried to flirt back. A little bit, anyway. She batted her eyelashes. *Totally lame.* And then it happened. The glue from the fakes Janelle had just applied must not have been thoroughly dried. The lashes on her right eye stuck firmly together. *Save me,* she thought, trying to pry her eye open. Nick didn't seem to notice. He just kept talking.

"And the men. As they are forced to watch the show with their girlfriends, and wives, they will want to be the one marrying you."

Mary Grace squirmed in her chair, fiddling with her lashes. *Success.* She got her right eye to open. She smiled a large and goofy grin.

"I love that smile," Nick said. "America will be so happy to plan a wedding for you. You are seriously my perfect *I Do* woman," he added, placing his hand on her arm. Mary Grace flinched. She didn't mean to, but it just happened. Nick immediately removed his hand and Mary Grace was sorry. Sorry she had flinched, and sorry he had retracted his strong, warm hand.

"I'm sorry if my touch made you uncomfortable, Mary Grace, but I just had to feel your skin. You are such a natural beauty; I wish I possessed what you have," he said.

"Oh," she said, no other words coming.

Once again Nick placed his hand on her arm. His grin was electric. His touch hot. This time Mary Grace didn't move.

"I don't usually have this kind of effect on people," Mary Grace said. *He is flirting with me,* she thought. *I was right.*

"Ralph is lucky," Nick said, the heat from his hand nearly burning a hole through Mary Grace's flesh.

Mary Grace tilted her head to the left, not sure what, if anything, to say. In her daydreams she was always glib and charming, but in real life, no decent words would come.

"Mary Grace?"

"Yes?" she said, certain Nick was about to kiss her and even more certain she would let him.

He looked at her, his head cocked to the left, his brow knit, his gaze intense.

She stared back into his dreamy eyes.

"I think you need to have Janelle work on your lashes," he said, pointing to her right eye. "Your right side is missing."

Mary Grace looked at herself in the mirror. It took all her strength to stifle a scream. *My eye is naked*, she thought. *I was just flirting with a naked eye. Where are my lashes?* She reached her hand up to cover her lashless eye, willing Nick to go away and leave her alone in her humiliation.

"Would you meet me for dinner this evening?" Nick requested with a velvety laugh. "I think you could use some extra work."

Mary Grace looked up at him, hand still covering eye.

"You need to work on relaxation. You're coming off too stiff," Nick said, his voice no longer dreamy, his head nodding toward the eyelashes on the floor. "I have some professional relaxation tips I can share with you."

"Yes, Mr. Charmin. Ralph and I can have dinner with you."

"Nick. Remember? And just you," he added.

Mary Grace was trying to come up with a response when she found herself saved by a new voice in the room.

"Hello, Miss Falcone. I am Owen from wardrobe. Oh honey, your eye. What happened to your eye? Janelle? Emergency," Owen shouted. "Nine-one-one," he said even louder. "And Mr. Charmin. You're not bothering this lovely girl, are you? Owen doesn't like his mannequins undressed before he gets a chance to dress them," he said, giggling like a schoolboy, charmed by the way he talked about himself in the third person.

Charmin glared at Owen. His eyes were squinted and his look was long and mean.

"Her eyelashes are on the floor," Charmin said, nodding toward the set of falsies on the ground. "Dinner, Miss Falcone. Nero's at eight. It's on the corner of Broadway and 64th." Charmin made a quick exit.

Owen grabbed Mary Grace's hand. "Don't pay one bit of mind to that cad. He thinks the world of himself. His head is so big, I'm surprised he fits through the door," Owen said, giggling again. "Now let's play dress up, baby. Owen can't wait to get his hands on those curves and teach you to work them. I am so sick of the skinnies. No meat is no fun. You, Mary Grace, are a dream come true. Janelle!"

Mary Grace just smiled a fake and pasted smile. She was out of her league. She stared at the engagement ring on her finger. *Was Nick flirting with me or not? Was he business or pleasure? Why in the world don't I know these things and what in the world am I, and my naked eye, doing here? Maybe Jayde was right after all. Engagement rings make women more desirable. Could it be?*

CHAPTER TWENTY-THREE

"Last year my birthday cake looked like a prairie fire." RODNEY DANGERFIELD

One hour later, dressed in Owen's clothes, sporting Maxine's haircut, and wearing Janelle's makeup—including a new set of thoroughly dried eyelashes—Mary Grace was taping the test episode of *I Do*. Mary Grace Falcone, the average kid from Newville, New Jersey, was gearing up to appear on national television. This sort of thing doesn't happen every day. Some mothers dream of their children attending Princeton. Some mothers dream of their children becoming doctors or lawyers or even President of the United States. But not Angela Falcone. Her dreams included television and trivia and game shows, and culminated with Mary Grace as the winning contestant.

Mary Grace learned at a young age to pack everything in her purse, from buffalo head nickels to dental floss, thanks to *Let's Make a Deal*. And her mother frequently tested her on the cost of cat food, aluminum foil, and new cars, thanks to *The Price is Right*. And as a knee-jerk reaction to *Wheel of Fortune*, Angela made sure Mary Grace was a wiz at hangman, initiating at least ten games a day. And then there was music, *Name that Tune*, and trivia, *Jeopardy*, and cards, *The Joker is Wild*. Mary Grace spent her days in an endless fog of mindless learning with Angela reminding her, "Mary Grace, this could be you one day. You need to be ready, because someday you'll be on one of these shows and I don't want you stuck without a paring knife in your purse!"

Mary Grace dutifully obliged. Most of the times the games were fun. But when she got bored or tired or just plain disinterested in the day's gruelling game show routine, she always thought of her father and what he had taught her: keep Mommy happy. So Mary Grace did.

When Mom sees me on television, she won't be able to contain herself; all her life's dreams for me, her little girl, will have come true.

"Are you watching, Dad?" Mary Grace whispered under her breath as she looked up toward heaven. "Because this is some cozy sweater."

It was nearly time to begin. On television everything about the *I Do* set looked big and grand and, quite honestly, perfect. But live and in person the stage shrunk to the size of Angela Falcone's kitchen and the furniture looked nearly shabby. There was the metal podium behind which Nick stood, and the base was nicked and dented as if it had been in some accidental foot-on-the-gas-instead-of-the-brake fender bender. Then there were the two red velvet chairs that flanked Nick. The seats of both chairs were nearly threadbare. *A show that makes this much money can't afford to reupholster?*

Nick Charmin took his place behind the modern, metal podium. He was such a natural fit to the live television scene, and looked as comfortable as if he were sitting in his own den. Mary Grace and Ralph each sat in one of the red velvet chairs. *Physically, Ralph looks good,* Mary Grace thought. *I wonder who did his makeup, hair, and wardrobe. He's almost stud-like. He looks better than he's ever looked in his life.* His clothes were right: faded jeans with some shreds and rips, and a black buttoned-down shirt left un-tucked. His hair was messy but done up; kind of gelled but not too spiky. And his teeth, they were so white.

Mary Grace wondered how Ralph handled everyone poking and pawing him, tugging his clothes this way and that, putting on makeup, handling him like chopped meat. A lot of Purell, and perhaps a Xanax. Mary Grace wasn't much of a fan of the poking, and she didn't share Ralph's neurosis. She felt bad for him.

She could tell by the look in Ralph's eyes that he appreciated her physical look, too. *Clothes and makeup do wonders,* she thought. *But who has the time to put this much effort into an "effortless look" every day?*

After the show's opening music, which was something akin to "Here Comes the Bride" on steroids, Nick Charmin introduced himself as the host of the most watched reality television show since *Millionaire*. "I'm your host, Nick Charmin." He smiled that movie star grin, parading his stubble around like the Olympic gold medal of good looks. *He is so handsome*, Mary Grace thought. *Like, best looking kid in the high school class, or stud on campus, good-looking. Men like that don't go for me.* Her mind raced again, curiosity her death sentence. *Was he really hitting on me*, she wondered, *or just being nice? Am I really supposed to be meeting him at eight? Should I? And would that be considered cheating on Ralph? Why, if I'm about to be marrying Ralph, on live television no less, would I be interested in a date with Nick Charmin? It's not a date. Like Nick said, it would be all about the show. I need extra work. Professional relaxation work.*

Owen had disagreed. He said Nick always hit on the ladies. But Mary Grace didn't want to believe she was being hit on. She wanted to believe there was some sort of connection. *No! No connection*, she reminded herself. *This is all about the show.* Suddenly, she heard her name.

"Mary Grace Falcone," Nick Charmin shouted.

She was startled to hear her name. Lost in her world of Nick Charmin, she had almost forgotten they were taping. She pushed herself out of the red velvet chair and moved to where Ralph was already standing. He reached for her hand and she obliged.

"America, this is our couple. Over the next eight weeks you will be planning their wedding. For them, I hope it is the wedding of a lifetime. Now, Mary Grace, tell America, why are you marrying Ralph?" Nick said.

Mary Grace was certain she saw him look at her in a way that said more than "reality show contestant." But since nobody had ever looked at her that way before, how could she be certain?

"Because I love him," is what she said. *Because he asked*, is what she thought.

"And Ralph, why are you marrying Mary Grace?" Nick prompted.

"Because Mary Grace is the one for me. Life without Mary Grace would be like living without food. Or water. Or air. Without her I would shrivel and die," Ralph said. And those were the exact words he meant.

I don't deserve him, Mary Grace thought. *He's too good for me.*

"Okay, you two lovebirds, let's just pretend you are perfectly matched. For now. You know the way this round works. I'm going to ask you each some questions; questions we gathered after interviewing your family and friends—who, by the way, are quite, shall we say, unique." Nick Charmin chuckled a long, velvety television laugh.

"The number of correct responses you provide," Nick continued, "equals the number of choices America gets to choose from for your wedding location. With no correct answers, a mystery pick from Worst Weddings ensues. Are you ready?" Nick smiled as if he were admiring himself in a mirror. "I said, are you ready?"

"Yes," Mary Grace and Ralph said.

"Good. Then Ralph, despite the fact that ladies go first, we're starting with you this round. And remember, I'm not Regis," Charmin said, doing his best Regis Philbin impression. "And this is not *Millionaire*," he continued, clearly pleased with his clever improvisation, his eyes darting for approval from Ralph to Mary Grace to camera three. "We don't do multiple choice and there are no lifelines." Returning to his own voice, Charmin asked the first question. "Ralph, can you tell us the nickname your fiancée's mother uses for her?"

"That's easy," Ralph said.

"Do you see that chemistry?" Tess said from inside the sound studio, where technicians were sitting in front of boards full of buttons and lights, wearing headsets and talking what could only be thought of as code. "Their magnetism is raw."

"Ralph and Mary Grace?" Gabriella asked.

"No! Mary Grace and Nick," Tess said. "Look at him; he's practically drooling over her in a Chuck Woolery sort of way. What was the name of his sidekick on that obscure game show with no prize money?"

"*Lingo?*" Gabriella guessed.

"Yes. That's it! Now, what's the blonde girl's name?"

"Shandy. She was a former Miss USA or something."

"You are good, Gabriella," Tess said. "The way Chuck drooled over Shandy made people want to watch the show just to see them flirt. I think our chemistry here is even better. More subtle. Maybe even more grown up, which is perfect for prime time. See the way Charmin's eyes linger on Mary Grace? And you can practically see her mind turning. She is wondering if it's real or not. It's brilliant. We have ourselves a winner here."

"Gracie," Ralph said. "Angela's nickname for Mary Grace is Gracie."

"Ralph, you speak the truth. And now, you are guaranteed one wedding location for America to choose from, and you have cleverly avoided a pick from Worst Weddings. Congratulations," Nick said, running his fingers through his hair. "He's good, Mary Grace, isn't he?" Nick asked. "No wonder you're marrying him. Are you ready for your first question, Miss Bride-to-Be?"

"I'm nervous," Mary Grace said, working hard to push the words out. "But ready."

"Good. Ralph is an English teacher and lover of books, right?"

"Right," Mary Grace confirmed. "So I got my first question correct?"

"Not so fast. What is your fiancé's all-time favourite book?"

"I know that one," Mary Grace said.

"Good. Then you can share it with us…" He hesitated for a moment before issuing his signature phrase. "Après pause," Charmin concluded, grinning his grin, furrowing his brow, and sweeping his hand across his face.

"Oh my God, this is golden. The signature phrase. The grin. The girl. This is the money, baby. We can retire on this connection," Tess said. She could feel herself, normally relaxed and calm, professional and polished, getting tense and tight with anticipation. Her naturally smooth voice raced a bit, fast and high.

"Remember, Gabriella, it is better to be lucky than good," Tess said. "My mother is friends with Mary Grace's mother. Did you know that? Our mothers are cut from the same cloth, although to be honest, I think Miss Mary Grace has it worse. Her mother basically lied to her to get her to do my show. Told her I needed her. My show would go bust without her. What a laugh," Tess added with a sarcastic snort.

"Basically, I got Mary Grace on a fluke," she continued. "And it turns out, I do need her. Maybe our mothers know more than we think they do." Tess stopped a moment to consider what she had just said. "Nah, probably not. Now Gabriella, get a little powder on Ralph. Fast. He's beginning to sweat."

"And we're back. So you think this one's easy, do you? You can, without a shadow of a doubt, name your fiancé's all-time favourite book? Think carefully before responding, because another correct answer gives America another option to choose from for your perfect wedding location."

"I know this one, Nick," Mary Grace said. "It is *The Catcher in the Rye*. That's Ralph's all-time favourite book."

Ralph's eyes lit up at her response. One look into Ralph's eyes, and Mary Grace could easily have confirmed the right answer. The only problem was, she wasn't looking into Ralph's eyes; she was looking into Charmin's.

"You speak the truth!" Nick said.

Finally, looking at Ralph, Mary Grace got giddy. *Two locations*, she thought. *Two possible locations for our wedding. It is amazing how sucked in you can get into something you didn't like in the first place.* And then she noticed them.

Nick's eyes were on her again. Was this her imagination, or was it for real? Oh God, she needed to know.

"Two more questions for this category," Nick said. "You're halfway there."

"Did you catch that last look, Gabriella? I think Charmin saw Mary Grace naked. I can't wait to see this show played back. Make sure America will see what I'm seeing," Tess said.

"If you see it, Tess, America will, too," Gabriella confirmed.

"Powder that sweaty boy up again, Gabriella. I've never seen anyone sweat like that. Now!" Tess screamed, letting go of any last shred of Zen she possessed.

"Are you ready, Ralph? This question is for you, and it is hard. It is a bit of obscurity, and obscurity is what we like around here," Nick said.

"I'm ready, Nick. There's nothing about Mary Grace I don't know," Ralph said, filling his lungs up with air.

"Okay, then. Back when your fiancée was a little girl and she lost her first tooth, she was scared of something," Nick said.

Still feeling confident, Ralph thought, *The tooth fairy. She was scared of the tooth fairy. What little kid isn't?*

"The tooth fairy," Nick continued.

Am I good or what? Ralph thought.

Oh my God, Mary Grace thought, a panicky feeling surging through her body. *They're going to tell this story in front of America? Where did they find out about this? I didn't tell this story in the interview. Did I ever tell Ralph this story? I must have. But who, who told Tess?* With one clear ah-ha, Mary Grace knew. *My mother!*

"So Mary Grace was scared of the tooth fairy. And she couldn't fall asleep because she kept visualizing a strange fairy flying into her room, taking her tooth, and leaving a quarter. Is this true, Mary Grace?" Nick said, aglow with lusty adoration.

Mary Grace nodded.

"And so she kept getting up and going to her mother, asking questions like, what time does the tooth fairy come? How long does the tooth fairy stay? Will she like me? Will she wake me up? What if she doesn't come?"

Mary Grace continued to nod, remembering this story as if it had happened yesterday, when in reality it was about twenty-five years ago. *I'm on television talking about a story that happened twenty-five years ago; only in America*, Mary Grace thought. Ralph's eyes became vacant, having no clue where this story was going or what Nick was even talking about.

"And so, after about one hour of this behaviour, Mary Grace's mother had had it. Is that right, Gracie?" Nick said, using her nickname and painting an even more familiar picture for him and for America. Mary Grace smiled, returning the familiarity. "And what did your mother finally say, Gracie? Do you remember?"

"Yes, I remember," Mary Grace said, catching that look in Nick's eyes and still wondering if it was for real.

"Do you want to tell America what she said?" Nick asked.

"Not really," Mary Grace said.

"Then I will," Nick said. "Your mother, Angela Falcone, said, 'I'm the tooth fairy. It's me. Now go to bed.' Is that right Mary Grace?"

"Every word," she said.

"Are you following along with us, Ralph?" Nick asked. Ralph nodded but remained lost as to where this whole story was going. He wiped his forehead, noting the heat of the studio lights and feeling, perhaps, that it was getting to him.

"If you, out there, are anything like me, you're now picturing a little girl marching back up to bed for the final time. But it didn't happen that way, America. Little Mary Grace had one more question. Did you hear me? One more question. She popped up one more time. And Ralph, here's where you come in, so pay close attention. Mary Grace asked her mother if she wore what garment, when she pretended to be the tooth fairy? What garment, Ralph, did Mary Grace want to know if her mother wore during her midnight fancies?"

Ralph looked blank.

I guess I never told him this story, Mary Grace thought. *If this show had a lifeline, Ralph could call Jayde. Jayde would know the answer.*

"I need an answer, Ralph. But I need it… après pause," Nick said.

"This is magic," Tess exclaimed. "Ronnie, does this look as good as I think it does?" Tess said to the man with the thick, stubby fingers who was working some piano concerto magic on the soundboard.

"I don't know, Tess," Ronnie said. "I see the connection, but check out Ralph. I'm worried about the son-of-a-bitch. There's sweat pouring out of every orifice, including his asshole."

"Gabriella, change the lighting. Fast. We need less shine. Ronnie's right. He's still sweating too much. Son-of-a-bitch. If he ruins this for me I'll kill him."

Ronnie smiled at what live television could do to people, including the otherwise unflappable, self-assured Tess Lunt.

"Check his pits and see if he needs a new shirt. Tell him to relax, too. This is all supposed to be fun, goddamn it," Tess snapped. "Remind him he's supposed to be having a goddamned good time."

"I'm on it," Gabriella said, dashing out of the sound booth and into the studio.

"Must I do every last thing around here? Including stopping hapless bastards from sweating?" Tess demanded. "I swear to God, if Ralph—"

"Let it go for now," Ronnie said calmly. "Just let Gabbie change the lighting… adding a blue hue might help. You'll check the test scenes out later. Gabbie can work wonders."

"Yeah, right. But if—"

"Tess! Just watch," Ronnie shouted, already tired of his psycho-boss' split personality.

"Okay, Ralph. We're back and we need an answer," Nick announced. "Think about it. What garment did Mary Grace think her mother wore when morphing into the tooth fairy?" Nick repeated the question for Ralph, who was now wearing a new shirt, despite it being the exact same as the old one, so that all of America wouldn't know.

"I honestly don't know," Ralph admitted, his disappointment palpable.

"You're best off at least taking a guess," Nick encouraged.

"A fairy costume?" Ralph tried.

"Oh, I am sorry," Nick said, making each word longer than it needed to be. "Your answer is incorrect. Mary Grace, can you tell us what you thought your mother wore?"

"Her wedding dress," Mary Grace said. "I asked her if she wore her wedding dress when she put the money under my pillow."

"Is this girl adorable or what, folks? She thought her mother wore her wedding dress. And guess what we have here, right now, courtesy of Mary Grace's mother, Mrs. Angela Falcone? If you guessed her wedding dress, you are correct! Suzie?" Nick said.

And from stage left, long-legged Suzie, draped in a skin tight, thigh length, black sheath and wearing six-inch heals, cat walked out holding a cleaned and pressed wedding dress. And this was the dress worn by none other than Angela Falcone on her wedding day.

"This is beautiful," Nick said. "Would you like to wear this when you marry Ralph?"

"I don't know. Somehow, I always pictured wearing my own dress," Mary Grace said.

"We'll see what America has to say," Nick said with a wink. "Perhaps they'll want to see you in it? Or Ralph?" Nick laughed. Ralph just looked wide-eyed. "Just kidding, buddy. But speaking of Ralph, you got that last answer wrong, which means you still only have two options for your wedding location. It is up to Mary Grace to provide a third. Are you ready, Mary Grace?"

"Ready, Nick."

"It's no secret Ralph is a bit of a germaphobe. Is that true, Mary Grace?"

"Yes," she said, looking at Ralph to see if he was okay with this line of questioning. The sweat pouring off his face told her he wasn't. *And he just changed shirts*, Mary Grace thought.

"You have a friend Jayde, correct?"

"Correct," Mary Grace affirmed.

"And Jayde has a nickname for Ralph. She calls him the CEO of something. What exactly is Ralph the CEO of?"

"Oh Nick, that's not a good question. Jayde's nickname is all in fun. She means no harm by it," Mary Grace said.

"Then what is it?" Nick pushed, still undressing Mary Grace with his eyes.

"I can't," she said.

"You can't, or you won't? Either way, you lose another wedding location…"

"Antiseptic Hands," Mary Grace blurted out before Nick could even complete his sentence. "CEO of Antiseptic Hands."

"You have funny friends, Mary Grace. And, more importantly, you speak the truth. Another wedding location will be coming your way."

"Sometimes they're funny," she said, with hesitation in her voice. "And sometimes they're not." Mary Grace peeked at Ralph to gauge exactly how upset he was with her, Jayde, and that question. On a scale of one to ten, she decided he was a nine. *Not good*, she thought. *This is not good*. Ralph appeared to be on the verge of sweating through another shirt. *I hope they have a large supply of those shirts back there.*

"Three out of four questions correct. Not bad, you two. I'll bet you're dying to see where your wedding might be, aren't you?"

"Yes," Mary Grace said. "I can't wait."

"But you'll have to. Because we'll find out…"

"Après pause," Nick, Mary Grace, and Ralph said together, only because the cue card girl held up a card demanding them to read it.

"Get Ralph cleaned up, and fast," Tess said. "And I don't care what you do to him. Use glue if you have to. But stop him from sweating."

Ronnie laughed. He was flipping switches this way and that, but he still had time to laugh.

"This is no joke," Tess said.

"I know. But stopping a guy like Ralph from sweating is like stopping a guy with a cataclysmic case of the flu from puking. Impossible. Some things, Tess, are out of your control."

"Nothing is out of my control," Tess snapped, storming out of the sound room and into the studio.

"You guys are looking great out here. You're up to the good part now, no more questions. Did you hear me, Ralph? No more questions. Can you try to stop sweating? Promise me you'll try," Tess urged.

"I'm trying. But I'm a sweater," Ralph said. Maxine had stripped him down to nothing and was helping him put his arms through a new black shirt.

"This is our last shirt," Maxine said.

"Get more. Pronto," Tess demanded.

"From where?" Maxine asked.

"That's your job. Do it." Tess scrutinized the stage. She scrutinized the contestants. She scrutinized Nick. "You all look good. Keep it that way. This taping is almost over."

"These lights are so hot," Ralph said. "That's why I'm sweating so much. Can't you turn them off? Or at least down?"

"No," Tess said. "Get ready. In five, four, three, two, one."

"Welcome back. With three out of four questions correctly answered by America's sweethearts, Mary Grace and Ralph, we can spin our lucky wheel three times," Nick said. Upon uttering the words, the lucky wheel—a gigantic, silver wheel of fortune—was lowered from where it had been suspended to the ceiling.

"Three spins. Three wedding locations. C'mon, Mary Grace, use all your strength and give this wheel one gigantic pull." Mary Grace pulled the wheel. The "Wedding March On Steroids" theme song was playing in the background.

"Round and round she goes, and where she stops—finish it for me, Ralph," Nick said.

"No one knows," Ralph finished, obliging Nick Charmin as the wheel ticked round and round.

"Aruba. The first wedding location you landed on is Aruba. Hey, I'd like to take you there, Mary Grace," Nick said. He was laughing, playing it off as some sort of funny joke, but as the words exited his mouth, he wished they hadn't. *Idiot*, he thought. *Total idiot*. "Just kidding. Ralph Ichy is the lucky guy who gets to escort Gracie to Aruba, or to whatever fantastic wedding location America decides on. Step on up here, Ralph, because it is your turn to spin that wheel," Nick said.

Ralph stretched his arms up high. His pit stains, even with the new shirt, were visible. Using both hands, he gave the wheel a gigantic pull, but somehow, he forgot to let go. The force of the wheel, and the force of his pull, threw him to the ground. Mary Grace covered her mouth with her hands, her eyes wide with shock. And as hard as he tried not to, Nick Charmin laughed. Not just a smile. Or a giggle. But a full-bodied, uncontrollable laugh. He reached his arm to help Ralph up, but was laughing too hard to be any good to him. His efforts to suppress his laughter resulted in tears streaming down his face. Ralph, now holding Nick's hand, gave it one hard pull, and *bam*, Nick was on the floor, too.

"What'd you do that for?" Nick Charmin demanded, the amusement gone from his face and the laughter gone from his voice.

"It was an accident. I–I didn't mean—"

"Cut," Tess screamed into her headset from inside the sound booth. "Cut. This is a disaster. I can't have my host and contestant on the floor. Ronnie, do we have enough footage before the fall to edit this out?"

"Yup," Ronnie said, also laughing. "Blooper shows will pay a lot of money for this clip."

"I don't give a damn about those shows right now. I just want mine to work. Do you hear me? Mine. To. Work." Tess' voice was louder than Gabriella and Ronnie had ever heard it before, and her tirade more aggressive, too.

Tess began again. "Mother fu—"

"It's working, Tess," Gabriella interrupted, attempting to calm her boss with a strong, soothing voice. "It's working. Did you see what happened before the fall? Nick Charmin practically asked Mary Grace out. This sexual tension is better than when *Moonlighting* was at its best."

"Yeah?" Tess began tugging at her hair. "You think so?"

And then, through the sound system, Tess began yelling again.

"Get up! All of you! And stop arguing. Just continue my show. Please. Nick, you're the professional. Just start in with the location. Ready? In five, four, three, two…"

"Rome. Our lucky couple landed on Rome, Italy. Now we need one more spin of the wheel and the rest is up to America. I'll do the honours this time," Nick said, giving the wheel a final spin. As the music played, Ralph,

Mary Grace, and Nick watched the wheel go round and round until, with one final tick, it came to a stop.

"Greenwich, Connecticut. And there you have it, America. The third location for the wedding of Mary Grace Falcone to Ralph Ichy is Greenwich, Connecticut."

Mary Grace smiled, but Ralph knew the smile was fake. And Nick tried to catch her eye, wanting to use telepathy to tell her they wouldn't end up in Connecticut. Nick prayed it worked.

"To recap, we now have our three locations: Aruba, Rome, and Greenwich. The voting is up to you, America," Charmin said, rattling off the appropriate number to text or call.

"Remember, America," Charmin continued. "Our results show is tomorrow at eight o'clock and you have until midnight tonight to vote. Until then, may all your weddings bring bliss," Nick signed off. Mary Grace and Nick waved to America, while Mary Grace mouthed the word "Aruba."

"If we get stuck in Connecticut, I don't know what I'll do," she whispered through a smile to Ralph.

"If I make it out of here alive, I'll be thankful," he whispered back.

"It wasn't so bad," she tried to assure him.

"Not if you're blind," he replied.

"And we're off the air," Ronnie said.

Tess ran out from the sound studio to the stage set. "Okay, guys, good job for today. Television isn't easy, especially taping a first episode. This was an excellent test run. Ronnie and I will watch this show frame by frame tonight and see if we can work with what we have. Ralph? Can you try not to sweat so much?" Tess implored.

Mary Grace eyed Ralph, who was already embarrassed enough. His face turned a brighter shade of red, if that was even possible. She linked her arm through his and gave him a gentle pat.

"I'll expect you both here at E-leven tomorrow morning. E-leven," Tess repeated, looking from Mary Grace to Ralph, putting the emphasis on the first "e" in "eleven," and making the word longer than necessary. She appeared to have traded tugging her hair out for this new, strange vocabulary.

Mary Grace couldn't help but smile. "E-leven," she whispered in Ralph's ear, mimicking Tess Lunt. Ralph was grateful for the diversion.

Tess gave them a curious look. "That's when you'll find out if you're our couple or not. For now, though, you're free to leave."

"Thanks, Tess. Thanks so much," Mary Grace said, unlinking her arm from Ralph, and freeing herself to shake Tess' hand. "This was actually fun. I hate to say it, but my mother was right."

"I agree," Tess said. *Your fiancé sweats more than a three-hundred-pound man in spin class,* she thought, her face fraught with worry.

As Mary Grace was pulling her stuff together to leave, Nick Charmin sidled up to her and began whispering. She was startled by his presence, and even more so by his words and the way his breath felt against her skin. She jumped, her eyes darting around for Ralph. He was grabbing his briefcase. Mary Grace was relieved that she had some space. She noticed the hair on the back of her neck stand up.

"You are made for television, Miss Falcone. Remember, tonight. Nero's. Eight o'clock," he said.

Before she was able to answer, Nick was gone. "Smooth" was the best word she could use to describe him. She put her hand to her heart and could feel it beating.

"What did that idiot Charmin just whisper to you?" Ralph asked. "Was it about me and how bad I was? Is he mad I took him down with me? Because he deserved it. He laughed right in my face."

"It was pretty funny," Mary Grace said. "It reminded me of *The Price is Right.* Remember when the old lady fell under the wheel as she tried to spin for the dollar? My mother and I saw that show together. They play it on all the blooper shows. I have to admit, we laughed."

"Now you're comparing me to an old lady?"

"No. I'm not comparing; I'm just saying sometimes when people fall it can be funny. That's all. And besides, you weren't bad. You just sweat a lot. It doesn't matter, so long as they have all those black shirts. Nick Charmin thinks we'll be a hit. That's what he said." Mary Grace licked her lips before running her top teeth over her lower lip.

"Now let's get back to New Jersey, where we can pretend to be ourselves again," Mary Grace said, handing Ralph a bottle of Purell from inside her purse. "E-leven," she mimicked Tess again. "We have to be back here at what time, Ralph?"

"E-leven," he copied, enjoying the joke he and Mary Grace shared.

Ralph refused to hail a cab, preferring to walk the twenty some odd blocks to Penn Station, claiming the exercise was what he needed to clear his head when in reality Mary Grace knew it was all about the dirty cabs. He had had enough aggravation today, and sitting in a dirty cab that thousands of people had sat in before would not be the best thing for his mood. With no energy to fight, Mary Grace just went along. She had a lot to think about, anyway. A walk would be useful.

How had she allowed herself to even fantasize about going on a date with Nick? She was marrying Ralph. She was wearing his ring. She was appearing on the pilot episode of a reality wedding show. She was leaving the city, but seriously contemplating returning on a secret jaunt to meet Nick Charmin at Nero's. *What's wrong with me?*

Just a week ago she had been teaching her students, marvelling at how far they had come since September. But that was last week. So much can change in a week. In a year. In a life. *Are we predestined to be what we become, or, at any time can we change our course? Am I destined to marry Ralph? Or not?*

"Faster, Mary Grace. We don't want to miss the train. Then we'll be stuck in disgusting Penn Station until the next one comes along," Ralph urged, grabbing her hand and pulling her hard.

"I'm going as fast as I can," she said, leaping over a puddle of mucky New York water, but focusing more on what Ralph had just said than on missing the train. "Until the next one comes along." *That's pretty profound.* If you wait long enough, the next one will come along. The next train. The next meal. The next opportunity for success. The next man.

Mary Grace needed a meeting, but there was no time for MexTexas tonight.

CHAPTER TWENTY-FOUR

"I've always thought with relationships, that it's more about what you bring to the table than what you're going to get from it. It's very nice if you sit down and the cake appears. But if you go to the table expecting cake, then it's not so good." ANJELICA HUSTON

Wearing a fluffy pink robe, matching slippers, and a towel wrapped turban-style over her wet hair, Mary Grace plopped into her beanbag. The shower had done wonders to refresh her body, but nothing for her mind, which was still playing the same old tape. She reached for the phone, dialled, and waited for an answer. As soon as she heard a voice, she began talking without the luxury of even a breath.

"It's me. I feel so selfish calling you for advice right now, when all you need is for me to be supporting you. I'm sorry. But I need you," Mary Grace said.

"Don't be sorry, Mary Grace. I don't have the entire market share of problems. You're allowed to have some, too," Annie reassured her. "Besides, John and I are working things out."

"You are?"

"We're trying. We're in counselling. It will be a long time before I ever trust him again, but I'm not ready to throw in the towel."

"Is he home?" Mary Grace asked, trying to remember how many days it had been since she had talked to Annie.

"As of last night. I was going to call you but I knew you were busy taping the show. Was it fun? What's Nick Charmin like?"

"Let's conference in Jayde, and I'll tell you both about it at the same time. But first promise me that you're okay, Annie. Promise me you're making things work because you want to make them work, and not because you think it is the right thing to do."

"It's hard to separate the two. Making my marriage work is the right thing to do and I want to do the right thing. It's so intertwined. Nothing is a stand-alone. You can't just put your life into little compartments. One for marriage. One for friends. One for children. One for right. One for wrong. It's more like one of my kids' finger paintings. All mushed together, with no clear definition of the reds or blues or yellows. Sometimes it's just brown, but you have to trust, underneath it all, the pretty colours do exist."

"And you trust that?"

"Colour I trust. John I don't. But once he was a pretty colour, and I believe he can be again. Does that make any sense?"

"More than you'll ever know," Mary Grace said, taking the towel off her head and tousling her hair.

"Want me to conference in Jayde?" Annie offered, dialling her number before Mary Grace had a chance to reply.

"Jayde, Mary Grace, you both there?" Annie asked. They were.

"Why don't we head to MexTexas?" Jayde suggested. "I could use a margarita and a meeting."

"No babysitter," Annie said.

"No energy," Mary Grace said. "Besides, I'm in a robe and I was invited to Nero's tonight, but I have nothing to wear."

"Ralph is taking you to Nero's? Ralph Ichy is heading back into that big, bad, dirty city? After spending the entire day there?" Jayde marvelled. "What is he? An addict now?"

"It wasn't Ralph who invited me," Mary Grace said.

"What are you talking about?" Annie asked.

"It was Nick Charmin," Mary Grace said, overcome with guilt just by uttering his name.

"Nick Charmin? Back up, Mary Grace Falcone, and start from the beginning," Jayde instructed.

"Jayde is right. There are too many missing pieces here. Tell us everything," Annie added.

"I don't know where to begin. It's all so weird, and, well, I don't even know if it's real."

"What? What is real?" Jayde inquired.

"Just begin at the beginning. We'll help you figure it all out," Annie said.

"Oh, but don't—" Mary Grace began to say before being interrupted by Jayde.

"Don't what? How can we don't anything when we have no idea what you are about to tell us? Just dig in, Gracie," she said, using the words Ralph had recently used on her.

"Well, this morning, after my hair and makeup, he comes to see me."

"He, Ralph?" Annie cut in.

"No. He, Nick. Nick Charmin comes into the room, and I'm not sure, but I think he begins flirting with me."

"What do you mean, you think? He either is or he isn't. You would know," Jayde said.

"No. You would know. Me? Not so much. Nobody's ever really flirted with me before. I don't know how the whole dance goes. But he told me I looked hot. He told me I was a natural woman. And he sort of told more than asked if I would meet him at Nero's at eight, but he played it off as a chance to get to know me better for the show. And then I lost my eyelashes. And he found them. And I didn't think it was flirting anymore. It was just jibber jabber," Mary Grace said.

"That jibber jabber is flirting," Jayde affirmed. "Confirmation, please, Annie."

"Flirting. Go on," Annie said.

"So we tape the show and Nick can't stop looking at me. Me. Mary Grace Falcone. It's like he's looking so hard at me he's burning a hole through my heart. It was weird. And poor Ralph, all he can do is sweat. He sweat clear through two shirts. Wardrobe had to strip and change him at the breaks."

"No," Jayde said. "Nobody sweats that much."

"Apparently, Ralph does. And by the way, I've already shared too much. I mean, I am sworn, contractually bound and everything, not to discuss the details of the show with you."

"Who cares? Go on," Jayde urged, anxious to hear more of the story.

"I have to care," Mary Grace said. "I'm not kidding. There was this whole big meeting with lots of lawyers and important, androgynous people in dark suits. And they told us all about leaking. And I'm not talking Pampers, Annie. I mean accidentally leaking information to the press. Accidents like that can ruin a show. And ultimately can be considered criminal."

"You would be eaten alive in jail, Gracie," Jayde speculated. "They'd have to put you in solitary confinement just to save you from the bitches."

"Very funny," Mary Grace said. "Besides, it's not exciting anyway, except for my sweaty Ralph."

"Don't skip right over Nick Charmin," Jayde exclaimed.

"Be patient. I'm getting to that part," Mary Grace said. "So the taping of the show is over. We're all about to leave and, out of nowhere, he's at my side."

"Ralph or Nick?" Annie asked.

"Nick. And I didn't see or even hear him coming. He was just sort of like, there."

"A sideler?" Jayde said.

"Exactly. And he tells me I'm made for television and then reminds me about Nero's at eight. He tells me he hopes to see me there," Mary Grace said. "I don't know what to do. Is he asking like a date? Is he asking for the show? And why do I care or even want to go? I'm engaged to Ralph."

"It's real," Jayde confirmed. "And if this happened one week ago, I'd be all over it, telling you to go and find out if Nick is your destiny. But after talking to Ralph, I'm certain he's your destiny. Gracie, he is a good man. He is one of the few good ones. Annie?"

"I don't know, Jayde. I thought I had a good one. And look at me now, struggling to make the thing work. I'm not saying it's not worth the struggle and I'm not telling you to meet him, Gracie, but things aren't always what they seem."

"But does wanting to go make me not ready to marry Ralph?" Mary Grace asked.

"Yes," Jayde said.

"No," Annie interjected. "At different points in your married life, there will be some wanting, but trust me, it's the acting on it that sucks."

"So you're telling me not to go?" Mary Grace asked.

"You're not married," Annie said.

"No. But you're committed," Jayde said. "And if you give up Ralph for Nick Charmin, I'll have you committed. This is Jayde talking, Gracie. I've been with a lot of men. And I don't say that with pride. I already told you I'm jealous of what you have with Ralph. What more do you want?"

"Maybe I want a little of what you've got?" Mary Grace offered.

"Shit. Why is it we always want what we don't have?" Jayde said.

"Because what we don't have appears so much better and newer and fresher and more exciting than the things we have and already know about," Annie stated. "It's human nature."

"I don't care about human nature right now. Just tell me. Do I go to Nero's or not?"

"Don't go, Mary Grace. Please don't go. Make a cake instead. I'll come over and we can eat it," Jayde said. "And we can talk it through some more. Talk about Ralph, and why he is the one."

"Don't come over now. I still don't know what I'm doing. Annie? What say you?"

"Same thing I always do. Follow your heart," Annie said.

The women hung up their phones and Mary Grace, still in her robe and slippers, splayed out in her beanbag chair, was no better off than before the phone call. *Do I love Ralph because he is easy and comfortable and what I know? Or do I love him in the way that says I want to spend the rest of my life with him? And why do I want to meet Nick Charmin?* Mary Grace lifted herself from the slouchy chair and, with both heavy foot and heart, walked into her kitchen looking for cake. *Jayde's right*, she thought, *I'll bake a cake.*

CHAPTER TWENTY-FIVE

"Birthdays are nature's way of telling us to eat more cake." ANONYMOUS

"Mary Grace, this is your mother. Pick up, Gracie. It's your mother. You didn't call me. I'm waiting to hear about the show, Mary Grace. You should be home by now. Are you home or are you dead in a ditch? This is your mother—"

Mary Grace, her head buried in the refrigerator looking for a substitute in a cakeless house, listened to her mother talk. Dead in a ditch sounded pretty good right about now. Easy, even. Dead in a ditch people don't have to make life-altering decisions. Those sorts of life-altering decisions have already been made for those lucky enough to be dead in a ditch. Unable to even follow her own twisted logic, she concentrated on the grating voice of her mother, who, by her own calculations, had about one more minute of time left on the machine.

"Gracie, if you're home, I want to hear about the show. Pick up if you're home. This is your mother, Gracie..."

Unable to last the full minute, Mary Grace picked up the phone. *Mom wins again.*

"Mom, it's me. Stop talking, Mom. This is me. I'm here," Mary Grace said.

"Where were you? I thought you were dead in a ditch, you took so long to answer."

"I just got out of the shower."

"What's the matter, Gracie?" Angela said, without giving her daughter enough time to finish her not-so-well-planned-out white lie.

"Nothing, Mom. Nothing's the matter."

"I hear it in your voice. A mother knows these things, Mary Grace. What is the matter?"

"Mom, listen to me. Nothing is the matter. Do you want to hear about the show, or not?" Mary Grace said, picking at her curls.

"Of course I do. Ha! *I Do*. I've been waiting all day to hear about the show. How come you didn't call me?"

"We're talking now, aren't we? So listen. You know I am bound by a legal contract not to disclose the details of the show?"

"They don't mean mothers when they talk about all those legal things," Angela said with a confidence that perhaps she was born with.

"They do, Mom. In fact, there is a special clause written specifically about mothers. It says something like, 'You are extra sworn not to divulge any of the day's happenings to your mother,'" Mary Grace said.

"So what can you tell me?"

"I can tell you it was fun. And it was hot. There are these bright, hot lights shining on you the whole time. And before the taping, professionals do your hair and makeup. You're going to like my look, Mom," Mary Grace said, trying to keep the topic as benign as possible.

"What were the questions?"

"Can't tell you."

"So tell me about Nick," Angela said.

"He's okay." Mary Grace concentrated on trying to swallow.

"Just okay?"

"He's good looking, I guess, in a host sort of way. And Ralph looked good, too, Mom."

"Of course he did. Ralph is already good looking. He doesn't need a show to look good, Mary Grace."

"You think?"

"I know. He has a strong chin, Ralph. Strong chins are good. And he is good to his mother. You can tell a lot about a man by the way he treats his mother. A man who treats his mother well will be good to his wife. Your father, may his soul rest in peace, was a good son, too. Good sons make good husbands."

"Mom?" Mary Grace scratched her neck. She could feel herself breaking out in hives. Nerve bites, her mother used to call them. She scratched some more, deciding how to phrase her next question. "Mom?" She hesitated, unable to push the words out. She looked down and noticed the hives spreading to her arm. The phone tucked between her shoulder and her ear, she ferociously scratched her forearm. Finally, she asked, "Did you ever regret marrying Daddy?"

"Regret marrying Daddy? Never. And I hope he didn't hear you ask me that. I hope he was too busy playing Pinochle with Uncle Mike, Uncle Sal, and Nestor."

"I'm sorry, Mom. It's just…"

"Cold feet, Gracie. You have cold feet. It's normal. Go put some thick socks on. I gave you thick socks, didn't I? Put them on and count your blessings that you won't be spending the rest of your life alone. I was always worried about that, Gracie. And now I don't have to worry anymore. Tell me more about the show."

"That's really all I can reveal, Mom. You'll love it, though. But I've got to go. I'm still wet from the shower. And I don't want to catch a cold."

"Go, Gracie. Go. But remember to call your mother."

Mary Grace hung up the phone and reopened the refrigerator.

"Damn it. Why don't I have any cake in here?"

Mary Grace rummaged through the kitchen pantry, looking for a cake mix. Chocolate. Vanilla. Strawberry. She was willing to admit that sometimes, when it was on sale, she did buy strawberry cake mix. It wasn't her favourite, but a sale was a sale. With the speed of a shark playing Three Card Monty, she moved the peanut butter, pasta, and shredded wheat. She shifted the spices, crackers, and jars of sauce. She even checked behind the box of plastic cutlery. The well was dry. Not one cake mix. Not one can of frosting. She let out a huge sigh and then glanced at the clock. It was seven twenty. If she hopped in the car now, and there was no traffic, she could be at Nero's a bit after eight. But she couldn't hop in the car now. She was still in her robe and slippers. She hadn't dried her hair. And she had no cake.

But she wanted to go. She wanted to meet Nick Charmin and find out what he was all about. What it was all about. What was it like to be wanted by a Nick Charmin? What was holding her back? Ralph? Her robe and slippers? Fear? Mary Grace thought about her high school days and hanging on the fringe of Jayde's beige suede jacket. Literally. Nobody in high school wore suede, let alone suede with cowboy-like fringe hanging in a "V" pattern on both the back and the front. Nobody but Jayde, that is. And Jayde pulled it off. Jayde looked cool. And Jayde had every guy in school imagining what it would be like to be her boyfriend. First it was Mike Nuggio. That didn't last too long. Then there was Jeff. *Oh, what was his last name? Why can't I remember Jeff's last name?* Mary Grace wondered. Oh well, that didn't last long, either. Next up was Dean Smythe. Jayde and Dean were together for a long time. He wrote plays, played music, and smoked a lot of weed. He was a nice guy. Smart. *I wonder what happened to him?*

Mary Grace remembered Jayde and Dean together, mostly because she remembered being their sidekick, tagging along to the movies or the diner or a Battle of the Bands. They were both really nice about it. And Dean even paid most of the time. Well, his parents did, anyway. They were loaded. During the Dean Days, Mary Grace developed an unwavering crush on Dean's best friend, Ozzie. Joey Ozerealla.

Where Dean was dark and mysterious and artsy, Ozzie was loud and funny and cute. But Ozzie wasn't interested in Mary Grace. Instead, he went through a string of girlfriends, kind of like Jayde in reverse. Occasionally, if Ozzie had nothing going on, he would join Mary Grace and Jayde and Dean at the diner. Mary Grace would actually pretend they were dating. *What a pathetic thing I was.*

Mary Grace kept telling herself how good she would be for Ozzie. How, when he came to his senses, he would realize how perfect they could be together. He would be loud and funny. She would laugh at his jokes. She would bake him cake. He would eat it. She was certain those other girls couldn't bake a cake.

"They might not bake cake, but they probably give head," Jayde said during one of their infinite conversations about Ozzie.

"That's disgusting," Mary Grace said. "Do you think they do?"

"Of course they do," Jayde replied. "Stop being so naïve. Stop pining for Ozzie. And most of all, stop being so down on yourself. If you opened your eyes, you would see there are more guys out there than just Ozzie."

"But Ozzie is the only boy for me. He has the Jane Asher Factor."

"You and that stupid Jane Asher Factor. I wish my brother had never introduced you to the Beatles. Why do you have to get so obsessed with things? Why can't something just be what it is? Like a record? Or a crush on a boy?"

"I don't know."

"Well I do. You know, I'm starting to think the only reason you really want Ozzie is because you know you can't have him. And you are just afraid of the boys you can have."

"Stop thinking so much, Jayde. Thinking doesn't work for you," Mary Grace said.

And so Mary Grace never went out with Ozzie. And after that she never went out with Billy, or Clyde, or Tom, Dick, or Harry. And now she had a chance with Nick and she was blowing it.

If given a chance to meet Ozzie ten years ago, she would have jumped on it. She would have been at Nero's so fast. So what was holding her up now? Being engaged to Ralph? Suddenly the phone rang, the common noise startling her in an uncommon way. She jumped before checking the caller ID.

"We just hung up, Jayde," Mary Grace said.

"I don't care what you said, I'm coming over," Jayde replied.

"Thank God. I'm losing it over here. I'm taking your advice and baking a cake."

"Good girl."

"But I have no cake mix. I have to make a cake from scratch. I'm going to find Angela's recipe and make Anytime Cake."

"I'll be there before you put the cake in the oven," Jayde said.

"Jayde?" Mary Grace asked, sounding all at once like the little girl Jayde had met on the playground all those years ago.

"What?"

"How is it Annie can survive infidelity and I can't survive a simple invitation to a restaurant?"

"Because you're Mary Grace Falcone," Jayde said, matter-of-factly.

"Thanks a lot."

"I'll be over as fast as I can."

Mary Grace opened the kitchen's junk drawer and rummaged through scissors, tape, coupons, hair ties, cards, shoe laces, and such before finding an index-sized recipe card with little orange carrots at the top, and the words, "Recipe: Anytime Cake; Given By: Mom." Holding the card to her chest, Mary Grace felt something she could only label as relief. She began mixing and measuring flour, sugar, salt, and baking powder. She glanced at the clock again. It was after eight. She couldn't help wondering about Nick.

CHAPTER TWENTY-SIX

"I learned basic cookery from my mom, taught myself cake techniques and then got fed up with my own cakes not looking as good as the ones in the shops." JANE ASHER

M ary Grace's Anytime Cake was in the oven and her apartment was beginning to reap the benefits of a warm, cakey smell. She inhaled one long, deep breath, allowing her lungs to fill with the comforting, scented air. *Thirty minutes and this cake will be mine*, she thought as she pulled out the confections for the frosting. As she added a touch of milk to the confectioner's sugar, she began mentally listing all the cake quotes she could think of. *That's the icing on the cake. Let them eat cake. You can't have your cake and eat it too.* Mary Grace stopped at three. Three quotes. *There must be more*, she thought. With an intensity usually saved for a college thesis, or final exam, Mary Grace ran to her computer and Googled the words "cake quotes."

Mary Grace was astounded by exactly how many cake quotes there were.

But the one that was most shocking wasn't surprising because of its words, so much as its author. Jane Asher.

"Having cakes as a business certainly changes things for me—I don't now sit at home doing a cake for the fun of it anymore. But it's an extremely happy and pleasurable business to run because people are generally buying cakes for celebrations." Jane Asher. *Jane Asher as in Paul McCartney's first girlfriend? One of the beautiful people? The object of the Jane Asher Factor?* Mary Grace wondered. Unable to believe it was true, Mary Grace Googled further and found it was. True. They were one and the same. Paul's first girlfriend now made special occasion cakes.

Most normal people don't even know who Jane Asher is. But me? Not only do I know who she is, I know what she's doing now, AND I created an entire theory after her! Where are you, Jane Asher? Making cakes? Want to have tea, Jane Asher? Because I would like to ask you, am I supposed to end up with Ralph? Does Ralph have the Jane Asher Factor? Aren't you supposed to end up with Paul? I mean, really, does Paul have the Jane Asher Factor?

Afraid she was seriously losing her mind, Mary Grace sat down at her desk chair, took a deep breath, and tried to rest. She even closed her eyes. But it was useless. She couldn't relax. Her brain wouldn't stop. She began filing through it for old Beatles tunes. *Rocky Raccoon. Let it Be. Hey Jude. Yellow Submarine. Yesterday.* And then it came to her: *The Long and Winding Road.* She ran through the lyrics. *Did Paul write that for Jane? Is the "you" the road leads to supposed to be Jane for Paul? Me for Ralph? Can you experience true love more than once? Did Paul truly love Linda? Or were all his experiences leading back to Jane? And where does Nick Charmin fit into all of this? He doesn't fit. I can't let him fit. If Jayde doesn't arrive soon, I will go certifiably bonkers,* she thought.

Before heading back to the kitchen, Mary Grace read one more quote, this time from Cynthia Nixon. "Your good friend has just taken a piece of cake out of the garbage and eaten it. You will probably need this information when you check me into the Betty Crocker Clinic." And that summed up how Mary Grace felt. When Jayde arrived, she would simply ask for a ride to the BC Clinic. *Where was that, anyway? If the Betty Ford Clinic was in California, was the Betty Crocker Clinic close by? It has to be some place with no humidity,* Mary Grace thought, still sopped with sweat from the Haze Craze and disgusted with her hair every day since before school let out. *If I'm going to the BC Clinic, at least I deserve good hair.*

CHAPTER TWENTY-SEVEN

"I'll do almost anything for cake—even trample little children!" GAYLE KING

The doorbell rang and Mary Grace was grateful for Jayde. Jayde would entertain all her crazy thoughts, help her sort them out, and piece her back together, like a well-loved puzzle. And soon, Mary Grace would be all together again. She exited the kitchen, pulled her robe just a bit tighter, and then walked through the living room and easily opened the front door, ready to explain her frightening Google experience to her best friend. *Jayde won't judge.*

"Hello, Mary Grace," Nick Charmin said.

"Nick? What are you doing here?" Mary Grace clutched her robe together with her right hand, trying to fluff her wet hair with her left. Her heart was beating so fast she thought it would pop right out of her chest.

"I think a better question is, what are you doing here?" Nick said. "You were supposed to be meeting me at Nero's at eight o'clock. It's almost nine thirty. Do I smell cake?"

Mary Grace went from frazzled schoolgirl to angry woman so fast she didn't even see it coming herself. All she knew was that he was intruding on her world, forcing her hand, and she wasn't sure she liked it.

"You show up at my door uninvited and the best you can do is 'do I smell cake'? I'm in a robe, for crying out loud."

"I don't mind the robe."

"I do! You'll have to do better than that," Mary Grace said, her neck beginning to look like a relief map of New Jersey thanks to her overworked nerves.

"I do better in front of a camera."

"Well, I don't."

"So you don't want a camera crew here?"

"Just hurry up and come in, would you? Stay right here," she said, pointing to her living room couch. "Don't move. I'm going to put some clothes on."

Mary Grace locked the door to her bedroom, just in case. Then she stepped into the denim shorts that were hanging on her chair. She pulled them off just as fast. *They make me look too fat.* She opened her closet door and got out a cute white skirt and black top. *This will have to do,* she thought, slipping the outfit on, then feeling her legs to see if she had remembered to shave or not. *Smooth,* she thought, *that's good. Why do I care?* she wondered, trying to remind herself she was pissed. *Nick Charmin just intruded on me and my world.* She grabbed her hairbrush. It was sitting on a small antique wooden box, inside of which were the paper napkins from her night of empowerment with Annie and Jayde. True to her promise, she had never read what her friends had written, but her own words? They were tattooed on her brain. She thought about them as she ran the brush through her hair. The words were hers, and yet they were no help at all. Mary Grace remained confused. *Just what is best?* she wondered as she put the brush down and then pinched her cheeks for colour.

"What's your deal?" Mary Grace demanded as she returned to the living room. "Video this encounter to boost the ratings?"

"Bite your tongue, Mary Grace," Nick said, despite being secretly intrigued by the idea.

"Then why are you doing this to me? I'm marrying Ralph. On the reality show *you* host, no less."

"I'm not trying to do anything to you," he said, walking toward Mary Grace. "I'm trying to determine if our chemistry is real. I feel it, Mary

Grace. I felt it the first time I met you. At the interview. You're not like other girls, Mary Grace. Do you feel it? Because if you do, you can't marry Ralph."

"I don't know what I feel. I wasn't going tonight because I didn't really want to find out."

"That's not being honest. In fact, it's worse. It's lying to you, to me, and to Ralph. And if there is one thing you aren't, it's a liar."

"How can you say that? You've only known me for what? A minute? You have no right to say things like, 'if it's one thing you are,' or 'if it's one thing you aren't.' You have no idea what I am or am not about."

"That's not true."

"What do I do for a living?"

"You're a teacher."

"That was too easy. You knew that just from my résumé. Or today's taping, even. We talked about that today, didn't we?"

Nick just hung his head. She was right.

"How old was I when my dad died?"

"I don't know, Mary Grace. But Ralph didn't know about your mother being the tooth fairy, either. Here's what I do know. I want to find out about you," he said. He brushed the hair off her face. "You are even more beautiful in your natural state, without all the fools from *I Do* fussing with your looks," he murmured. "I love your jumbled wet curls and the way you can throw on a skirt and look so heavenly."

"You do?"

"And I loved you in your robe, too."

"Don't give me that robe business."

"It's true. I'm not flirting. I'm speaking the truth."

"You are?" she asked, scratching at the hives on her neck.

"Yes. I am. And the truth is, right now, I want to find out what it would feel like to kiss you," he said, leaning in to Mary Grace.

"Oh my God," she said. "I have a cake in the oven. I have to check the cake." She turned her back on Nick and practically ran to the kitchen. She put her oven mitts on, opened the door, and peered in at the liquid cake.

Damn, she thought. *Not ready*. She shut the oven door, and when she turned around, Nick was right in front of her.

"How do you do that?" she asked.

"What?"

"Get places so quietly. It seems every time I turn around you're there, but I don't hear you coming."

"Magic," Nick said. Starting softly, he touched his lips to hers. This time, with no cake to check and no clothes to change into, she didn't resist. He pressed harder and she returned to him with gentle power, savouring the moment. As Nick continued kissing her, he walked backwards, guiding Mary Grace toward the living room couch. Once at the couch, Mary Grace took in a huge gasp of air, not willing to believe this was all happening.

"What's the matter?" Nick asked, his voice soft, his lips only millimetres from hers.

Mary Grace didn't speak. She just stared at Nick for a long thirty seconds. He was beautiful. When he kissed her again, he sat down on the couch, and she followed his lead, her eyes closed as she drank in all that was Nick Charmin.

CHAPTER TWENTY-EIGHT

"Just about everyone enjoys freshly baked, lusciously frosted cakes..." BETTY CROCKER

The first thing Ralph did after the day's fiasco and Manhattan was check on his mother. She was sitting on the couch, watching television with Celia, her day nurse, by her side. It had hit one hundred degrees today, and yet his mother was wearing a button down sweater. The sight forced the corners of Ralph's mouth down. Along with everything else, his mother suffered poor circulation. *It's just not fair,* Ralph thought. *Hasn't she suffered enough?* As if reading his mind, Celia smiled at Ralph and told him not to worry so much. His mother had a normal day. And as if to confirm Celia's observation, Ralph's mother's face lit up at the sight of her son.

"How was work today?" she asked.

"Good," Ralph said, in no mood to correct her, remind her it was summer vacation, or repeat where he was, for her, or himself, for the millionth time. He didn't need to be reminded of *I Do*. In fact, he was trying hard to forget about it. He had sweated through three shirts! Nobody does that. Nobody who is normal, that is.

"I'm just tired, Mom. And I need a shower. I'm glad your day was good," he said.

"How was work?" she asked.

Ralph just stared at his mother, nodded at the nurse, and made his way to his bathroom.

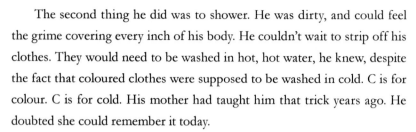

The second thing he did was to shower. He was dirty, and could feel the grime covering every inch of his body. He couldn't wait to strip off his clothes. They would need to be washed in hot, hot water, he knew, despite the fact that coloured clothes were supposed to be washed in cold. C is for colour. C is for cold. His mother had taught him that trick years ago. He doubted she could remember it today.

Finally naked, Ralph stepped into the shower, the hot water he had turned on only moments prior just waiting to clean his filthy frame. As the hot water pulsed down his back, he started to recount the events of the day. What he concluded was that he felt worse for Mary Grace than he did for himself. *I am forced to live with myself,* he thought. No choice there. Mary Grace, on the other hand, was merely agreeing to live with him by saying yes to his marriage proposal. *What was that poor woman agreeing to?* he wondered. *A life with a sweaty germaphobe? What had Jayde nicknamed me? The CEO of Antiseptic Hands? How can I ever make this up to Mary Grace?* he wondered.

His first gesture would be cake. After nearly thirty minutes in the shower, Ralph shut the water off, towelled dry, dressed, and headed straight for the expensive grocery store in town, hoping the bakery section would have at least one good cake left. He would have gone to the bakery, but it was nearly nine o'clock. The grocery store would have to do.

In the store, Ralph darted to the bakery section. Behind the thick glass case he immediately spotted Fourth of July sugar cookies, cupcakes with three feet worth of icing, and assorted pies: strawberry rhubarb, peach, blueberry, and cherry. None of this would do. He needed cake. He sidestepped to the next case and nearly pressed his nose to the glass when he saw it. A strawberry shortcake piled so high he was certain it would tip over. He was thankful to find a cake, any cake, but strawberry shortcake was not what Ralph needed. It was too light and fluffy. *I need a serious cake tonight for some serious eating.* Next he spotted a carrot cake with cream cheese frosting. It was okay, but the little orange carrot decorations with green frosted tops were just too cutesy. And finally, when he was just about to settle on the strawberry high rise, his eyes caught sight of the mother of all cakes. It was blocked by the shortcake, but it was well worth finding. It was a double chocolate, seven-layer cake. Big. Thick. And heavy.

The cake described Ralph's mood. He bought it right away, certain Mary Grace would be pleased with his selection. He was happy to watch the girl behind the counter carefully place the sinful cake into a white bakery box and wrap it with red and white string.

A smile, what he figured was the first of the day, naturally spread across his face as he carried the cake from the store to his car. He turned on the ignition and drove as fast as the speed limit would allow, anxious for the sight of MG, hoping his peace cake would make her forget those three black shirts he had sweat through today.

Ralph parked in front of Mary Grace's apartment, grabbed the cake, and practically skipped up her walk, light with anticipation. The night was dark, but he knew Mary Grace was awake because her apartment was bright and she was not one to waste electricity. And besides, he noticed she hadn't drawn the blinds.

Two steps up the walk and Ralph stopped dead in his tracks. He spotted Mary Grace on the couch. But someone was with her. *Who was that?* On closer inspection Ralph knew exactly who it was. But he just couldn't believe his eyes. It couldn't be, could it? Yes, it could. It was Nick Charmin. Mary Grace was on the couch with Nick Charmin. Nick Charmin! Like a train wreck, Ralph watched, unable to avert his eyes despite being disgusted by the picture before him. And then, as if seeing them sitting on the couch weren't enough to endure, he saw them kiss. Oh, so tenderly they kissed. More tenderly than he recalled his own kisses with Mary Grace to be, a fact that forced pools of tears into his sad, startled eyes.

So that's what Charmin was saying to Mary Grace after the show, Ralph thought, recalling the events of the day. *"I'll meet you at your apartment for a little tryst." I'm such an idiot.* He banged his hand—the one that wasn't holding the cake—against his head. Ralph, clean from his shower, and light with cake, started sweating all over again. He ran four steps closer to her door, his body filled with sadness, then once again stopped, uncertain what he would do when he got to it. *What would a man's man do? Barge into the apartment and take Charmin down. Beat him bloody for stealing his woman. Destroy his ugly face so he could never work in television again.*

None of this plan suited the deflated Ralph, though. He had lost. Again. He had endured Jayde's inquisition, Angela Falcone, reality television, and loving Mary Grace hard enough for the both of them. He had fought so hard for Mary Grace that he had no fight left inside of him. He was empty. He ultimately turned around, shoulders slumped, and staggered back to the car, dumping the cake in an empty trash can Mary Grace had left on the curb, not feeling like dragging it back to the house after the day's garbage pickup. The combination of the empty metal can and the heavy chocolate cake made for a loud thud. *That's my heart breaking,* Ralph thought when he heard the noise. For added emphasis, he kicked the metal can and watched as it crashed to the ground. *I will never see that woman again,* he thought. *More than that; I will never, ever let her see me.*

The sad reality was that it was over.

He wiped away the tear that spilled down his cheek and returned to his car with no idea where he would go.

CHAPTER TWENTY-NINE

"Bourbon does for me what the piece of cake did for Proust." WALKER PERCY

"What was that?" Mary Grace exclaimed, pushing Nick Charmin away.

"What?"

"That noise. Didn't you hear it?" she insisted, ears cocked, twisting her head back and forth and trying to determine what she'd just heard.

"No."

"Please don't tell me your camera crew is here," Mary Grace said, continuing to crane her neck left, then right.

"Why do you keep insisting I brought a crew with me?" Nick wondered, still secretly intrigued by the idea. "Now come back here," Nick added, pulling Mary Grace toward him. "Where were we?"

Mary Grace thought for a moment. Where were they? It was a good question. But she couldn't return to where they were. The noise she heard had startled her back to the reality that was her life.

"I'm fat," she said.

"You're voluptuous."

"My nose is too big."

"It's unique," he said.

"I'm marrying Ralph."

"Not today."

"Then kiss me again," she said. And Nick did. Longer and harder than before. Then he moved his hand down her back and she felt a shudder up her spine. She raised her hands to his cheeks and gently caressed them, not allowing their lips to part. His stubble felt so different and unfamiliar. *What am I doing?* she wondered, in full betrayal mode. This time, with no loud noise to startle her, she forced herself to push away.

"Do you think Jane Asher will ever return to Paul?" she said, blurting the words out so fast it sounded as if she were speaking a foreign language.

"What are you talking about?" Nick asked, trying to get back to the kissing.

"I just asked a question. Do you think Jane Asher will ever return to Paul?" she repeated, much slower this time, keeping Nick at arm's length.

"Is she the *I Do* contestant from season two?"

"Jane Asher? An *I Do* contestant?"

"Wasn't she the tall blonde?"

"No," Mary Grace said, not trying to hide her annoyance. "She was Paul McCartney's girlfriend before Linda."

"Why do you know that?"

"I don't know."

"I'm serious. Why do you know that? That's weird."

"I just do, okay? Do you think Jane and Paul have a chance at happiness?" Mary Grace asked again.

"I don't much care about Jane and Paul. I care about me," Nick said. "And you," he added quickly. Nick leaned in again, wanting nothing more than to continue kissing Mary Grace, while hoping it would lead to bigger and better things.

"Stop. Wait. This isn't right," Mary Grace said. "I don't speak your language."

"English?" he chortled.

"Love. The language of love is what I share with Ralph. I mean, I liked your kisses. I *really* liked your kisses," Mary Grace admitted, just shuddering at the thought. "And I imagine I would like what comes after, too, but the best way for me to describe it is it is foreign to me. I'm glad we sort of tried.

What I mean is, I'm glad you came to me. If you hadn't I would never have known."

"Known what?"

"Ralph possesses the Jane Asher Factor."

"We're back to Jane Asher?"

"I don't think I ever really left her. And thanks to you, and Jane, I know what I really want, more than anything else, is to become Ralph's wife. He speaks my language," she said, grateful to be able to come to this conclusion.

"I speak your language, too," Nick said. The more Mary Grace pushed him away, the more he wanted her. He, Nick Charmin, was supposed to end up with Mary Grace, not Ralph. He tried to kiss her again. "I want you," he said, pressing his body to hers.

"I don't want you," she said. "I want Ralph."

"But I'm so much better looking," Nick said, sounding more desperate than charming. "And I make a ton more money," he added, trying to caress her shoulder. *And I'm supposed to end up with the girl, not Ralph*, he thought, but didn't say.

Mary Grace flinched, then jumped up.

"What are you doing?" Nick asked.

The oven timer went off, signalling that the Anytime Cake was done. Mary Grace was relieved. The timing was perfect, or not, depending on how you looked at it.

"What's that?" Nick asked.

"Cake is done. And so are we," Mary Grace said.

"No. We're not," Nick said, trying to regain the upper hand. He turned a few ideas over in his mind before reaching for Mary Grace's hand. He tried to grab it, but she pulled away and walked toward the kitchen. Like a puppy dog, he followed.

"You know that camera crew you've been so worried about? The one you were afraid I had stalking our every move?" he said, feeling smug.

She gave him a curious look before pulling her cake out of the oven. She inhaled its healing smell before returning her attention to Nick.

"Yeah?" she said, attempting, unsuccessfully, to lead him back to her front door.

"You were right to worry. I don't go anywhere without a crew. They've been documenting our every move. All I have to do is walk out this door and I'll have no less than fifty compromising shots of you to choose from."

A huge grin spread across Nick's face.

"What do I care?" Mary Grace said, trying to remain cool. She could feel her heart racing.

"'Cause I'm Nick Fucking Charmin. That's why you care. These pictures make their way to the tabloids and you lose everything. Your job. Your precious Ralph. And perhaps, most importantly, your reputation."

Mary Grace swallowed hard, trying to hold back her tears. *What have I done?* It took her a moment to process what Nick had just shared. Could he really take her down? She turned the idea over in her head and worked hard to push the next words out.

"You wouldn't do that to yourself," she whispered.

"Don't test me. Remember, I'm the fucking star. The way I see it, this sort of scandal could be good for me. My ratings raise the roof and a rainstorm of money rests in my lap," he said, rolling each "r" off his tongue.

"You're a total sleaze bag. How'd I miss that?" Mary Grace shook her head, trying to push her brains back into place.

Nick threw his shoulders back, puffy at what he interpreted as a compliment.

"You wooed me and I let you. I let you," Mary Grace cried. "But you're disgusting."

Nick just smiled. He wanted what he wanted. *Nothing wrong with that,* he reminded himself.

"I want you, Mary Grace," he said, taking his voice down a notch; his personality, too. He flashed his famous smile.

"Don't give me that look. You don't want me. You don't even know me. You want the idea of me," Mary Grace said, pining for Ralph, wondering, if these pictures made it to the tabloids, how she could ever make it up to him. Even if they didn't, she had probably lost Ralph for good. "And for the love of God I don't know why. Why?"

Nick just shrugged. "I want you to be my girlfriend," he said.

"And what if I don't want you to be my boyfriend?"

"If you don't agree to date me then the pictures of you and me, I assure you, will be all over the tabloids by the end of the week. You can kiss Ralph, and life as you know it, goodbye."

Mary Grace began to sob. "Get out," she screamed. "I hate you. I hate *I Do*. I hate everything!"

"But me," Jayde said, running up the apartment stairs.

"Jayde! You're here."

"I told you I was coming."

"But—I—and he—" Mary Grace stuttered.

"Well put, Gracie," Jayde said, turning her attention to Nick Charmin. "You are a schmuck. Nothing more than a playground bully," she said, getting in Charmin's face, and pinning him to Mary Grace's living room wall. "And here's a little tip. Don't fuck with the friends."

Somehow, next to Jayde, Nick looked tiny and almost helpless. "You were probably nothing more than a hapless nerd in high school. And now you act this way because you can. But guess what, asshole? You can't. I'm here," Jayde said.

"Mary Grace?" Jayde looked her friend square in the face. "Tell Mr. Charmin, please, besides cigarettes and fabulous mascara, what is the one item I always carry in this big, black Chanel bag of mine?" Jayde reached into her bag.

Mary Grace gave her friend a quizzical look, watching as she rifled through her bag. Nick and Mary Grace appeared equally intrigued. But as Jayde continued reaching in her bag, a light went off in Mary Grace's head.

"Your tape recorder, Jayde," Mary Grace exclaimed, her voice filled with delight. "For your interviews!"

"You speak the truth!" Jayde said, stealing Nick's signature line and pointing at Mary Grace like some sort of game show host, in honour of the dishonourable Nick Charmin. "As a fashionista, blogger, columnist, and reporter, I never leave home without it."

The colour drained from Nick Charmin's face, and his eyes filled with panic.

"That's right, asshole. You should look like that," Jayde said, nose to nose with Nick. "You think a scandal like this would be good for you and your career? Think again. I've got it all here on tape. Blackmailing a poor innocent girl like Mary Grace Falcone. It will be your end, not hers."

"Mary Grace?" Nick said, his voice pleading, his eyes begging, just waiting for her to get him out of this.

"Don't look at me," Mary Grace said. "I'm no fangirl."

"I don't even really have pictures," Nick admitted. "You kept insisting I had paparazzi here so I went with it. I made it up. All because I wanted you. I would do anything to get you."

"I'm not making this up," Jayde said, shaking her tape recorder in Nick's face. "So unless you want this on *Entertainment Tonight*, *TMZ*, or the fucking evening news, get your scrawny little butt out of here. Now." Jayde's voice was hot with anger and determination.

"Yeah," Mary Grace added. "Get out of my face. My house. And my life."

Like a remorseful schoolboy, Nick Charmin left, his head down, his walk dejected. He had been outplayed, something he didn't like to admit. *But at the end of the day*, he reminded himself, *I'm still Nick Charmin*. He thought about Tanjia, home in his bed, and didn't know whether to smile or cry.

"You saved me, Jayde. Again." Mary Grace hugged her friend so tightly Jayde thought she might never let go.

"The way I see it, we saved each other."

Mary Grace pushed away from Jayde, her eyes asking for more.

"You inspired me."

"How?"

"I called that old boyfriend of mine. Robert Altmann."

Mary Grace looked at Jayde with raised eyebrows.

"The lawyer? Remember? I gave his card to Annie?"

"I know who he is, Jayde. He's the one I said had the Jane Asher Factor."

"Yup. I couldn't remember why we broke up in the first place. I thought, perhaps, I was just being too critical. Thanks to you I decided to give him another shot. Maybe, just maybe, he is one of the good ones."

"Have you seen him yet?"

"Once. It was nice. Maybe I missed the good in him. I missed it in Ralph. I'm not perfect."

"Thank God. It's better now that you're a mere mortal, like the rest of us."

The girls looked at each other, and at the same time said the same word.

"Ralph!"

"Oh my God, Jayde, I have to find him. He is the best thing that ever happened to me. If I lose him now I will die."

"Go, Gracie. I'll stay here. Someone has to ice this cake. And eat it," Jayde added, picking at a piece and popping it in her mouth. "Oh, it's good."

"Did you know Jane Asher makes cakes now?" Mary Grace called over her shoulder as she began running toward the door. "It's true. Google it."

"Not as good as this one, Gracie. Now go get your Paul. And call me."

Mary Grace was equal parts happy and terrified. She, without a shadow of a doubt, wanted to marry Ralph. But she wasn't sure, after what she would reveal, if he would still have her. The thought made her sick to her stomach.

Reading her friend's mind, Jayde shouted after her, "You know, you don't have to tell him." As she heard the words exit her lips, she knew they weren't true. Of course Mary Grace had to tell Ralph. Everything. *This is going to be hard*, she thought, taking a lick of the frosting Mary Grace had whipped up. *Jane Asher makes cakes? Go figure.* Jayde continued icing the cake, instinctively knowing Mary Grace would need a huge hunk of it later that night.

CHAPTER THIRTY

"Made a lightening trip to Vienna eating chocolate cakes in a bag." LENNON AND MCCARTNEY

When Mary Grace pulled up to Ralph's house, she noticed his car wasn't in the driveway. A surge of panic raced through her body, the kind that makes you shake from the inside out. *He's not here? If not here, then where?* She dialled his cell and it went right to voicemail, indicating that it was off or dead. *Like me,* she thought, *off or dead.* She forced herself to try anyway: physically walk up to the door, ring the bell, and make sure he wasn't there. She couldn't be certain he wasn't in the house unless she checked it herself. She looked at her watch. It was late to ring the doorbell. Too late. His mother was probably sleeping. *But this is an emergency,* she rationalized. Ralph was missing and she needed to find him in the most urgent sort of way.

With wobbly knees and the threat of puking stuck in the top of her throat, she rang the doorbell and then held her breath. Celia answered the door, rubbing her eyes at the same time. She saw the panic that enveloped Mary Grace and tried to put her at ease.

"You didn't wake me," Celia said, her voice upbeat and firm. "Promise. I just got sucked into a movie, that's why I was rubbing my eyes. Too much television. And Mrs. Ichy is sleeping peacefully. Are you okay?"

"I'm looking for Ralph," Mary Grace said, the words coming out of her mouth nearly silent and fractured.

"He's not here," Celia said, using her softest voice. "He left here around nine and asked me to spend the night with his mom." She glanced down at the watch on her wrist. "Said he was going to see you, Mary Grace. You haven't seen him?"

"No. He said he was seeing me?"

"Yes."

"But I haven't seen him, Celia," Mary Grace said.

Celia shrugged her shoulders, unsure of how to respond. Ralph hadn't looked good to her earlier that evening, but Mary Grace looked even worse.

"I'm so sorry to disturb you. Thanks," Mary Grace said, her voice cracking. She darted to her car, opened the door, jumped in, and slammed the door shut before losing it. She sobbed like a baby, shoulders heaving up and down, head bobbing. *The best thing in my life is Ralph*, she thought, *and I ruined it with a sleaze bag like Nick Charmin. I don't deserve Ralph. I don't deserve happiness. I don't even deserve cake*, she thought, unable to stop the tears from falling. *What did I do? Oh God, what did I do?* With a few deep breaths, Mary Grace tried to regain her composure. She dialled Jayde, but still couldn't speak.

"Mary Grace? Is that you?" Jayde asked, having checked the caller ID on her cell. She heard sniffling. "Why are you crying? Stop it. You're scaring me," Jayde said. "Take a deep breath. Tell me where you are."

"Ralph," Mary Grace blurted out. Then she took one long deep breath before pushing the next words out. "He's not here. He's gone."

"Okay. Take another deep breath. How do you know he's gone?"

Jayde heard Mary Grace breathe in, long and loudly. "Celia—"

"Who the hell is Celia?" Jayde interrupted Mary Grace.

"His mom's nurse." Mary Grace sniffled the words out. "He asked her to stay the night. Said he was going to my house. He's not there, is he, Jayde?"

"Nope," Jayde said, turning her head around the apartment just to confirm.

"Do you think he knows I kissed Nick?" Mary Grace yelled at Jayde.

"No, he doesn't know. How could he know?"

"Then where is he?"

"I don't know, Gracie, but I'm on it," Jayde said, devising a quick plan, wondering if, in fact, Ralph did know about the kiss. *Impossible,* she thought.

"Jayde? You there?"

"Still here. I've got a plan. You check the gym and the diner."

"The gym's not open," Mary Grace started to argue.

"But the parking lot is. Just check it."

"Okay," Mary Grace whimpered. "I have to find him, Jayde. I can't lose Ralph. He's the best thing that ever happened to me."

"We'll find him. I promise," Jayde assured her.

"Where are you going?"

"Your mother's."

"But—" Mary Grace started to say.

"Just go. Now," Jayde said, once again not letting her finish. "Call me with updates."

Jayde took another quick look around Mary Grace's apartment, sort of like an inventory to make sure Ralph hadn't snuck in without her noticing. She laughed at herself before grabbing her purse. She shook the bag to make sure her keys were in it, and then, after hearing them tinkling on the bottom, she plunged her hand in to find them. With a smile painted on her lips, Jayde exited the apartment, possessing a pretty good idea of where a confused and missing Ralph would go. It wasn't Angela's. Or the gym, either. She had just sent Mary Grace there to give her something to do. Jayde wanted to get to Ralph first, because Mary Grace could not lose him, and she, Jayde, would make sure that didn't happen.

CHAPTER THIRTY-ONE

"I wanted to buy a candle holder, but the store didn't have one. So I got a cake." MITCH HEDBERG

With her mind on Ralph—losing Ralph, getting Ralph back, and assorted versions of *what the hell was I thinking*—Mary Grace backed wildly out of her parking spot in the complex. She didn't remember looking behind her. When that thought came to her, she shook her head in disbelief. *Concentrate, Mary Grace,* she told herself. *The last thing I need is an accident.* Her personal scolding lasted only a minute or two before her mind took over again. *Where would he go? Why did he go? Does he know? Did he sense something between Nick and me? I'm an idiot.* She could feel the tears running down her cheeks. She wiped them away with the back of her hand. When she replaced her right hand to the steering wheel, she suddenly remembered she was driving.

Shit! Where am I going? The gym. Jayde told me to look for Ralph in the gym parking lot. When she looked up at the street sign, she realized she was heading in the wrong direction. She checked in front of her and in back of her, and with no traffic visible, pulled a u-turn right in the middle of the street. *There,* she thought, *at least I'm going in the right direction now.*

Mary Grace had been travelling north on Main for only a moment when a police car, in all its police glory, pulled up behind her, sirens blaring and lights flashing. Mary Grace peeked several times in her rearview mirror to confirm what was behind her. *Me? He wants me?* Riddled with problems,

Mary Grace started to cry again, or perhaps she had never even stopped. There were so many tears it was difficult to tell. Her heart started racing with a surge of police-infused panic, and she could feel her anger boiling, too. *I don't have time for this,* she thought as she pulled her car to the side of the road. *This distraction could mean the difference between me finding or not finding Ralph. My future is at stake.* She thought about peeling out, pushing away, dissing the cop. But she would do none of that. Instead she rolled down her window, and when the cop approached her car, she cried even harder.

"Good evening, Ma'am. I'm Officer Reynolds. License and registration, please."

Mary Grace was crying so hard she couldn't speak—not even to ask why he was pulling her over. Her hands were trembling as she tried to fumble in her purse for her license.

"Have you been drinking, Ma'am?" the officer asked, giving Mary Grace a curious look and official once-over.

"No. I swear." She pushed the words out, keenly aware of what a sight she was. "You can even do one of those... those... those tests on me," she said, her hands shaking as she passed him her license.

"I'll need your registration, too. But you don't look well. Are you sick?"

"Not with the flu or anything," she said as she leaned over to the glove box, although she did feel like puking. She swallowed hard to get rid of the sensation and pulled out the registration card. She handed it to the officer and tried to smile, but even the tiniest of grins wouldn't come.

He looked at her picture and then at her in the flesh. Something didn't add up. "Wait here," he said before walking back to his car to run the appropriate vehicle tests.

Mary Grace sat in the car, her leg pulsing with nerves, hives breaking out over her body. *I have to go. I have to go. I have to go,* she repeated in her head, wondering exactly how long this whole procedure would take, and exactly what he was ticketing her for. After several long minutes, Officer Reynolds returned to the car.

"Your vehicle checks out okay, but really, you don't look too good. What are you sick with?"

"Seriously?"

He stared at Mary Grace with steely blue eyes and a look that said, "very seriously."

"A broken heart," she said before taking one long, deep breath and letting the next string of words pour out. "The man I'm supposed to marry, the most wonderful, gentle, kindest man in the world, has figured out that I'm not worth marrying. He is too good for me and he knows it. I'm afraid I may have broken his heart along the way, only I don't know for sure if he knows what I think he does, and if he does I can't figure out how, and if he really is hiding from me, I don't know where that is, so me and my best friend Jayde are out looking for him. She is checking my mother's house and I'm supposed to be checking the gym and—"

"Gym?"

"Yeah. The YMCA. It's just around the corner."

"You got a lot going on, lady. I'm not sure you should be driving around. And the Y should be closed at this hour anyway."

"That's what I told Jayde but she told me to check the parking lot. And then the diner. And I can't argue with Jayde. I can't argue with my mother. I can't argue with anyone. All I want to do is find Ralph. I have to make things right with him or else my life is over. And I'm not just being dramatic. I swear. If I lose Ralph I lose myself. I don't know why it took me so long to figure that out. But it did. And now I'm stuck here with you— no insult intended—for doing God knows what, and I'm risking missing Ralph–and–"

"A u-turn, Ma'am. You can't just make an illegal u-turn in the middle of the street. But you got me on a slow night and I'm a sucker for a good love story. So follow me," the officer said.

"Follow you?" Mary Grace asked, her eyes teary and sad.

"Please. I'll escort you to the gym. If your guy is there you can make up. If not, we'll check the diner. But then I am escorting you home. You are in no condition to be riding around out here," he said, handing her back her license and registration. "You seem like a nice lady. I want it to work out for you. But I have to keep you safe. Follow me."

"Thank you, Officer—"

"Reynolds. Officer Dean Reynolds," he said with a nod of his head. "Glad to be of service."

Officer Reynolds got in his car and kept the flashing lights on. With Mary Grace behind him, he drove carefully to the gym. Ralph was neither in the building, which was locked up for the night, nor the parking lot. Just as he promised, Officer Reynolds escorted Mary Grace to the diner. She felt hopeful upon entering the diner, the cop by her side, thinking Ralph just might be there, eating a large piece of chocolate cake.

"We eat a lot of cake," she told him as they walked in. "You know, cake can solve a lot of problems. My mother always says there is no problem in life that can't be solved over a nice hunk of cake. Did you know Jane Asher, Paul McCartney's girlfriend before Linda Eastman, is a baker of cakes now? It's true—"

"I'll check the men's room," Officer Reynolds said, silently relieved to pull away from Mary Grace for a moment, leaving her to scour the diner.

"But how will you know it's Ralph?" Mary Grace asked, breaking out of her cake talk.

"I'll ask," he said with a tiny smile.

Mary Grace and Officer Reynolds met back at the cash register. Neither one had found Ralph.

"I'm sorry, Miss Falcone," he said. "But I think you should call that friend of yours. What was her name?"

"Jayde."

"Call Jayde and have her meet you at your house."

"Apartment."

"Apartment." Officer Reynolds repeated the word, rolling it over in his mouth, as if it were a word of significance. "I'll bring you home now," he added, waiting for a long diatribe from Mary Grace. Instead, she steadied herself against the cash register in silence.

"Okay?" he prompted with a softness in his voice, attempting to confirm that Mary Grace understood him.

With no energy left, all Mary Grace could do was nod.

CHAPTER THIRTY-TWO

"A party without cake is just a meeting." JULIA CHILD

Jayde had a good idea of where Ralph was, and felt a tad guilty for sending Mary Grace on a wild goose chase. But Jayde knew it was best to keep her friend busy; alone in her apartment, Mary Grace would lose her mind. Jayde couldn't help but smile when she saw Ralph's car in the parking lot. His ratty automobile wasn't hard to spot, being that it was the only one there. She parked next to him, turned off the ignition to her Bimmer, and sat still for a brief moment. She entertained the idea of calling Mary Grace first, just to let her know she had found him, but changed her mind. Fast. She needed to take a pulse of the situation. Find out what was on Ralph's mind. See if it could be repaired.

She lit a cigarette and exited the car, practically in one motion. The long drag she took soothed her nerves and helped her compose her thoughts. She peeked into Ralph's car, making sure he wasn't catatonic in the back seat or something. He wasn't, so she trotted toward the building—Minot High School—and took one more drag of her cigarette before flicking it to the ground and running up the steps. She pulled the door open. *Damn. Locked.* She tried all four front doors with the same results. *I know he's in there,* she thought as she ran back down the steps, devising a new plan.

She walked the perimeter of the building, trying to remember which side of the school his classroom was on. When she got to the side closest to the football field, she breathed a sigh of relief as she noticed one lonely classroom light was on. *Ralph*. Jayde bent down and scooped up a few pebbles from the ground. She even plucked a giant rock, just in case. She walked closer to the lit window, positioning herself underneath. She threw her stones at the window, pleased at her marksmanship, and glad to hear the pinging noise they made. After shooting five stones, she waited, impatiently, for Ralph to appear at the sill. He didn't. She was afraid she had gotten the whole thing wrong. *He's got to be in there*, she thought. *His car is in the lot. He's here, with his books and papers, to seek refuge. I know it.*

She threw two more pebbles and waited, her mind suddenly filling up with horrible thoughts. She turned the big rock over in her hand, ready to hurl it at the window and smash it open, when she heard her name.

"Jayde?" Ralph said as he peeked out the double hung window and leaned out over the sill. "What the hell are you doing here?"

At the sound of her name, Jayde felt the deepest sense of relief she had ever experienced. She looked up and saw Ralph's face, and knew she could help him. Help them.

"Don't jump!" Jayde said. "It's not that bad."

"It's only the first floor," Ralph reminded her, confused.

"That's why it's funny, Ralph. If you were, say, at the top of the Empire State Building, it wouldn't be funny," she said, regretting having to even explain her joke. "Help me in there," she instructed, reaching her hand up toward him as she got closer to the window.

"No. Go away. I want to be alone," Ralph said. "Wait; how'd you even know I'd be here?"

"Help me up and I'll tell you," Jayde said with a smile.

"Just go, Jayde. There are some things even you can't fix."

"Bite your tongue. I can fix anything."

"Except yourself," Ralph said with more venom than he intended. Venom meant for Mary Grace.

"Ouch." Jayde reached into her purse and pulled out a Barnes & Noble bag. "That was below the belt."

"Sorry. But I can't do this, Jayde. Leave me alone. Please?"

"I promise to leave you alone if you just let me in for one minute. Sixty seconds of Jayde-time and then I'll get out of your hair."

"Seriously? A bald joke?"

"No! No joke. Just a bad choice of words. C'mon. Help me up." She tried, unsuccessfully, to hoist herself up to the window. "At least let me show you what's in the bag." Jayde shoved the bag she had just pulled from her purse toward the window with grand, dramatic effect.

Ralph eyed the bag curiously.

"Fine." He caved, as Jayde knew he would. "But just go to the front of the building and I'll let you in."

"No way! Hoist me up," she said, shoving the bag back in her purse and flinging it over her shoulder, freeing up her hands. "This will make a much grander story for your little Falcone-Ichy children."

"You're nuts," Ralph said. "You can make the story as grand as you want, but there will be no children. At least not mine." Ralph grabbed Jayde's hands, helping her scale the side of the building. "Maybe Falcone-Charmin kids," he added as Jayde tumbled into the classroom.

Jayde laughed hysterically as she pressed out her shirt and collected her things. "That was fun, Ralph. Right out of a movie."

"Glad you find my life so amusing," Ralph said.

"Oh, stop being so tragically serious. Your life is not amusing. But me, tumbling into your classroom, that's amusing."

"Sorry I don't see the humour. And pardon my foul mood, but I'm busy grieving here, seeing that Mary Grace dumped me for Nick Fucking Charmin."

"I've never heard you swear before."

"I've never been dumped before. Correction. I've never even had a girlfriend before."

"Mary Grace didn't dump you, Ralph. She's out searching for you right now. We both are. I just got to you first. What's going on? Tell me."

And he did. He told her about buying the cake. And walking up to the apartment and seeing the love of his life kissing Nick Fucking Charmin.

And Jayde told Ralph about Nick "The Dick" Charmin. And how he tried to blackmail Mary Grace. And how Mary Grace was a wreck; a miserable, horrible wreck, convinced she had lost the best thing that ever came into her life.

Ralph watched with intensity as Jayde spoke, his eyes begging her to tell him more, his heart praying that what she was saying was the truth.

"But if everything you are saying is true—if Mary Grace loves me so much—then why did she have to kiss Nick Charmin?"

Jayde paused for a moment; long enough to take a fake drag from a non-existent cigarette. She tilted her chin up and blew out her breath in a long, slow stream. Then she looked Ralph squarely in the eyes.

"She needed to be certain."

Ralph took a handkerchief from his pocket and wiped his tearing eyes.

"She is," Jayde added.

"It's too late." Ralph took a deep breath. "I just can't do it. You say she wants me, but the thing is, I don't want her. I never want to see her again. I mean it. Don't bring her here to apologize or beg. I never want to see her again," he repeated, this time emphasizing the word "never."

Jayde felt her stomach turn sour, Ralph's words making her sick.

"She takes too much out of me," he continued. "Loss is painful. I'm better off alone." Ralph shoved the hanky back into his pocket.

"Sometimes, Ralph, you have to fight for what's worth having. There is no sin in putting on the boxing gloves."

Ralph sighed. "There's no sin in surrendering, either." He stared at Jayde for what seemed like an eternity, refusing to divert his gaze. She accepted the challenge and kept his stare. It was Ralph who looked away first, and when he did he uttered the words, "Can you leave now?"

"Not until I show you what's in this bag," Jayde said, reaching for the Barnes & Noble bag she had pushed back into her purse.

Ralph stared at the white bag with green lettering and listened, his ears fixated on the distinct crinkling noise it made. He was curious. He watched as Jayde pulled out what was in the bag.

"*The Catcher in the Rye.*"

Ralph raised his eyebrows in disbelief.

"Well, you made it sound so intriguing I thought I may have missed out on something really great. I thought maybe, after I finish, we could discuss it?"

Ralph nodded yes.

"Good. I'll leave now. But promise me something."

A long pause followed.

"Don't you miss out on something really great."

CHAPTER THIRTY-THREE

"I've always told my children that life is like a layer cake. You get to put one layer on top of the other, and whether you frost it or not is up to you." ANN RICHARDS

Annie was sleeping, but not soundly. Never soundly. Since becoming a mom she always slept with one ear opened, just waiting for the cry of a child who couldn't sleep, had a nightmare, or was feeling sick. She didn't mind it, mostly. Sometimes rocking a child back to sleep was the most peaceful part of her day. But after John's affair, things changed. She found she wasn't sleeping with one ear opened; she just plain wasn't sleeping. Insomnia. Not sleeping left her with a desperate feeling, wanting something so badly that she wasn't able to attain. It also left her angry. Lying there, her husband sleeping soundly next to her, was maddening. *He's the one who messed everything up, how come he gets to sleep like a baby?*

She rarely used getting out of bed as a tactic to fight her sleeplessness. More often than not she just lay there, quietly, reminding herself that resting was just as good as sleeping. She was in that state—that resting is just as good as sleeping state—when the phone rang, startling her the same way it would have if she had been in a deep, sound sleep. *Who died? Is my mother okay?* Her mind always focused on the worst possible scenarios. She fumbled for the phone, noticing the blaring ringing hadn't disturbed her husband's sleep in the slightest.

"What's the matter?" Annie demanded, her voice cracked and anxious.

It was Mary Grace, apologetic and in the middle of a Texas-sized panic attack. Ralph was missing. She kissed Nick Charmin. She nearly got a ticket from a cop who escorted her around town searching for Ralph. They couldn't find him but Jayde was still out looking for him and calling Jayde's phone was useless. Straight to voicemail every time. And she was pacing, pacing, pacing around her apartment with no idea what to do with herself.

Annie kept the volume of her voice low as she tried to talk Mary Grace off the ledge. She glanced over at her husband, who remained peacefully sleeping, and realized the volume of her voice made no difference to him. She could whisper. She could shout. He wouldn't wake up unless she physically nudged him, nearly rolling him over. He puzzled her. After all the shit they'd been through, he could still sleep like a baby. He shatters the marriage, and she gets insomnia. There was something wrong about that, and yet she wanted some of what John had. *What is it? The ability to compartmentalize?* She often wondered if he wanted some of what she had, only she couldn't figure out what that was. *I love him. I hate him. It is a thin line,* she thought, *one Mary Grace is walking right now.*

"I'll be there in ten," she said, hanging up the phone and knowing how badly her friend needed her. She nudged John until she was certain he was awake; certain he understood what she was telling him. She was heading to Mary Grace's. Her friend was having a panic attack. The boys were sleeping and her phone was on.

"Be safe. You're a good friend, y'know. And wife," John said dreamily before rolling back to sleep.

Annie smiled. That thin, thin line. It got her every time. She threw on jeans and a T-shirt, slipped into her flip-flops, and was out the door.

By the time Annie arrived at Mary Grace's, Jayde was already there. They were sitting at the kitchen table in silence. Annie shot Jayde a look of concern, kissed Mary Grace on the cheek, and slid into the open chair.

Still silence.

The only thing between them was the cake Mary Grace had prepared earlier in the evening, although earlier in the evening felt more like weeks ago.

"She didn't want me to talk until you arrived," Jayde said, finally breaking the silence. "For two reasons—"

"I wanted your support," Mary Grace said, not letting Jayde finish, and looking at Annie with a smile. "And the longer I don't know what really happened, the longer I can pretend everything will be okay," she whispered.

"So you found him?" Annie asked, looking at Jayde, who nodded in agreement.

"Where?"

"Minot High School."

"I wanted to go there but Jayde didn't think it was a good idea," Mary Grace said. "I couldn't bear to hear why."

"Okay, honey," Annie said gently. "We're together now. Let Jayde tell us everything."

"Jayde?" Mary Grace prompted.

"I'm not certain it's good news," Jayde said, gazing down at the table while tugging at her long black hair.

Annie gasped, sucking just a bit of air in, but Jayde heard it and so did Mary Grace. *Try to be soft*, Annie's gasp said. When Jayde looked up, she saw a look of horror in Mary Grace's eyes.

"But it's not all bad, either," Jayde quickly added. She looked down again, this time focusing on her hand, the one she'd been using to tug at her hair. There, between her fingers, were a few loose strands. She shook her head in an attempt to dislodge the pain of the conversation.

"Just tell me," Mary Grace said.

"He loves you."

"He said that?" she asked.

"Yes."

"So," Mary Grace hesitated before asking, "what's the bad news?"

"He knows about Charmin. He saw you, Mary Grace. Through your picture window. He's pretty devastated."

"What'd he say?"

"Something like—"

"Not something like. Exactly. Exactly what did he say?"

"He never wants to see you again because—" Jayde stammered, pulling out more of her hair, "because–because–"

"Say it," Mary Grace shouted.

"It hurts too much."

"Ouch," Mary Grace said, a shiver running through her. Annie reached for one of her hands and Jayde took the other. Mary Grace pulled away, folding her arms across her body instead.

"This isn't good," she stated. "I singlehandedly managed to screw up my entire life while hurting the best man I've ever known. Shit!" Mary Grace slammed her hand down on the kitchen table, sending cake crumbs flying. "My mother was right all along. I will die alone."

"You'll never be alone," Annie said. "You'll always have us."

"She's right," Jayde agreed, cutting a big piece of the cake, putting it on a plate, and pushing it toward Mary Grace, who just shook her head no.

"No?" Jayde asked.

"No," Mary Grace whispered.

"In my entire life, I have never seen you turn down a piece of cake. Especially during a crisis," Jayde said. "I'm worried."

"About me not eating cake or Ralph not taking me back?"

"Natch, the cake," Jayde said.

Mary Grace smiled, but Jayde wasn't sure it was directed at her joke, because after she said it, a long pause ensued. Annie shot Jayde another in a long line of is-she-going-to-be-okay looks. Jayde nodded yes despite her own uncertainty.

"You know what's weird?" Mary Grace finally said, staring at the unwanted piece of cake in front of her. "I think I'm all cried out." And then she just nodded, as if she were agreeing with herself, but not saying a word until she finally spoke again. "You should have seen me when that cop pulled me over. I couldn't stop the tears," Mary Grace said, idly picking away at the chocolate cake, making a mound of crumbs before her. "Now? I feel nearly catatonic. No tears. No grand emotions. Just—"

"Exhaustion," Annie said, glancing at the clock on the wall. "It's three in the morning, Mary Grace. You've been awake for nearly twenty-four hours. Twenty-four long and turbulent hours."

"Gracie," Jayde added, "there's nothing we can do tonight that will change anything. I honestly think the best thing for you right now is sleep. We can all look at the situation with fresh eyes in the morning."

"I'm too agitated to sleep."

"Do you want an Ambien?"

"No. I want Ralph. I need Ralph. Oh my God. Ralph. We were supposed to be back on the *I Do* set at e-leven tomorrow. I mean, e-leven today," Mary Grace said, glancing at the clock.

"Why are you saying 'eleven' that way?" Jayde asked.

"It's a Tess Lunt thing. It made me and Ralph laugh," Mary Grace explained, smiling at the memory. "It also worked to sear the time in my brain. E-leven. Today. What am I going to do?"

Jayde and Annie eyed each other.

"We'll go with you," they said.

Upon hearing that news, Mary Grace felt immediately calmed. The unwavering friendship of Annie and Jayde was the smoothest sort of Valium a stressed out, anxiety ridden, hot mess of a human being could take. Their brand of meds soothed her frazzled nerves, and their unwavering friendship seemed bottomless. They insisted on sleeping over, knowing they had to help Mary Grace make it through the night.

Mary Grace didn't argue, rationalizing with herself that if she was going to be alone for the rest of her life, it was best not to start tonight. After searching for new toothbrushes, offering clean washcloths, sharing bottles of Advil, and pouring big glasses of water, the girls tucked themselves into Mary Grace's queen sized bed and offed the lights. The room was pitch black, *like my heart*, each woman thought, though for differing reasons.

Jayde was sad she couldn't repair what was broken between Mary Grace and Ralph. Jayde fixed everything, but this time she couldn't, and her powerlessness and uncertainty of the future were alarming.

Annie was unsure of what the demise of Mary Grace and Ralph meant for her and John. She was having a hard enough time trying to piece her marriage back together and learn to trust again. She tried to picture John when she'd last seen him, as he'd whispered, "you're a good wife." But regretfully, the only picture she could come up with was John in bed with the blonde skinny bitch. *What would happen to them all?*

Mary Grace, in the middle of her two friends, felt safe—for the time being. She didn't know what the future would bring, or how she would manage without Ralph, or even if she could ever forgive herself for hurting him so irrevocably, but she would work on it all later. For now, as she lay awake, rolling the events of her life over and over in her brain, she would let herself feel the security her best friends brought her despite having no crystal ball to predict the future.

"I haven't stayed up this late since college," Annie said.

"I have," Jayde said with a sordid laugh. "Mary Grace, don't even try to spoon me," she added. "You know I don't like being touched when I sleep."

Annie laughed, but Mary Grace didn't say a word.

"You sleeping already, Gracie?" Jayde asked, leaning over to look at Mary Grace, but unable to see a thing in the darkness.

"Nope," Mary Grace whispered. "You guys remember our night of empowerment?" she asked, not waiting for their answers. "I have our napkins. Remember? The ones we wrote on? With Annie screaming at us to just do it?" She chuckled. "I doubled back and took them. I wanted proof that our night of empowerment happened. I guess I never knew how much I would need the proof. I swear to you both I have never, ever looked at them. Not even my own. I just wanted to have them."

Mary Grace waited a moment to see if either friend would get mad at her for what she had revealed. Nobody spoke, so Mary Grace continued.

"You want to look at them? Together?"

"No," Jayde said. "I remember mine clearly. I don't need to know yours," she added, her voice not angry, but very firm and certain.

"No, honey," Annie agreed. "I like your proof the night existed. Maybe someday we could add some other treasures to the napkins and bury them in a time capsule in the ground. But for now, let's let the napkins rest."

"Yeah," Mary Grace whispered. "Sometimes not knowing is nice."

CHAPTER THIRTY-FOUR

"My mother still sends a cake to my office for my birthday." DAVID ULEVITCH

When Nick Charmin finally returned to bed it was three a.m. He was certain, because the neon red numbers on his alarm clock were shouting at him. He thought about picking up the clock and hurling it across the room, but even as drunk as he was, he knew that wouldn't make it not be three o'clock in the morning, or even change the events of the night. Instead, he promised himself he would get a new clock, one that wasn't so mean and aggressive.

He was a stumbling, slurring drunk, and his horrific evening had left him exhausted with a large side of humiliation. He was Nick Fucking Charmin. He got what he wanted, when he wanted it. *What had that bitch of a friend said? "You were probably a nerd in high school and now you act this way because you can."* He felt like glass; not the frosted kind that allowed you to decipher only shadows and shapes, and not the tempered kind that was strong and non-shattering, but regular, good old-fashioned glass—transparent and breakable. Mary Grace and that friend of hers had seen right through him; since his summer of reinvention, that had never happened.

He slipped back into bed, right next to Tanjia, who remained sleeping. *Was she even aware I left? Worse, is she aware of the real me?* If he truly wanted to meet someone like Mary Grace, someone honest and true and beautiful, he would have to become more authentic. It wasn't impossible. He could just re-reinvent himself. Again. Even drunk, he laughed at his own stupidity: just the idea of becoming more authentic seemed to negate the concept of authenticity itself. But he would do it. If anyone could, it was Nick Fucking Charmin. He would, come hell or high water, become a genuine person, and then Mary Grace would regret ever losing him.

"Goddamn it," he shouted out loud, partly because he was drunk, but mostly to confirm his beliefs.

"Oh, honey." Tanjia rolled over and stroked his hair. "You sound so forceful," she said in a sleepy, sexy voice. "It's kind of exciting," she added. "I think I was just dreaming about us doing some pretty naughty things."

"Oh?" Nick pressed.

"Really naughty."

Nick raised his eyebrows and groaned. He could feel himself becoming aroused.

Tanjia worked her hand down and lightly brushed the hair on his chest.

"I was hoping you could take me shopping tomorrow, Nicky," she said in the same sexy voice she used to talk dirty.

He groaned again. It didn't matter what this girl said—it all came out of her mouth sounding hot—and yet his mind still wandered. *If I'm going to re-reinvent myself as an authentic man who dates girls like Mary Grace, do I have to dump Tanjia?*

"Do you want me to show you what I was doing to you in my dream?" she offered.

"Yes," he whispered, answering both Tanjia's question and his own. Dumping Tanjia was an essential part of the plan, *but nobody said the plan has to start now.*

For now, he would let Tanjia work her magic on him, the way his worked on her.

CHAPTER THIRTY-FIVE

"My policy on cake is pro having it and pro eating it." BORIS JOHNSON

When Ralph opened his eyes he couldn't remember where he was. It didn't take long for the reality of his dismal situation to flood back to him. He was in his classroom at Minot High School. Mary Grace had disappointed him. Jayde had shocked him. Life had deserted him.

He had only put his head down on his desk for a minute, just to rest his burning, tired eyes. He must have fallen asleep because now it was—he checked the watch on his wrist—eight o'clock in the morning. What time had he actually fallen asleep? Three? Four? Six? He remembered a crazy dream he had. It, like him, was blurry and hard to make out. Holden Caufield was in it. In an attempt to remember more of the dream, Ralph shook his head, as if that sort of action would dislodge his brain's memory card. It worked. His dream was coming back to him. Not in full, more like tiny shards of glass he could attempt to piece together.

Holden was his student. And they were in what was referred to as the teaching meadow.

"This grass is burned out," Holden said.

"I see that," Ralph said, picking up a clump of dried-out grass. "The board of education should do a better job preserving the meadow."

"You know, I could care for the meadow, Mr. Ichy," Holden said.

"Just take care of yourself, Holden. That's enough," Ralph said.

"I'm not really doing a good job of that," Holden said. "Just look where I landed."

Suddenly they were no longer in the meadow but at Ralph's home, and instead of his mother in her "sick" bed, Holden had taken her place. Ralph was confused.

"I know you're not well, Holden, but where is my mother?"

"She's doing great, Mr. Ichy. She has that meadow greener than an Arnold Palmer golf course."

Ralph gave Holden a puzzled look, the kind you see in a comic strip, where the eyebrows are painted on like question marks. He cocked his head to the left, for dramatic effect. And then he squeezed his eyes tightly and tried to return to the meadow to find his Mom, but he couldn't get back there. So he squeezed his eyes even tighter, but when he opened them he was still at home, and Holden was still in his mother's bed. He could feel himself begin to cry, at which point he started to realize he was stuck in a dream. The meadow wasn't real. Holden wasn't real. His mother wasn't missing. *Bam.* He opened his eyes. The dream, the night, Mary Grace— they all took so much out of him. If possible, he had woken up more tired than when he had let sleep take him in.

Ralph stood up and stretched. He got up on the balls of his feet and reached his arms up to the ceiling. He let out a large groan, the kind that goes perfectly with that first morning stretch, coupled with that sense of deep depression. He needed to face the reality of his new life. His life as a permanent bachelor; a bachelor who takes care of his sick mother. It was a grim picture, but he would get used to it. He knew in the long run it would be better to keep his heart safe than to ever give it away again. *Loving people is too painful,* he thought.

He would start his new life by going home and relieving Celia of her day's duties; after all, she had already spent the night with his mother. He, himself, would prepare his mother a hearty breakfast and serve it to her wherever she wished: in bed, at the kitchen table, or in her favourite reclining chair. He alone would make her happy.

When he stepped outside, he thought the day belied his mood, because this appeared to be the first perfect day in weeks. Could it be that the Haze Craze was finally over? There was no trace of humidity in the air, just breezy blue skies, Ralph noticed, looking up. *Where are the grey skies when I need them?* he thought as he walked to his car, ready to drive right off Holden's cliff and right into his new normal.

CHAPTER THIRTY-SIX

"Some things are just wonderful, like friendship and chocolate cake." UNKNOWN

Mary Grace was supposed to be the first to wake up. That's what they had decided in the wee hours of the morning. She would put on a huge pot of coffee that they would all desperately need, shower, and then get her friends going. In theory it was a decent plan, but it didn't work out that way. Jayde, who required very little sleep, was up first, showered, and looking city perfect, wearing an old dress of Mary Grace's that hung on her skinny frame and made her look like a waif model from the magazines. She paired the paisley dress with her own black ankle boots. With her long hair slicked back in a tight, low ponytail, she was ready to go. Annie took a shower, just to wake herself up, but with no need to impress anyone, she wore her jeans, T-shirt, and flip-flops from the night before, and took on the most important responsibility of all: brewing the coffee.

It was Mary Grace who couldn't wake up. Annie gently shook her. Jayde played loud music from her iPhone, but Mary Grace wouldn't budge. Jayde couldn't help but wonder if her friend had snuck one of her Ambiens after all.

Finally, Annie went to the kitchen to get a bowl of cold water to dunk Mary Grace's fingers into. It was in those few moments that Mary Grace stirred, with Jayde by her side. She looked at Jayde, then the clock, then back at Jayde, before panicking.

"Why didn't you wake me?" she screamed.

Jayde screamed back, "I tried! Annie tried! She's getting cold water right now to pour on you."

"Forget the cold water," Annie shouted on her walk back from the kitchen. "I've got something better. Coffee," she said, holding a tray with three mugs of steaming coffee on it.

"E-leven!" Mary Grace said, not paying attention to either friend. "If Tess Lunt said it once, she said it a million times. E-leven. There's no way we'll make it."

"Honey, did you sleep?" Annie asked Mary Grace, putting the tray down and pushing a mug of hot coffee in front of her. "Drink this. It will help. Jayde," Annie continued, nodding toward the closet, "pick out an outfit for Mary Grace. Let's get it on her. And here's your coffee." Annie pushed another mug toward Jayde.

"In control. I like it," Jayde said, walking toward the closet and purposefully pushing through Mary Grace's clothes. "Maybe. Maybe. Definitely not," she said to the clothes, before turning back to Mary Grace. "And we are not going to be late. I ordered a car service. The driver will text me when he's here."

Mary Grace sat up in her bed and sipped her coffee. It was good. She pulled out the drawer of her bedside table, grabbed two Advil, and washed them down with a large swallow. Lucky for her, her friends seemed to have her disastrous life under control. *Too bad it wasn't all a horrible dream.*

The girls picked at the cake for breakfast, and poured large amounts of coffee into Mary Grace's to-go cups. Jayde received a text from her driver that he was in the apartment parking lot, and after a quick inventory of their respective to-do lists—Annie texted John, Jayde hit the send button on her HuffPost article, and Mary Grace called her mother, telling her she was heading to *I Do* for day two, leaving out the small detail that Ralph was not joining her—they exited Mary Grace's apartment. Mary Grace was ready to face the wrath of Tess Lunt upon arriving on-set without her fiancé.

The first thing Mary Grace noticed when she stepped outside was the lack of humidity in the air. The temperature actually felt comfortable, but the bright sun hurt her tired eyes. She hung her head and rubbed her eyes so hard she could see the colours of the rainbow behind them. When she was done, she looked up. Was she seeing clearly, or was her vision muddied from the rubbing? Was it really him? Ralph? She closed her eyes and swallowed hard to make sure she wasn't dreaming. When she opened her eyes again, he was still there. It wasn't a dream.

A wave of relief washed over Mary Grace. Ralph was alive and he was back. *Or is he? Perhaps he's here to break it off in person. Tell me what a horrible human being I am. Confirm what I already know.* She felt her knees tremble. She didn't know what to do. Run up to him? Wait for him to come to her? Someone gave her a slight push. She was uncertain if it was Annie or Jayde. If she were to bet, she would have put her money on Jayde.

She trotted toward Ralph, who was leaning against his car, just waiting for her.

As she was moving closer toward him, he looked at the watch on his wrist and said, "E-leven, Mary Grace. We need to meet with Tess at E-leven."

She couldn't help but smile, and smile big. Ralph returned her grin and moved toward her. They embraced. Annie couldn't help herself. She clapped, like she was watching the end of some Broadway show. Jayde smacked her arm and gave her a look. *Cut it out,* the look said.

"I'm hurt, Mary Grace."

"I know," she whispered. "I'm so sorry I was the one who did it."

"I told Jayde I never wanted to see you again."

"She told me." Mary Grace took a deep breath. "I'm sorry you saw what you saw," she continued, gently touching the hair at Ralph's temples. "I'm even more sorry I let him kiss me."

Ralph groaned, the pain in his voice palpable.

"I thought my life was over, Ralph. I was out looking for you all night. And when I finally came home, it was Annie and Jayde who convinced me to let you have some space."

"I thought *my* life was over," he said. "I wasn't coming here. I was going home. Ready to start a new life by myself. Mom and me. But almost without my consent, I came here instead."

Mary Grace just stared at Ralph, a smile on her face and relief in her heart.

"I have one question." Ralph turned his head to the left, staring into Mary Grace's eyes. Her look begged him to ask away.

"Did that son-of-a-bitch kiss you like this?" Ralph put his lips on hers and gently pressed himself to her, laying his hand on the small of her back. It was light and long and lovely. Ralph was speaking the language Mary Grace understood. She basked in his warmth, letting it envelop her entire body, before breaking them apart.

"No. Not like that, Ralph. Not at all like that."

Ralph looked disappointed.

"I mean that in the best possible way." Mary Grace smiled. "Nick Charmin was a foreigner to me. His kiss wasn't your kiss. And it was at that exact moment I knew I only wanted you. If you'll still have me."

"Forever, MG. You're easy to love."

"Now I have a question," Mary Grace said, cocking her head the way she had seen Ralph do only moments earlier. "Do you think Paul McCartney will ever get back together with Jane Asher?"

"His first girlfriend?"

"You know who Jane Asher is?"

"Doesn't everyone?"

"No. Not everyone."

Ralph shrugged.

"So, what are the odds?"

"Odds?"

"That they'll get back together?"

"Not good, MG. Not good. He seems very happy with Nancy."

Mary Grace just stared at Ralph for a long second. She smiled. "Yes he does, doesn't he?"

Annie nudged Jayde, a huge smile on her face. "You think they made up?" she asked. "They look like they did, don't they?"

"I think if they don't take my car right now they will never meet Tess Lunt at e-leven," Jayde said, walking toward Mary Grace and Ralph. "I hate to break this up," Jayde called, "but…" She looked at a non-existent watch on her wrist.

Mary Grace and Ralph hopped into the car, prepared to say a final goodbye to *I Do* and Tess Lunt.

CHAPTER THIRTY-SEVEN

"For me it's been a good season, but we've only made a cake. Now we need to put the cherry on top." RAFAEL BENITEZ

Everything about commuting to Manhattan was different.

The weather was different. The sky was the colour of the Mediterranean, and cotton clouds appeared to be suspended in midair with only nylon fishing wire holding them up, confirming what all the weather personalities had been spewing all morning: the heat wave was over.

Their transportation was different. Instead of riding into the city on a filthy train, which brought out the worst in Ralph's OCDs, they were sitting in a lovely limo that was new and clean and sparkling.

In fact, Mary Grace and Ralph were different. Their love was deep and true and real. Ralph knew for certain that Mary Grace loved only him. And, for her part, Mary Grace was confident in her love, too. She didn't just love Ralph because he loved her first. She wasn't marrying him because he was the only one who had asked. She wasn't marrying him to make her mother happy. In some strange way, thanks to the unwanted but entirely welcomed advances of Nick Charmin, she was no longer desperate. She was marrying Ralph because she wanted nothing more than to spend the rest of her life with him, and it showed. It showed in her walk, in her face, in her entire demeanor.

Seconds after arriving at the *I Do* building, Gabriella met Ralph and Mary Grace in the lobby. Gabriella looked surprised when her eyes landed on her *I Do* test couple. She reached out her hand to shake Ralph's and gave Mary Grace a quick hug.

"Follow me," she said, trotting toward the elevator. She glanced at them over her shoulder. "Can I be honest with you?" Gabriella asked, entering the elevator, and holding the door open button until Mary Grace and Ralph were securely inside. She hit the button for the fifteenth floor. "What was I saying?" she wondered. "I just lost my train of thought."

"Honest," Ralph offered.

"You asked if you could be honest with us," Mary Grace added. "Please do."

"Right. You guys look like shit. What the hell happened to you last night? Too much tequila?" she quipped, flipping through the notes on her clipboard. She didn't look at either of them but continued talking. "Tess is a busy woman. She was up all night reviewing tapes of the show. Tweaking it here and there. Did you know it's harder to do season five of a show than to launch a brand new one? Some people will tell you otherwise. Don't believe them," Gabriella said. "She looks like shit, too. Tess. Were you drinking tequila together? Perhaps with Mr. Charmin? He won't even leave his office this morning. I've never seen him so grumpy." Gabriella took a moment to think about what she had said, and then laughed. "Correction: heard him so grumpy. He's just barking orders through the door. I haven't seen him. Nobody has."

The rest of the ride was silent, until Gabriella said, "We're here," stepping off the elevator.

Ralph and Mary Grace followed two steps behind Gabriella, walking down the narrow hallway and sending each other cryptic, puzzled messages with their eyes. Gabriella opened the door to Tess' interview room and, voila, Tess was seated in the wicker chair, legs curled under her, sipping tea. *She doesn't look so bad*, Mary Grace thought.

"Mary Grace, Ralph, so good to see you. Have some tea. I was up all night. Some people need peace and quiet. Me? I need peace and tea. Join me? Gabriella, that will be all for now," Tess said with a nod. Gabriella slipped out of the room.

Ralph and Mary Grace took their obligatory places on the overstuffed love seat. The room felt less comfortable than it had during the interview. It was missing something. *The ocean smell, that was it,* Mary Grace thought. Today the room didn't smell of the ocean, only of herbal tea, a scent Mary Grace didn't particularly enjoy.

"You two look different today," Tess said, pouring the tea.

"None for me, thanks," Mary Grace said. "Ralph?"

"I'll have some, thanks," he said, reaching for the tea Tess had originally poured for Mary Grace.

"Yes. What is it? You look so different, but I can't put my finger on it. Perhaps it's me not seeing you in wardrobe. I've been looking at the two of you all night, but the couple I was looking at was done," she said, using her fingers to make quotation marks when she spoke the word "done." *Just like Nick Charmin,* Mary Grace thought with a laugh. They must learn that in television school.

"My attention was particularly focused on the one of you who was sweating."

Ralph hung his head.

"Look, your chemistry was great. Particularly between Charmin and you, Mary Grace," Tess said with a laugh.

Ralph lifted his head and glared at Tess.

"Sorry, Ralph, but it's true," Tess said.

"I know," he said, giving Mary Grace a sideways glance. This time it was Mary Grace who hung her head.

"If I could, I would bottle and sell that shit, and probably make a billion," Tess added, taking a long sip of her tea. "But we have a huge problem." Tess took a long pause.

"Ralph? You sweat too much," she finally said.

Just this conversation was making Ralph nervous, and perspiration beads were beginning to form on his forehead.

"It's not your fault. I'm not blaming you. But I need a hit with this show. And I'm afraid the profuse sweating will be a real turn-off to America. I think Americans like to see a guy sweat when he is doing something athletic, like perhaps enduring a challenge on *Survivor*, but not sitting idly in a chair. That kind of perspiration is a turn-off. I thought we could mask the problem with the shirt changes. I was banking on it. But the tapes I watched proved otherwise."

Mary Grace and Ralph stole a quick look at each other. Mary Grace allowed her shoulders the tiniest of shrugs and her mouth an even tinier smirk.

"And so, it is with much regret I must enact section five-point-three of the contract you signed when you agreed to do the test show. It reads, 'blah, blah, blah, if for any reason contestants are not right for the show, blah, blah, blah, they can be dismissed at the discretion of, blah, blah, and be requested to leave by, blah, blah, blah, the show's producer.' That's me," Tess said. "And despite the good chemistry, there was just too much, um, chemistry."

"You mean we're off the show?" Mary Grace asked. "You're kicking us off the show?" *We don't have to quit*, she thought but didn't say.

"We're not getting married on television?" Ralph asked. "We can get married where we want, when we want, wearing what we want?" A feeling of relief washed over him.

"Pretty much, yes," Tess said, confused about why her news was making Ralph and Mary Grace so happy. She assumed they would be disappointed—devastated, even—to be off her show.

"Oh, Ralph—" Mary Grace began to say, but was interrupted.

"Please tell me you are going to say this is the best news ever," Ralph said, a hint of fear in his voice.

"You read my mind," Mary Grace said.

"No hard feelings," Tess said, her voice forced and awkward.

"Hard feelings? Never. This show gave me something I could never live without," Mary Grace said. "Ralph."

Tess raised her eyebrows.

"Tess," Mary Grace began, looking directly into the producer's eyes, "Ralph and I will be planning our own, grand wedding. And we would love it if you would attend." Mary Grace shot a quick glance at Ralph, who was nodding in agreement.

"Lord knows your mother will be there," Mary Grace added with a laugh.

"It will be my honour," Tess said, eyes darting between Mary Grace and Ralph, before taking a huge gulp of tea.

"You know you two were the favourites around here," she said, leaving her producer self behind, pleased her news didn't leave the favourite couple with a sour taste in their mouths.

"Everybody loved you," she added. "So how about we have Maxine do your hair and Janelle do your makeup the day of your wedding? I know they would be honoured to be a part of your big day. Even on your terms."

Mary Grace smiled in approval but before she could spit out the words "thank you," Ralph spoke.

"Who are you getting to replace us?" he asked, genuinely curious, as he rose to leave, grabbing tightly to Mary Grace's hand.

"You know I can't reveal that," Tess said with a wink. "Remember the contract?"

"Remember it? I'm going to be thanking God for it for the rest of my life. And for my hyperhidrosis."

Tess gave Ralph a curious look.

"You know, my overactive sweat glands… the reason I went through two shirts."

"Three," Tess said with a laugh.

"And I'll be thanking God for Mary Grace, too," Ralph said, pulling her toward him and nearly running out of Tess' office.

"Forever," he whispered in Mary Grace's ear.

CHAPTER THIRTY-EIGHT

"We once created a birthday cake for a lady's party which was a model of her in the form of a naked marble statue." JANE ASHER

*W*hoever thought it was impossible to put together a fantastic wedding in just *two weeks' time was wrong,* Mary Grace thought at t minus one day and counting. Mary Grace hired a three-piece band. A photographer. And ordered flowers. Owen from *I Do* helped her shop for a dress, and Angela Falcone didn't even object. Instead, she tagged along on their Manhattan garment-district shopping spree, and willingly, Owen dressed the mother of the bride, too. Angela's years spent as a devoted parishioner of Our Lady of the Valley secured Father Jack, who agreed to preside over the nuptials and offered his assistance in last minute Pre Kana classes. And MexTexas's owner, Carlos, was more than happy to rent the top floor banquet room to his favourite regular.

With yards of toile, Annie decorated the restaurant, giving it a light and special feel. Chairs were set in five rows of ten, leaving ample space in the middle, wide enough for a bride and her wedding party to glide through. Invitations were printed on Ralph's computer and delivered by the hand of Mary Grace to the intimate friends and relatives included in the festivities. She stuck to only one tradition: the groom could not see her in her dress before their wedding day. Ralph begged and pleaded. He even tried ordering her, but it came out so funny the two of them fell on the floor in fits of laugher.

Ralph was dying to see what his future wife would look like as his bride, but Mary Grace insisted he wait. And she was right, because the moment he set his eyes on her, his bride, on their wedding day, he became entranced by her beauty, and a grin spread across his face that filled him with a love and wonder that tingled from his toes to his fingers. And that was the moment he had waited for his entire life.

A pianist whom Carlos had hired started to play, fingers tripping lightly over the keys. But it wasn't the traditional wedding march he played; it was "The Long and Winding Road." The song selection gave all those in attendance pause to smile. *Leave it to Mary Grace*, they thought. Annie walked down the MexTexas aisle first, holding the hands of her children, who flanked her on either side. Despite her marital problems, her genuine smile confirmed to Ralph that marriage was a trip worth taking. Annie easily felt her husband's gaze on her and locked eyes with him. She loved him and had promised, for the sake of her children and the sake of herself, that, with counselling, they would make it work. She gave him a breezy, it-will-be-all-right smile while she tightened her grip on the hands of her children.

Behind Annie walked Jayde. A confident, radiant Jayde, who didn't smile so much as laugh as she trotted down the aisle. There was no slowing this girl down; she wanted a wedding and she wanted it now. She allowed a giddy, happy feeling to take over her body.

The pianist ended the Beatles tune and paused for one lengthy second before beginning the Wedding March. And then Mary Grace appeared. And that exact moment was the one for which Ralph had waited a lifetime. Mary Grace. Gracie. MG. Hair, compliments of Maxine, was piled high atop her head, with soft tendrils framing her face. Makeup, compliments of Janelle, was painted on lightly, only used to enhance her natural wedding day glow. Mary Grace took tiny steps down the aisle, wanting the moment to last forever. She made contact with nearly everyone in the intimate crowd: Tess, Janelle, Maxine, Owen, her aunts and uncles, and then her mother. She fixed her eyes on her mother and mouthed the words, "I love you." Her mother mouthed back, "Me, too," and then as the tears streamed down her face, she whispered words only Mary Grace could hear: "Your father is proud."

And finally, Mary Grace allowed her eyes to feast on Ralph, the man who in moments would be her husband. She was in love with him, despite the fact that he was, and still remained, the CEO of Antiseptic Hands. Or maybe it was because of it that she was ready to spend the rest of her life with him. And, more than anything, she was ready to dive into their wedding cake, made compliments of Angela herself, who called it Anytime Cake With a Twist.

With Father Jack at the helm, the service was short. Ralph went first, and agreed with everything the good priest said. Next, it was up to Mary Grace. Father Jack spoke about loving and honouring, and sickness and health, and 'til death do you part, and cherishing one another all the days of their lives. Mary Grace smiled and nodded and held on to Ralph's hands with all her might. And the last words anyone could hear, before the clapping, laughing, and pianist's playing filled the room once again with happy noise, were the words spoken loud and clear by one Mary Grace Falcone.

"I do."

EPILOGUE

September meant another school year for Mary Grace and Ralph. But the start of this new year was even more exciting than usual, because they were doing it as newlyweds. Her new third grade class was filled with wide-eyed and wonderful children. And one crier who was having a terrible time separating from his mother. Mary Grace didn't like to favour any of her students, but from somewhere deep down, she couldn't help but shower some extra love on this little boy. Her students, especially the ones with older siblings, were trying to get used to her new name, Mrs. Ichy. But so was Mary Grace. They would all get used to it together.

Mary Grace was puttering around the kitchen of her new house—which was technically not a new house, but Ralph's old one. She was setting her mother-in-law's breakfast dishes out for the next day. She was happy to help Ralph care for his mother, and it gave her more insight into her husband and his good nature. She had realized her mother-in-law thrived on routine. *Not unlike my students*, Mary Grace thought. She was also cutting two slices of the Anytime Cake she had baked the day before. She set them on a tray along with napkins, forks, and milk.

"Ralph," she said, carrying the tray into the family room, "is *I Do* on yet?"

"Just about. Hurry up and sit down," he answered, patting the seat next to him. Mary Grace obliged and set the cake tray atop her left leg and Ralph's right, making sure it was steady before they bit into their first pieces. The theme song started. It was still the Wedding March on steroids. And there was Nick Charmin.

"That could have been us," Ralph said, laughing.

"You sad?" Mary Grace asked.

"Not one bit."

"Ralph! Do you see who the couple is? Do you recognize them?" Mary Grace exclaimed as the show continued its run.

"No."

"That's the tall skinny girl."

"I can see she is tall and skinny."

"Don't tell me you don't remember her. We met her at the interview. What's her name again?" And then Charmin introduced the couple as Rhonda Flemming and Ian Moskovitz.

"Rhonda," Mary Grace said. "That's it. She told us to stay away. She was making it big someday."

"Help me, Rhonda," Ralph sang to the tune of the Beach Boys' song.

"Shh. Let's listen," Mary Grace said as the telephone rang. "Let the machine get it."

"Mary Grace. This is your mother. Pick up, Mary Grace. Ralph? Are you there? This is your mother, Angela Falcone. The show is on. Are you watching? No. You can't be watching. You're not there. Are the two of you dead in a ditch somewhere? If you're not dead, call me. This is your mother."

"Do you want me to pick her up?" Ralph asked.

"No, let her talk." Mary Grace gave Ralph her best, tiny smile. *While life brings on tremendous changes, it is comforting, in the strangest of ways, that some things stay exactly the same.* "I'll call her after the show." Mary Grace put her cake aside for the moment and curled up into Ralph's waiting arms.

Hail Mary, full of grace, thanks for Ralph's warm, strong embrace, Mary Grace thought, but didn't say.

AUTHOR'S NOTE

While my writing is a solitary activity, I hope your reading of my writing is not; if you like a word, a sentence, a paragraph, a chapter, or hey, the whole book, let me know. Better yet, share the word, tell a friend, or host a book group (a Book Club Guide follows). Have fun, make a cake, eat it with your friends, and talk about *Love, Reality Style*. Sounds like fun to me.

ABOUT JUDITH NATELLI MCLAUGHLIN

Judith Natelli McLaughlin is an author/illustrator whose work crosses over many genres. Her novel, *This Moment*, appeared on the Amazon bestseller list. Her children's poetry has been published alongside idols like Shel Silverstein, Jack Prelutsky, and Judith Viorst. Her children's classic, *Poems on Fruits and Odes to Veggies – Where Healthy Eating Starts with a Poem*, is a staple in the world of healthy eating, making good food choices fun. Her middle grade novels include *Dear Diary, E.P. Thompson Here*, and the first in her chapter book series, *Mackenzie Goode Makes a Mistake – A Big One*, was published in 2015. She lives in the Garden State with her husband, Brian, three daughters, Katie, Lindsay, and Maggie, and a Westie named Duke. She is proud to call herself a New Jersey native.

BOOK CLUB GUIDE

Make a cake. Don't fuss over it. Use your preferred boxed mix and icing from a can. Here's a favourite story. I brought just that sort of cake to a cocktail party: yellow cake with chocolate frosting. During the evening I heard one of the guests was looking for the "cake maker." She found me, held my hands in hers, and proceeded to tell me, with tears in her eyes and a cracking voice, that my cake tasted just like the cake her grandma made when she was a little girl. "Can I get the recipe?" she asked with wonder. We still laugh about it. It's not the cake (well, maybe it is); it's the experience you have while eating it. So make a cake, gather your friends, and discuss:

1. What part of Mary Grace Falcone can you relate to the most; her friends, her mom, or her love life?

2. Do you find Ralph Ichy to be a likeable character or do his idiosyncrasies make him unlikeable? What are some of his phobias and can you relate to any of them?

3. Mary Grace, Annie, and Jayde have a unique friendship. Do you have friends in your life like these women? If so, think about a time in your life when you were most grateful to have them.

4. When Mary Grace, Jayde, and Annie have the napkin ceremony at MexTexas, Annie makes them write three things on their napkins:

    1. What you believe about yourself.
    2. What you want to believe about yourself.

3. What you would like to change about yourself.

What do you think each woman wrote? What would you write?

5. When the women have an opportunity to read each other's napkins, they turn it down. Why? Would you?

6. When talking about her faltering marriage, Annie says, "You can't just put your life into little compartments. One for marriage. One for friends. One for children. One for right. One for wrong. It's more like one of my kids' finger paintings. All mushed together, with no clear definition of the reds or blues or yellows. Sometimes it's just brown, but you have to trust, underneath it all, the pretty colours do exist." Do you trust the pretty colours exist? Why?

7. Throughout the book, trust is a running theme; how so? If someone breaks your trust, can they win it back? How and how long would it take?

8. How does Mary Grace's past shape her present? Think about your own past and ways it has made you the person you are today.

9. As a teenager, Mary Grace became obsessed with the Beatles and particularly the love between Paul McCartney and Jane Asher; if you were in true love, your mate had "the Jane Asher Factor." (In fact, a working title of this novel was The Jane Asher Factor.) Think about your teenage self. What sorts of themes, games, ideas did you and your friends make up? What would you tell your teenage self now?

10. Do you believe in happy endings? Why?

WRITE FOR US

We love discovering new voices and welcome submissions. Please read the following carefully before preparing your work for submission to us. Our publishing house does accept unsolicited manuscripts but we want to receive a proposal first and if interested we will solicit the manuscript.

We are looking for solid writing—present an idea with originality and we will be very interested in reading your work.

As you can appreciate, we give each proposal careful consideration so it can take up to six weeks for us to respond, depending on the amount of proposals we have received. If it takes longer to hear back, your proposal could still be under consideration and may simply have been given to a second editor for their opinion. We can't publish all books sent to us but each book is given consideration based on its individual merits along with a set of criteria we use when considering proposals for publication.

Thank You For Reading Love, Reality Style